If at First

By Grant Williams

HALA
AlaHala - "oh my God!"

Thank you to Sara, Logan, and Evie for being patient during this endeavor.

Thank you to Camille, Susan, and Nick for all of your help putting this

together.

Chapter 1

As I stood atop the American National Bank building, my thoughts moved like the cars forty stories below me, erratically from one thing to another. The things I had done in my life felt like a weight dragging me down. The things I hadn't done and the few personal relationships I had were the only things keeping me on the ledge, and they weren't making much of an argument.

Though I had never been on top of the ANB building before, the scene was surprisingly familiar to me. I had tried to kill myself several times before. Most of my attempts were what experts would call 'a cry for help'. An overdose of aspirin, cuts, even the old 'keep your car running in the garage' attempts had failed. Even I was starting to wonder if the failures were cleverly timed ruses, but this time I had chosen the tallest building in town. This time, even if it was a cry for help, no one would be up here to hear it.

I closed my eyes to take in the last sounds I would ever hear. The pulse of traffic was hard to recognize from this height. Up here, the sounds of planes were more prominent. I reopened my eyes to gaze upon the world for the last time. I had never seen the world from this perspective; the view was different when there wasn't a big office window separating you from it. It was prettier than I thought it would be. The sun was just rising on a fresh Friday morning in the middle of September.

My mouth crept open slightly. A deep breath filled my lungs. I held it, long enough to feel pressure build up in my chest. I relaxed my diaphragm and let the imprisoned air escape. My hand came up to smooth the red paisley tie that flapped in the wind. Understanding how futile it would be to make my tie stop flapping, I tried to smooth my hair down. It was so short it didn't change much. I wiped both hands down my face, feeling the clean shave from the morning. I inhaled as I wiped and exhaled as my hands slid down my chest, smoothing out the jacket of my suit.

Despite being an off the rack suit, it hung nicely on my frame. Considering I spent more time in the library than the gym I was in decent shape. I had the body of a lazy swimmer; good shoulders and arms, but not a lot of definition on the torso. At least everything was still visible in the shower. It was more a being blessed with good genes and luck than effort.

No point looking like a slob when you die, I thought. Most people look a mess when they commit suicide. I glanced down just far enough to make sure I had my jacket buttoned properly. On any other day, I could have been mistaken for someone far more successful. While I understood the implications of a forty story free fall, I imagined the suit would lend my death some sort of poetic attachment; the beauty of ending the ugliness of my past. I was always looking for meaning where there was none.

I began humming a tune in my head. I couldn't remember the name of the song but I recognized it as a nursery rhyme from my childhood. The words weren't in my head any more either; all I had were the vague memories of the melody. I was trying to center myself. I was working up the courage to take the easy way out.

"Jump." The words left my lips as I rocked up to my tip-toes and pushed myself into space.

Out of reflex, my eyes clamped shut. A shock passed through my body. I could feel my heartbeat in my teeth. The realization that it was finally over hit me as gravity took ahold and pulled me towards the earth. The noise was deafening. The wind rushing past me pushed my skin back tight and screamed in my ears. It seemed like an odd thing to notice, but I could feel my ear lobes fluttering. For the first time in weeks or months or years, I had a moment to think. Unfortunately, that moment ended quicker than I had anticipated.

My left arm hit first, breaking the bone on impact and then about four feet later, the rest of my body made contact. I kept my eyes shut thinking that death was just around the corner. Forty stories didn't feel how I thought forty stories would feel. The pain shooting through my entire body had me wondering what was taking so long. Outside of my control, a scream of agony let out. That scream was abruptly followed by another scream of pure terror.

The second scream wasn't from me. When I finally did open my eyes, the first thing I saw was Jesus. At least that was what his name tag said. From the look of the man standing as far away from me as he could on the scaffolding, the 'j' was probably pronounced like an 'h'. I closed my eyes again. The harsh reality that I had failed yet again set in. The immediate shock was wearing off and was being replaced with excruciating pain. I writhed around on the cool metal floor of the window washing platform waiting for the hurt to stop.

"You okay?" a surprisingly soft but shaky voice asked in a Spanish accent.

I rolled over and considered pushing myself off the unit to finish the job. A glance over the edge made me realize that approximately thirty-seven stories stood between me and my goal and that I had suddenly developed a fear of heights and the pain accompanied with failure.

"Fuck," I moaned, scooting away from the edge as much as one could in a four by ten space. "Fuck! Fuck! Fuck! Fuck!"

"Sir?"

"What?" I yelled. I wasn't mad at the man, but I wasn't ready to be bothered.

I used my right arm to pull myself to a standing position and flattened myself against the railing closest to the building. One wet sock indicated that I had lost one of my shoes on impact. I then wondered why

I was wet. Looking at the shivering Spaniard before me, I noticed that we were both soaking wet and covered in soap suds.

The man in front of me was just about my height, only a slightly chunkier build and wore a bright yellow jumpsuit that made him look like a six foot tall banana. Over his right breast pocket was a white name tag with a half torn off black Brother Label with white lettering that read 'Jesus N'.

"Where did all this water come from?" I asked straining to get my breath back while trying to make polite conversation in an awkward situation.

"My bucket," Jesus replied with a degree of confusion.

"Where's your bucket?"

Jesus maintained his grip and cocked his head to the side, indicating that it went over the edge.

"I am, truly, sorry about your bucket. If you would lower us, I'll get your bucket when we get down."

"I think it's broke," Jesus looked over the edge. "It's a long ways down."

Irritation was welling up inside me. "I'll buy you a new bucket, then. Can you please just lower us? I think I need medical attention. In case you didn't notice, I've had a bit of a fall."

"We go up. You didn't notice the wench?" Jesus replied pointing to the sky.

I looked up three stories and saw the apparatus holding the cleaning scaffolding and the cables running down. I felt foolish that I hadn't noticed it before. Of all the buildings to throw myself off, I picked the one that had a safety net.

"Whatever."

Three stories going up was a much longer trip than the three stories going down. It gave me more time to consider the foolishness and selfishness of my actions. The cart stopped at the roof level and I opened the gate and stepped off. Jesus cleared his throat to grab my attention.

"Yes? Oh, thanks for the lift."

"My bucket."

"Oh, right." I dug into my pocket and pulled out my wallet. I placed the billfold into my stationary left arm. I dug through it looking for a twenty, but I was disappointed when I only found a hundred. Benjamin Franklin was placed there for the first guy who found me on the ground. It was a bit of gratuity for the trouble. After all, I wasn't mad at the world. My troubles were my fault.

"Do you, uh, have change for a hundred?"

"No."

"You didn't even check."

"Sorry. No cash on me," Jesus said, scratching the back of his head.

Begrudgingly, I handed over the bill and grabbed my wallet from my left hand to put it back in my pocket. I turned to walk back to the roof access door. Jesus stepped off the cart and followed me.

"Where are you going?" I asked as if it were my business. I wanted to make sure he wasn't following me or going to tell the police.

"I need to get a new bucket."

Jesus strode off in front of me and grabbed a full bucket of soapy water from behind an air conditioning unit. I stood still and glared at him as he got back on his cart and disappeared beneath the roof level.

There were no elevators that went to the top floor, so I had to hobble with one shoe down a flight of stairs to get to the floor with the elevator. Luckily, there were no occupied offices on the very top floor so I was able to get to the elevator unnoticed. I had no such luck once the elevator doors opened; a Middle Eastern woman stood against the back wall.

I took long enough contemplating whether I should enter or not that the elevator doors started to close. The woman reached out and stopped the doors. I first noticed the deep red fingernail polish on well-manicured nails on the ends of long elegant fingers. Those fingers attached to hands that vanished into the sleeves of a black suit jacket, covering ample breasts held back by a white button down with long lapels opened a button further than was probably prudent. The white from the blouse only accentuated the bronze color in her skin. The bottom of the blouse led to a black skirt that hugged her hips and tracked down to just below her knees. Sprouting out of the bottom edge of the skirt were two perfectly toned legs ending in a pair of black heels.

Her face was even more striking than the rest of her. From her look, I assumed she was a very well taken care of late thirties, but her features were so soft she could have passed for her twenties. Even more impressive was that everything appeared natural, though I dared not stare enough to come to a definite conclusion.

"In or out?" the woman asked. She looked down at her smart phone. Sheets of thick shiny black hair poured down to the top of her breasts.

"In... I guess," I said stepping inside. I wasn't sure why I was 'guessing'. I was clearly rattled from the fall, but for some reason, my senses seemed a little more off kilter than I thought they should be. Once inside, I turned and faced the control panel. None of the floor buttons were lit up. "Did you need to get off here?"

"No," she replied, "lobby is fine."

I had to reach around her to press the button for the lobby. I took a step back stared at the floor hoping to not make conversation for thirty-nine floors. We travelled six before she spoke.

"Where's your shoe?"

I glanced down. "I lost it on the roof."

"How do you lose a shoe?"

"It fell over the edge."

"Did you go with it? You look like hell. And if you went over, how are you up here and not dead?"

"Lucky, I suppose."

As if it wasn't bad enough I just tried to kill myself, I now had to deal with the critique of strangers. I decided the best course of action would have been to pretend she hadn't said anything at all.

"Look, I didn't mean to offend, but you really do look like hell." She touched my shoulder softly. "Do you need a ride somewhere? The hospital, maybe?"

"No, I'm fine. Thank you."

The doors opened to the lobby and I stepped out without a word. She smiled at me and watched me walk away. After a few steps in the marble floored lobby, I became irritated by my one shoe clacking and my wet sock squeaking. In my frustration, I balanced on my right foot to take my shoe and sock off, but had to sit down in a lobby chair to take the sock off my right foot with my one good arm.

The woman in black strode by me on her way out the door. At the door she stopped and turned to face me.

"You sure you don't need a ride?"

It felt like everything she was saying was to mock me, but in a playful way, so I dismissed the thought. My gut was telling me to take the ride. My mind was telling me not to. As was usually the case, my mind won the argument.

"Yeah, I'm fine. My car is just around the corner," I said, desperately yanking on the wet sock clinging to my foot. It was a lie, and she knew it, but she let the issue drop.

I had taken a cab to the ANB building. An inconvenience was the last thing I wanted to be remembered for, and having to pay impound fees on my car that would eventually be towed seemed like more than my family should have to deal with. If nothing else, I thought I was courteous.

The woman chuckled and half-heartedly waved good-bye as she disappeared through the revolving door. My shambled appearance was starting to gain attention from the workers and patrons in the lobby. My wavy dishwater blond hair lay haphazardly around my head. The small trickle of blood that had crept out of my nose had gone unnoticed by me, but likely stood out plainly on my clean-shaven face. The now wrinkled black suit was particularly shiny from the moisture still trapped inside the fabric. To top it off, my pale bare feet stood out against the contrast of the black pants. I quickly dumped my socks and shoe in the nearest trash can and left through the same doors my pushy new friend had gone through.

Stepping out into the cool air felt good. I hadn't stopped sweating since the fall. My nerves were finally settling down, allowing the breeze to lower my temperature. It was the first real relief I'd had since I woke up that morning.

The pain radiating out of my broken arm made me reconsider asking the woman in black for a ride, but a brief scan of my surroundings showed that she was gone. I flagged down a cab, but as the car pulled up next to the curb, I remembered that I had just spent all my money on a new dime-store bucket for Jesus. I waved the driver on with my good arm.

The thought crossed my mind to call my girlfriend April, but if I had, what would I tell her; that I had just tried to throw myself off a building? Cover story first, girlfriend second. It wasn't that she was a pain in the ass, quite the opposite, but I was ashamed of what I had done. She knew about my past, she knew about my previous attempts. In hindsight I should have called her that morning. She would have been there. She always was.

Bare foot and soaking, I headed for the hospital. I couldn't afford the insurance where I worked, reducing my options to visiting either the doctor's office at the health department or a non-profit hospital. I chose the non- profit, because the thought of waiting all day at the health department scared me more than whatever the bill was going to be at a regular hospital. I wasn't a snob, but I had spent plenty of time in government-run institutions and I made it a point to avoid them whenever possible.

I walked on in a daze. My trance broke when I stepped into a puddle about a block from the bank. I looked down to see a blue plastic bucket, broken nearly in two. That should have been me, I thought, smearing my toes around the sudsy puddle. I grunted and moved on.

The further I walked, the more my arm ached. The adrenaline had all but left my system and the only thing left in its place was more regret. I just wasn't sure if it was regret from failing again, trying again, or the same feeling that took me up to that roof in the first place. Every car that passed by was another wasted opportunity for me to finish the job, but I couldn't muster up the courage to be a coward again.

According to the law, I had paid my dues. Eight years. It should have been eighty as far as I was concerned. I thought for a moment that they were the lucky ones; the ones that died. It was a stupid selfish thought. If I could just finish the job, I wouldn't have to miss them anymore. I wouldn't have to wear my guilt like a scarlet letter. Instead, all I ended up with was an eight inch scar down the left side of my ribcage and head full of ghosts.

"Asshole," I called myself out loud, drawing the attention of fellow pedestrians. Until that moment, no one noticed my bare feet or my shambled appearance. I was just another prick in just another crowd.

I made a quick turn to mix in with another crowd. Luckily it was reaching lunchtime, so the further I walked, the thicker the crowds became. The thicker the crowd, the less attention I drew to myself. Less attention was better for me.

I never wanted to be the center of attention. The few times attention was drawn to me, it was either because something bad happened, or was going to, usually by my own doing. Since I got out, I just wanted to live my life just like everyone else. Get up, go to work, rinse, repeat. Except, of course, those times when I couldn't imagine wanting anything more than to stop living my life altogether.

A short pudgy man with a bald head and a dated brown on brown suit sneezed behind me, spraying a fine mist of God knows what on the back of my neck. I wheeled around to confront the gentleman, but without missing a stride, the man side-stepped me and was on his way, with no remorse. I used my sleeve to wipe the back of my neck.

I found a small measure of amusement in the fact that I just got done throwing myself off a forty story building, lived to tell the tale, but worried about getting germs on me. It was a justified concern. Being sick is just another reminder of how miserable life can be.

Living in a big city, I had become accustomed to walking to get to places, but after a couple of hours, it started to take its toll on me. I had stepped on just about every conceivable piece of garbage that someone can leave on the street. Topping the list was chewed gum. A lot of chewed gum. Spit was probably next on the list followed by spilt beverages, a variety of foods, one lukewarm dog shit, and random bits of broken glass. I became half-jockingly concerned that by the time I reached the hospital they would have to cast my arm and amputate my feet.

The journey did grant me time to make up an elaborate lie regarding the nature of my injuries. Of all the bad things I had been in my life, a liar was not one of them. The few times I had tried lying, it had usually resulted in me looking like an ass. Four hours of walking seemed like plenty of time to come up with a decent foundation to build a lie upon.

First I needed a location. I tried for over a mile to imagine where I would break my arm in a suit. I couldn't say work, because it would become a workman's comp case. A funeral popped into my head, but that seemed ridiculous. Secret agents wore suits, but they most likely had insurance. After coming up fruitless, I removed my suit jacket and tie and laid them in a dumpster. Maybe some hobo would find them. One less piece of the equation. I chose home for the scene.

Second, I needed an actual accident. That was easy. I went for a good old-fashioned slip and fall. That happens to people all the time; who was going to argue?

Third was the situation. Battered wives enter emergency rooms all the time claiming they fell. I had to have something better; something with at least a little back story. I didn't want anything too complex, though. Simple was the name of the game.

The official story I decided on was that I had taken the day off to clean my apartment, was in the process of taking my glass recyclables to the recycle bin, and on my way out I tripped over a neighborhood cat that hangs out on the front steps of my apartment complex. Because of the vast amount of breakables, I had to land on my forearm to avoid smashing down on a bag of glass. To top it off, the door had locked behind me as I went out and my shoes were inside. It was believable enough. I would add details as needed, but for the most part my lie was constructed and ready for testing.

I called April. I thought it better to test my fabrication on my girlfriend. If she believed it, then anyone would. I stopped at a filling station near the hospital and used a calling card I kept in my wallet to call LaRose Financial's billing department. April worked as a bill collector there. Larry, my best friend, or my 'best black' friend as he liked to point out for no good reason, and I worked in the same building as bookkeepers for small businesses that outsourced their financials.

April being a bill collector made it very difficult for me to lie to her. She had been bullshitted in just about every conceivable way. Her genuine kindness often made me question her career choice and why she would be drawn to someone as broken as me. Perhaps it was just in her maternal nature.

"Thank you for calling LaRose Financial, this is April Klein, how can I help you?" April answered in her best professional voice.

"Well, hello, April. What are you wearing?" I dropped my voice an octave.

"Excuse me?"

I returned to my normal voice. "April, it's me, Steve."

20

"Oh, that guy that doesn't call his girlfriend anymore or come visit her at her desk?" She was joking, sort of.

"Yeah. The complete jerk who has been extremely insensitive lately and will make it up to you as soon as I get out of the hospital." Softening her up before the lie seemed like a solid plan to me.

"Oh my God! You've been in the hospital?" She was clearly feeling bad about bringing up the no phone call thing. At the same time, she had known me long enough to know that if I don't call her it means I'm having a hard time with something. She knew there was something wrong, but she was nice enough not to press it; she would get it out of me eventually.

"Well, no," I paused, "I'm actually on my way there now."

She hesitated because the first thing on her mind was why I hadn't called, but she knew it would be poor strategy to not ask why I was going to the hospital first.

"What for?"

"I was cleaning the apartment, because I thought it would be nice to have the place clean when you come over this weekend. Anyway, I was taking the recycling out, and I tripped over the cat that hangs out on the front steps, and broke my arm. I think."

"Since when do you recycle?"

"Thanks for the concern."

"Sorry." April softened her tone, "Are you okay?". She asked in a manner that made it sound like she wasn't asking about my arm.

"I will be. I'll call you when I get home tonight. Want to come over tomorrow?"

"Sounds good and yes. Call me tonight. But I've got to go. I haven't met my quota for getting called a bitch yet today."

We blew each other kisses through the phone and hung up. I considered the experiment an overall success. She questioned the recycling, but let the rest go. I knew she would grill me about the missing days later, and rightfully so, but I was free and clear for the moment.

About the time my feet decided they had endured enough filth, the Benton County General hospital came into sight. It wasn't one of the sprawling complex hospitals they show on television. This was the poor person hospital. It was one rectangular building eight stories high. Minus the emergeny room entrance and the ambulances parked out front, it could have easily passed for an apartment complex. In its day, it was probably a top-notch facility, but that day was a long time ago, and that notch had fallen a few steps.

Chapter 2

As I shuffled across the parking lot, a decade old white Ford Explorer with an orange spinning light on top cruised up beside me. The shield sticker on the side read "Benton County General Hospital Security". The tinted window rolled down and a late twenties gentleman with thin rimmed glasses and a rat like face stuck his head out the window. I continued walking. I wasn't going to stop if he wasn't going to say anything. Apparently, ignoring him was his hot button.

"Hey," he shouted louder than necessary.

"What?" I asked not looking at him.

I stopped and faced him. He had expected me to keep walking, so he rolled a little past me. I heard a 'damn it' from inside his vehicle, as the white lights came on and he backed up to meet me.

He pushed his glasses up so I could see the irritation in his eyes. "Can I help you with something?"

My mind was overburdened by my fear of doctors and hospitals, so the question was perceived as genuine and I answered accordingly. "Nope."

"Is that a fact?"

"Yeah, I'm fine," I responded. My response that time was more curt, as he seemed too eager to help, like a pushy salesman. The response on his face, enlightened me to the what he was really getting at. He thought I was a bum. It hadn't dawned on me that I certainly resembled one. Normally, I would cooperate, discuss, and resolve. I wasn't in a cooperate, discuss, or resolve kind of mood. I pretended he didn't exist and kept walking.

"Hey, I'm talking to you."

"No, you *were* talking to me," I said as I continued my journey.

The security guard slammed the vehicle in park. That was the first sign that I had screwed up. The second sign was that when he stepped out, he was considerably larger than I had expected. He struck me as the kind of guy that was picked on in high school and spent his collegiate years in the gym.

Before I knew what happened he had me up against his car with my broken arm behind my back and I was screaming like a girl. The good news was that my scream was genuine enough that he eased off. The bad news was that my arm hurt more than it had all day.

I did manage to get an apology out of the guard and an offer to drive me up to the doors. My humility in check, I graciously accepted and climbed in the passenger seat of the Explorer.

"So what did you do?" he asked.

"I tripped over a cat taking out the trash."

"Really?"

"Yeah. What's wrong with that?"

"I'm just saying," he paused and looked over his glasses, "I've heard better."

"What's that mean?"

"Nothing." he laughed to himself, but loud enough for me to hear. "We're here. Sorry again about, you know, your arm."

"It's fine. I deserved it."

"Yeah. You did. Good luck."

He reached across me and opened my door for me. It was a nice gesture but unnecessary; I still had one good arm. I nodded a goodbye and I stepped out of the vehicle. I bumped the door shut with my butt and headed for the automatic double doors leading to the emergency room.

Stepping inside, it took a moment for my eyes to adjust. For a few seconds, everything was monochromatic and out of focus. As the color filled in, the scene came together as I expected. The poor person hospital was always full of a colorful cast of characters. It really did explain the security guards actions.

I must have hit the pre-dinner rush. It looked like the waiting room in *Beetlejuice*, only not as funny. In the corner was a bum having a perfectly fine conversation with either himself or his imaginary friend. I couldn't hear what they were talking about, but it seemed they were arguing. Off to one side was a Mexican family waiting patiently with the father who had a blood soaked towel wrapped around his knee. A mid-twenties woman sobbing by the window was being watched by an elderly obese couple on matching oxygen tanks. A mom rocked her youngest son back and forth on her lap, while his older brother hobbled around in a leg cast, intentionally banging it off everything he could find.

It was hard to tell when most of the people had last showered. I started to question why I hadn't taken the shorter walk to the Health Department; the patrons were of equal caliber. Not that I was much better in my current state, but it was bad enough that I held my breath as I walked past certain individuals on my way to the admittance desk. It was a bad habit I had done since I was young. I had a real problem with breathing other people's air; after all, it had been inside them. It was gross.

I approached the admittance desk to greet the back of the male nurse working in that area. A huff let me know that he acknowledged my presence, but the Sudoku he was working on was of immediate concern. Without looking back, he leaned over in his chair, grabbed a clipboard with a stack of papers on it, placed a few x's on the front page, one on the next, and two more on the very last page.

He turned his chair enough to place the clipboard on the counter in front of me and then spun back around.

"Fill out all the blanks, sign where I placed the x's. Return the top sheet to me when you're done, take the clipboard and the rest of the paperwork with you when we call you back. Any questions?" He may as well have been a recorded message.

I didn't answer, because I knew it wouldn't matter. I slid the clipboard off the counter and took a seat a safe distance away from the crying girl. She appeared to have the best hygiene standards, minus the tears and snot, but I couldn't hold that against her.

I propped my left leg up on my right knee to form a table so I could fill out the paperwork. That was the first glimpse I had gotten at the underside of my feet. Crying girl also shot a peek at my feet and the face I made upon seeing them. She grinned a little through her sobs. We exchanged minuscule smiles, and she returned to her tears, only quieter. I returned to my paperwork.

I returned the top sheet to the nurse at the desk. He glanced over it to make sure I had followed his instructions, running his finger from blank to blank.

"So, no insurance?" he asked, knowing the answer.

"Nope."

"Have a seat."

I followed his new instructions. At twenty to thirty minute intervals, a different nurse would come out, call someone's name, and they would both disappear behind a set of heavy metal doors leading to exam rooms. For every person they took to the back, two more showed up through the front doors until eventually, I was surrounded by sick people.

The only thing I could find wrong with the gentleman to the left of me was that he smelled like urine and sweat and didn't know how to comb his hair. To the right was an elderly woman with white hair and pursed lips. She also smelled a bit like urine, but more like overwhelming old lady perfume. At least it lessened the urine stench.

Eventually, a tall, full-bodied black woman in her late twenties came through the doors and called my name. She must have just come on shift. Her scrubs were bright blue, still had pressed seams, her hair was perfectly curled and pulled back, and her lips were still shiny with gloss. Above all else, her attitude was the nicest I had run into that entire day.

"And what seems to be the problem, dear?" She chose not to look at my chart, instead opting for conversation to figure it out. "You look a bit...uncomfortable."

"A little." I responded, like all men do, diminishing the wound's severity in athinly veiled effort to sound manly.

"By a little, do you mean a lot?"

"Pretty much."

Approaching a row of exam rooms created by metal frames and sliding curtains hung from the ceiling, she pulled one curtain back and stuck her hand out, inviting me inside. I graciously nodded my head upon entry.

She followed me in to get some basic questions out of the way. She removed a blood pressure gauge from a three drawer plastic cart and slid it over my right arm. After a few pumps, she stared at her watch and started counting as she eased off.

"Your blood pressure is a little high, 138 over 74. Is it usually high?"

"I honestly have no idea."

"It could be from the pain, but you might want to have that checked out later. Let's get this arm checked out, Steven."

"Steve. Just Steve. My dad calls me Steven."

"Okay, Steve. Dr. Vasanta should be in to see you shortly."

"Thanks."

She gave me a perfect smile. Her teeth looked brilliantly white against her glossy lips and dark complexion. I reciprocated with my usual crooked smile. I used to smile normal until I lost one of my back teeth and couldn't afford to get it fixed. I was reduced to ensuring my teeth were closed when I smiled and if I did show teeth it was my left side.

I propped myself up on the bed and tried to find a comfortable spot. The crinkling of the paper cover was loud enough that I gave up and leaned against the side of the bed. The room I was in didn't have the things typically seen in a doctor's office. There were no posters on the ceiling of Garfield saying something witty. No pictures of Corvettes hung from the walls. Even the model organs that come apart in four pieces to show you what a diseased one looks like against a healthy one were nowhere to be found. I was flanked by blue curtains, showered in fluorescent lights, and bathing in the stench of hospital air. Nothing in the room was even remotely entertaining, let alone comforting.

Lost in thought, I jumped when the doctor pulled the curtain open to enter the room. I stood up, as if I wasn't supposed to lean on the bed. The wrinkled paper gave me away.

The doctor that entered was far from what I expected. There was a good chance that I had five years on him and as many inches. He was a short Indian man with thick black hair, copper skin, and a smooth face. His white coat seemed to swallow the tiny frame that carried it.

"Okay, Steve, I'm going to need you to drop your pants," he said not looking up from his clip board.

"Excuse me?"

He released a scripted chuckle. "I was just making a joke. I do not need you to drop your pants. Just your guard. I'm Dr. Vasanta". His hand extended out.

"Oh. Well, that's good. You had me worried." I made an exaggerated motion of wiping my brow before shaking his hand.

"So, you're experiencing some arm pain. Is that correct?"

"You could say that."

"Would you?"

"Well, yes. I would."

"And what were you doing when the pain started in your arm?" he asked with a smile on his face telling me he was expecting a smart ass answer.

"Falling on it," I replied.

He smirked, apparently satisfied with my answer. Even with his heavy accent, he was easy to understand and surprisingly pleasant to talk to. I would have traded this for every Garfield poster and car picture in every office I had ever been in.

Dr. Vasanta informed me that the nurse would be back in to take me to x-ray, inquired about painkiller allergies, and assured me he would return after the results. He proceeded to hand me a couple of pills that he was carrying in his pocket and left the room.

Within minutes, a new nurse entered the room with a small paper cup of water. Once I took the pills she led me to x-ray and waited for the completion of the procedure, though it seemed more so she could talk to the handsome x-ray technician than out of concern for me. When it was done, she returned me to the room and disappeared.

Dr. Vasanta returned frowning. "I'm afraid it is broken my friend."

"My arm?"

"Yes. Your radius and your ulna are both broken. There is some good news though."

"Really, what's that?" I asked.

"You get to pick your color of cast."

"Black."

"Except that. If you get it in black, it is difficult to sign."

That hadn't occurred to me, but at that time I didn't really care. At best, April would sign it, Larry would sign it, and then the people at work who act like they gave a shit would ask to sign it and I would let them. I wasn't up on cast etiquette, but I was certain it was rude to tell people they couldn't sign your cast, even if they were jerk offs.

"Blue."

"Actually, I only have white, glow in the dark, a very bright green, purple and pink."

I contemplated for a moment, before making my decision. I wasn't in the mood for fun, but if my cast lit up in the dark, it could be a constant reminder of what got me to that point in the first place. It was childish symbolism, but some symbolism was better than nothing.

"Glow in the dark, then."

"That's good. I had you pegged for a white one."

He left the room, and came back with a cart full of cast-making items and another nurse.

"About that arm," Dr. Vasanta started, "how did you fall on it?"

"I tripped over a cat taking the trash out."

"That is unfortunate. It must have been a very hard fall. I almost had to reset the bones." He was pushing. It was obvious he didn't believe me.

I stood my ground. "Yeah. It sure was."

"Did you hit anything specific when you fell?" He asked while wrapping the first layer around my arm.

"Not that I can remember."

"Hmmm."

He worked silently until the cast was complete. When it was done, the nurse left the room but Dr. Vasanta hung around. I knew a lecture was coming. It didn't bother me, because as little as I knew him, I knew he wouldn't be rude about it.

"Look, Steve," he coughed, "it isn't my place, I mean, it is my job to fix your bones, not your life, but typically only people with bad cover stories, neck tattoos, and eight year old boys ask for black casts. Whatever is making you feel this way, it probably isn't worth it."

"No offense, doctor, but you have no idea what's making me feel...whatever I'm feeling."

"But you are sad."

I gave him no response.

He continued. "Here is a card for a group that may be able to help." He reached into the same pocket where he kept the pain pills and pulled out two business cards. He tapped them in his hands before handing them over. "Put one on the refrigerator at home, maybe put the other in your wallet. You never know when things will get to you."

"Thanks." I looked at the cards without reading them and put them in my back pocket.

In the room next to me, a commotion began. It started with a few beeps, then a long tone. I could hear sneakers squeak on the floor as nurses scattered. The black nurse that had looked so clean and fresh before, popped her head in the room. Her lip gloss was gone, her hair was still in good shape, but fading fast, and the pleasant smile from before had turned into a grimace.

"Doctor, we need you over here, now." She did her best to appear calm.

"Certainly."

Dr. Vasanta left the room without another word. I was left in the room alone again. I wasn't sure if I should leave or stay, so I hung around. I could feel the tension next door escalating. The nurses talked less and the doctor yelled more. Even though I didn't understand what he was talking about, I knew it wasn't good.

From where I sat on the bed, I could see an open seam between two curtains leading into the room next door. My vantage point only allowed me to see the nurses scrambling and the patients arm, hanging limp off the side of the bed. I leaned back slightly and caught a glimpse of a salt and pepper bearded man in his mid to early fifties.

He briefly had a look of shock on his face, then he noticed me looking at him. For a moment, he just stared at me. Blue eyes stood apart from the paleness of his face. The wrinkles around them seemed to vanish. He almost looked comfortable. Then, he appeared to drift off to sleep. I felt a sensation run from the base of my skull down to my tailbone that felt like scolding hot water being poured down my spine. It quickly faded.

Dr. Vasanta stood on the opposite side of the bed, holding his other arm. He felt his wrist with one hand and was staring at an instrument mounted on the wall. The black nurse handed him a clipboard. He gently lowered the man's arm down to the bed and signed whatever was on the clipboard. As he walked out of my line of sight, another nurse pulled the sheet over the patient's head.

It wasn't the first time I had seen death. Hell, death was what got me put in jail. It was death that has haunted me since that day, and death was what I was chasing earlier that morning. It always seemed to elude me when I was looking for it, but was never a stranger when I wasn't.

I stared at the sheet and the man under it until Dr. Vasanta opened the curtain.

"I'm sorry, Steve, you probably did not need to see that."

"It's okay. I've seen worse. Is there anything else I need here?" I just wanted to get out. Fortunately, the pain had subsided, but I was exhausted and mentally numb.

"No, my friend. We are done. The cast should be ready to come off in about four to six weeks. As bad as the break is, I would probably keep it casted for at least the six weeks. When it's ready to come off, come in, and ask for me. I'll remove it, or see your primary care physician."

I nodded and headed back to the waiting room. I still had no money and no car. If I was going to get home, I was going to have to call April and explain why I didn't have my car or call Larry and explain how I broke my arm. Neither option sounded especially appealing, so I took a drink from the water fountain and began the long barefoot walk home.

Chapter 3

The buzzing sound of my doorbell stirred me from my solid slumber on

Saturday. I had covered my curtains with blankets to ensure no light would

enter my room, so when I woke, I was lost to the time of day. I flipped my

clock up to see 8:17 a.m. staring at me. My cast's luminescence had worn

off through the night, having nothing to charge it, but its presence was no

less obvious.

I rolled out of bed and placed my feet on the cool wood floor. The

buzzer went off again. The thought of putting pants on briefly crossed my

mind, but was quickly dismissed. If someone wanted something bad

enough to abuse my doorbell, they could surely deal with me in my

underwear.

I left my room and entered the living room of my apartment. The

living room consisted of the sitting area, dining area, and kitchen all in one.

The only wall separating them was the island between the kitchen and

dining area. The room's only windows were in the dining area. The glass ran

almost the full length from floor to ceiling and the windows were hidden by

the full length, deep purple blackout curtains. Much like my room, the only

way to tell if it was day or night was by the clock on the wall. I kept them

open most of the time, but the glare was counterproductive when it came

to reading books or watching television.

As I approached the door, the buzzer sounded again. I quickly

loosened the chain and turned the dead bolt. The door opened before I

could turn the knob. Thrusting her way in my apartment was April. She

was a few inches shorter than me, so I had to look down slightly to get a

full look at her. Her pulled back hair was a mess, was still in her Hello Kitty

pajama pants, a plain white T-shirt and blue plaid house shoes. While it was

clear that she hadn't done her full morning's regiment I could smell the

minty freshness of her toothpaste, and it made me insecure about my

breath when she wrapped her arms around me and kissed me.

"My God, I'm glad you're okay." she said.

"Why wouldn't I be?" I asked, though I knew damn well why I

wouldn't be.

"Last I talked to you, you were on your way to the hospital. You

said you would call me, but you didn't. I fell asleep on the couch, waiting,

woke up at six and have tried calling you since then, but you haven't been

answering. I was afraid something had happened, so I just came over."

"I appreciate the concern, but I'm fine."

"You're fine?"

"I am now." I tried to give her a smooth grin, implying that her

presence was the cause of my being 'fine'. I wasn't sure that I sold the idea

all that well.

We both stood just inside the doorway. The light from the hallway

barely lit my living room. April let loose of me enough to try to look me over and make her own medical judgment as to my condition. Not satisfied with the light, she flipped the switch by the door. She stepped in, forcing me to step back two steps. Her right foot slid back and shut the door behind her.

Using her hands, she moved my face left and right, picked up my right arm, then my left. She carefully grabbed my left arm above the cast and raised it so she could check it completely. I allowed the exam to continue. She turned me around, then back to the front.

With the exam complete, she gave me her assessment. "I suppose you're okay."

"Thanks, Doc."

"Don't be a smart ass," she said giving me a playfully disapproving smile.

"Is that how you treat all your patients?"

"Just the smart ass ones." She playfully gave me a push in the chest. "Now brush your teeth and get back to bed. Doctor's orders." She turned me again and started pushing towards the room.

We spent the rest of the morning floating around the apartment. April demanded that she make me lunch, to which I demanded that it be grilled cheese and tomato soup. She obliged, though it may have been due to a severe lack of groceries available in my apartment.

While cooking, she noticed the business card Dr. Vasanta gave me stuck to my fridge beneath a fridge magnet I bought at Niagara Falls with my parents in sixth grade. I noticed that she leaned in carefully to read the card and though she said nothing I could sense her wheels were turning.

"Can I ask you a question?"

"You just did." I had a feeling I knew what was coming, so I tried to divert with a smart ass comment. I was merely delaying the inevitable.

"Seriously."

"Yes," I knew what was coming and in a small way I wanted her to ask. "What's up?"

"What's that Fresh Start card on the fridge?" She knew what it was, considering it listed their services on the front of the card; the first being 'Counseling' in big bold letters preceded by a bullet point.

"It's no big deal. The doctor gave it to me. I think they have to hand so many out a month or something." I downplayed it. I was trying to act tough.

"So this doesn't have anything to do with the accident?" Her emphasis on 'the' and the way she softened the word 'accident' made it clear what she was referring to. She was talking about the accident that got me put in prison, ruined my life, and had me standing on the roof of the American National Bank building the previous morning.

Just mentioning the accident was enough to bring it to the surface, where it was still sensitive. When I kept the thought in the back of my mind it was a dull ache. When I actively thought about it, even after years had passed, it felt like a fresh wound. April knew it. She also knew that once brought up, it would consume me while the memory forced its way to the forefront. She sat silently, waiting to console me.

It happened early September, the first day of my senior year in high school. My best friend Ross Scott, his girlfriend, Kathy King, and my longtime girlfriend Michelle Fletcher thought it would be a good idea to skip school to start the year. Like all bad afterschool specials begin, we also thought it would be a good idea to go out to the country with as much pot as we could scrape together.

Most of my friends were poor, so coming from a bit of money, I was the only one with a car. My prized possession was a baby blue 1981 Camaro Z28. It was the last year the Camaro looked good. I bought it out of a salvage yard for $300 dollars, wrecked beyond belief, but with a good motor. My dad and I spent two years putting it back together.

My friends and I made it out to the country and parked in a field almost completely surrounded by trees. We weren't doing anything particularly stupid to start out with. We smoked our pot, broke off into our respective couples and made out in the trees. It seemed so much better than a day at school.

Around two, we decided it was time to head back home. We would get back home around the time school let out, and no one would be the wiser.

I zipped down the dirt roads, music blaring, using my emergency brake to make tight corners, never dropping below third gear. The girls were screaming, but they weren't asking me to slow down. The longer they went without saying stop, the more daring I became.

We popped over a set of train tracks. The car seemed to sprout wings. When we landed in a cloud of dust, everyone insisted we do it again. I should have called it good, but my need to impress girls overrode my sensibilities. I pulled the emergency brake and cranked the wheel. The car spun around facing the tracks again.

I carefully returned the transmission to first gear and revved the engine. I popped the clutch and was off. Second gear came and turned to third in an instant. I was in fourth before I hit the tracks. I could feel the tires lift off the ground as the car took flight. This is the part in the story where everyone expects that a train hit us. It didn't. We landed safely. A thousand times I had wished it had been a train. If it was a train, I could blame fate, chance, or just bad luck. Instead, I was left to blame myself.

It was when I pulled the e-brake to turn again that things went bad, I hadn't checked my speed, and it sent the car barrel rolling down the road, throwing me out of the car. I don't recall anything after the third roll. I woke up six days later. No one else woke up.

I was charged with three counts of vehicular manslaughter. I got off easy. All three of my friends' parents sued mine, ruining them financially. Three sets of parents never got to hug their children again, and mine got to hug me during forty-five minutes of visitation a week. I was left carrying three ghosts and a million demons.

For a moment, I had forgotten that April was there. She allowed me the time to collect myself. Taking that time answered her question. I broke down. It wasn't the first time, but it was one of the worst in recent memory. I buried my face in my hands and tried to hold back everything wanted to come out. I failed. April sat quietly next to me and rubbed my back. There was nothing for her to do but let me work through it.

I composed myself and apologized. She apologized in turn. Neither apology was necessary, but it seemed like the thing to do.

"Are you going to call them?" April asked, scratching my back.

I had forgotten what had brought the subject up. " Who?"

"Fresh Start."

"I don't know."

"It might help."

"I don't need help, I've got you."

It was cheesy and lame and mostly true. She did as much for me as any therapist could. She usually was the one to catch the brunt of it when my past bothered me. I never spoke about my past to Larry or my parents. I had cost my parents so much, and not just financially, that when I spoke to them I always told them I was doing great. I wasn't fond of lying to them but I couldn't bear to be the cause of one more second of concern, pain, or disappointment in their lives. They already sacrificed too much.

She let it drop for the moment, though I knew she wouldn't forget about it. I changed the subject by mentioning that my cast glowed in the dark. She knew it was diversion, but played nice and acted intrigued. It wasn't what I was going for, but she suggested we go in the room and shut the lights out to test it. I wasn't going to argue.

We ordered take out Chinese food and rented two movies from the pay per view channel to cap off the evening. Sunday morning, she got up to go to church. Sometime after her wild days ended, she found Jesus. She wasn't the kind to bludgeon me with the notion of going to church, she just thought it might help. She hadn't sold me on the idea.

"You sure you don't want to go?" she asked smelling of perfume and brushed teeth.

"I'm good. You have fun." I replied, smelling.

"Call Fresh Start."

"We'll see. I doubt they're open on Sundays."

"Then call and leave a message."

"Fine, I will, now get out of here," I responded with artificial malice. "And have fun."

"I will. I'll call you tonight." She leaned over the bed and kissed me on the cheek and tossed what bit of hair I had.

She left and I was there by myself. The only sound in the apartment was the sound of the elderly couple on the floor above mine getting ready for Sunday brunch with their grandchildren. I knew if I was going to get back to sleep, I would have to hurry. Their grandchildren were very young and very noisy.

44

I pulled my comforter up over my head to block out any possibility of light and reduce ambient noises. Any other Sunday I would have been out in minutes, but there was too much on my mind. I tossed and turned. The thoughts of the accident, my latest suicide attempt, and Fresh Start rolled around in my head, noisier than any group of bratty kids could be.

The longer I lie there awake, the angrier I became. Sleep was one of the few pleasures in life I didn't feel bad for indulging in, and it was being stolen from me. After an hour, I resigned myself to getting up. I wrapped a plastic grocery bag around my cast and hopped in the shower.

Cleaned up, I put on a pair of shorts and positioned myself on the couch. I flipped through a few channels on the television before shutting it off. I paced back and forth around my place, looking for things to do to occupy my time, but nothing presented itself to me.

I opened and closed the fridge a dozen times looking for something to eat to satisfy the boredom. Each time I grabbed the handle, the Fresh Start card flashed in front of me. Eventually, I tried flipping it over to the blank side, but much to my chagrin, the card was double-sided.

Shifting to the cabinets, I finally found a box of cereal to munch on. I grabbed a bowl and prepared to pour and then I realized I would have to get back in the fridge for milk, so I decided to sit on the couch and eat from the box. Knowing the television was no good for entertainment, I turned on the radio. Six minutes passed and I hadn't heard a single song, so I clicked the radio off.

There I sat, on my couch, barely dressed, in relative darkness, with only the sound of crunching cereal and the pitter-patter of brat children in the apartment above me to keep me company. It appeared boredom was inevitable, much like the depression that usually accompanies boredom. Refusing to give up the fight, I strode back into the kitchen, grabbed the business card from my fridge, snatched up my phone, and dialed the number at the bottom.

I tapped my foot while the line rang. One ring, then two, then three before the other end picked up.

An automated message machine chimed in. "Thank you for calling Fresh Start. Our normal business hours are between the hours of 8 a.m. and 5 p.m., Monday through Friday. If you know your party's extension you may dial it at any time. If you wish to leave a message, press zero now."

I pressed zero. "Hi, my name is Steve, and I was given one of your cards at the doctor's office the other day and I was thinking about setting up an appointment or whatever." I proceeded to leave my number and the best hours to reach me.

I hung up the phone and tossed it on the couch. I followed shortly behind it. My message kept running through my head, mostly because I thought it sounded stupid. Every time I left a message on a machine, I spent the next thirty minutes analyzing if I sounded like an idiot. I was usually pretty sure I did.

46

Having a sense of accomplishment comforted me enough that I could settle down long enough to watch some television, and I even managed to doze off, until April called. She wanted to know if I called Fresh Start, which I assured her I did and backed it up by repeating the automated message. She even assured me that she didn't think I sounded like an idiot.

I spent the rest of my Sunday preparing myself for the next day. I packed a lunch, which consisted of ramen noodles and a soda, pressed my polo shirt, and shaved for the first time since Friday.

Monday morning came early. I awoke from my slumber at 4:37 a.m. The only light in the room was the red numbers on the alarm clock and an extremely faint glow from my cast. I tucked my cast under the blanket and rolled away from the clock, but sleep would not return. It was nerves and I knew it.

April hadn't pushed the issue too much, but she was just one person. I was about to head to work with dozens of people who have nothing better to do in life but converse about other people's misfortunes and shortcomings. Larry was sure to press me about why I was gone. Those who wanted to be seen as caring would ask if I was okay, if I needed anything, and that would lead into asking how it happened. The questions would be followed by people wanting to sign the cast. The cast was on the verge of becoming the focal point of the entire day. The guy inside the cast wanted to stay as far away from the limelight as possible.

The time for me to get up arrived before I could slow my busy mind. I rolled over to the alarm side of my bed and switched it off before it could sound. I huffed as I raised myself from the bed and headed for the shower. Before leaving the house, I put on an oversized black windbreaker attempting to conceal my cast. Other than the portion that covered my hand, it did a fantastic job.

My arrival at work was no different from any other day. I walked past the reception desk for the building and was greeted warmly by the elderly woman stationed there.

"Good morning. Have a great day."

That was her line. Every day, anyone that walked through the front doors at the LaRose Tower was greeted by a short twiggy white-haired woman, bidding them a good morning, then demanding that they have a great day. Nothing less than great would suffice. I often wondered if she secretly harbored a desire to tell people what she really thought.

"Good morning. Except to you. You're an asshole."

"Good morning, young miss. Did you borrow your business attire from a lady of the night?"

"Good morning. You do know that cologne is not the same as a bath, right?"

"Good morning. How was your failed suicide attempt, loser?"

48

These were all things I imagined her saying. It was probably that I wanted to say these things, but I had a long history of biting my tongue. Telling people what I felt was never my strong suit.

"Good morning," I replied as I walked by.

"What happened to your arm?" she asked at my back.

I paused for a moment to decide if I was going to answer. Had I not physically stopped, I would have pretended I didn't hear her, but it was too late. "Oh, just fell taking the trash out. Tripped over a cat. Just one of those things, I replied with a shrug.

"Well I sure hope you're okay."

"I'm sure I will be. Thank you."

Before the thank you came out, she was already bidding someone else a good morning. I seized the opportunity to escape into an elevator. Like most other mornings, the elevator was filled with people I didn't know who worked on different floors, and by the time I exited on the eighth floor, I was alone. Thank God for staggered schedules. The anonymity of the elevator gave me a brief period of rest before the next round of questions.

Once on my floor, I navigated the sea of cubicles, offices, water coolers, and motivational posters. The small business finance department was segregated by the time zones in which the customers resided. Therefore, the east coast department was already there, I was in the Midwest, but earlier than most of my coworkers. The west coasters, or

'Beach Bums' as their supervisor dubbed them in a big laminate banner hanging over their department, weren't due in for two hours, so I weaved through their department first.

Next were the mountain timers, or Rockies as they liked to be called. That wasn't what we called them, but that was the furthest thing from my mind. My only concern was to get to my cubicle unnoticed.

"Where the fuck have you been, Nancy No-Show?" Larry greeted me with his usual zeal.

He sat, chair turned facing my desk, impatiently waiting my return. His small size required that he lower his chair so his feet touched the floor while he worked. A fact I made sure to remind him of as often as possible. At thirty-five, he still looked to be in his early twenties, save a few random grey hairs on his short, curly, black hair. His face was always clean-shaven. It was his opinion that black people looked strange with facial hair. I was never really sure what gave him that opinion, except that he was raised by a white family that adopted him, so he felt it necessary to have some opinion about his heritage.

"Good morning, Sunshine," I said, placing my things on my desk. I reached under my desk and powered on my computer. The roundabout was going to take a while, so I decided to get settled before engaging in verbal combat. I draped my windbreaker over the back of my chair, exposing my cast.

"What's with the cast?"

"You know, you sure ask a lot of questions," I replied.

"So," Larry said bluntly.

I wanted to keep Larry at bay for a bit longer. "How was your weekend?" I asked.

"Fine. My girlfriend was over all weekend, but she brought her kids, so no sex for me. What's with the cast?" He rushed his answer to get to mine.

"Why can't you have sex while her kids are there? Aren't they both under five? Don't they take naps?"

"Dude, you've been to my apartment. Two bedrooms, walls like paper maché. Seriously, what's with the cast?" he pressed on.

"What are casts usually for?"

"Assholes that keep jacking with me. I know people." He shook his fist at me.

"Just because you're black doesn't make you a gangster. The closest you've been to the hood was that Starbucks on 3rd street, six blocks from the homeless shelter."

The closest he had ever come to being gangster was when he bought a small-caliber pistol to keep under the seat in his vehicle. He fired it once out in the country just to do it and the remaining five bullets remained in the gun, waiting to rust away.

"Doesn't mean I won't fuck you up."

"You wouldn't hit a guy with a broken arm would you?" I waved my cast in front of me.

"I'm thinking about it."

With the niceties out of the way, I gave in and recanted my tail of tripping over a cat. Larry confirmed his belief in the story by calling me a dumb ass. It was a title I couldn't argue with, though for a different reason.

"I'm glad it was that. I thought you were going to off yourself," he said jokingly. "You weren't yourself last week at all. And I would have called this weekend to check, but I'm not your mom and we aren't gay together."

"Thank God for that. Last I checked, breaking your arm was a really difficult way to kill yourself. Seriously, I was just taking a personal day, you know... my thing happened in September. Just needed to clear my head a bit," I said. He knew about my accident and completely understood. It was enough for him. He didn't mention it again.

The remainder of the morning was spent with random coworkers stopping by my desk casually, asking me about my arm, signing my cast, then wishing me well. Larry spent that time finding various office supplies to hit my cast with to see if I felt the impact. I obliged him in his experiment until he wanted to staple something to it. I had to draw the line somewhere.

When lunch came around Larry and I joined April in the cafeteria on the second floor. I had intentionally left the lunch I brought at my desk.

My appetite was returning after a few days of not wanting to eat anything and I thought a package of instant noodles wasn't going to satisfy.

Despite the fact that I could still use my left hand to hold my tray, April and Larry took turns treating me like an invalid. April refused to let me carry my tray. I had to pick the items, put them on the tray, and she would slide it down the line. Larry wouldn't let me get a fountain drink. April was being nice. Larry was patronizing me, and he mixed my soda with half diet.

Conversation was light, as the newness of my condition had worn off, we had already discussed our weekends, and it was too early on a Monday for anything interesting to have happened. Before we left, April asked if Fresh Start had called me back yet. I explained that it had only been twelve hours and that I was sure they would, but she needed to be patient. I was appreciative that she waited until Larry was out of earshot before asking.

The rest of the week went the same way, except as the week went on, April's insistence on me calling them back became more overbearing. My reprieve started on Friday, as April took a long weekend to fly back home to Indiana to visit her parents. At least I thought it was a reprieve until my phone rang at 6 a.m. on Saturday morning. The first time, I let it go to voicemail. When it rang again at 6:05 a.m., I stormed my way across the room to my phone and snatched it up.

I took a deep breath and a long exhale before answering to calm myself. "Yes?"

A soft, seductive female voice greeted me from the other end of the line. "Good morning, Steven. I hope I didn't wake you."

The gentleness of the voice disarmed me. I even overlooked her calling me Steven, though I distinctly remember using 'Steve' on the answering machine. "No, I was just brushing my teeth. With whom am I speaking?" I wasn't sure why I said I was brushing my teeth, nor was I sure why I said the word 'whom'.

Chapter 4

"My name is Hala. I'm with Fresh Start. I apologize for calling so early, but I didn't get your message until late last night and I would really like to arrange a meeting. I think I have an opportunity you might be interested in." Her voice was familiar, but I couldn't place it.

"Opportunity? I thought Fresh Start was a counseling group."

"Not exactly," she chuckled under her breath, "but I think we can help you."

"You don't even know what's wrong with me. What makes you so sure you can help me?" I was immediately on gaurd.

"The suicide attempt isn't why you called?"

The phone fell out of my hand and slid under my dresser.

"Shit."

I scrambled around on the floor looking for it. My room was still dark, and I found myself panicking. Other than Jesus, no one knew about my attempt, and I doubted anyone else could. I found my phone and it was still on. Hala was waiting patiently on the other end. I composed myself.

"What makes you think I tried to kill myself?"

"You received a card for a help line at a hospital emergency room. It would only stand to reason that you tried to kill yourself. That and the doctor said you weren't a very good liar; you were hiding something," she responded quickly. It was as if she had anticipated the question.

"But if you're not a real help line, what are you, and why did I get your card? What if I had really needed help? What if I was going to kill myself, hypothetically of course? It's been a week since I called you." The longer I talked, the more I wound myself up.

I could nearly hear Hala smile on the other end of the line. "Steven, listen. I know you have a number of questions. I have answers for most, if not all, of them. Over the phone is not the most appropriate place to discuss these things. I would like to schedule a meeting if that works for you."

"Sure. Why not? When?" As defensive as I was, I felt like I needed to meet this woman.

"I'm free all day. Why don't you go back to sleep, call me when you get up, and we can find somewhere to meet?"

"Do you not have an office?"

"I have a very nice office, I assure you, but it's Saturday. Do you like being in the office on Saturdays?" she asked.

"Good point."

She gave me her cell phone number so I could call her back. Having no paper handy, I scribbled the number on the bottom edge of my cast, mixed in amongst a few signatures. We exchanged goodbyes, and I crawled back into my cold sheets.

56

My bed offered me little comfort. I ran the conversation through my head a thousand times before I gave up trying to go back to sleep. I didn't call Hala back immediately, though. I didn't want her to think I hadn't gone back to sleep or that something was bothering me.

I piddled about, ate some toast, brushed my teeth, took a shower, and got half-dressed. Since I was up so early on a Saturday, I turned on the television and stopped at the first cartoon I found. I watched about fifteen minutes before I realized I had no idea what the hell was going on. I couldn't tell what any of the characters were supposed to be, what they were talking about, or if it was supposed to be funny. What ever happened to rabbits, ducks, and mice?

The clock struck nine before I called Hala back. I would have waited until ten, but I didn't want her to think I was a loser that slept days away. She answered after only a few rings.

"Did you get some more sleep?"

"Yeah, a bit." I said keeping my fib small.

"Great. I live outside of town, so it takes me a while to get in. What do you say to lunch at Bucci's say, around one thirty?"

"Is that the place at 73rd and Market on the East side?"

"Yes."

"Great. I'll see you then."

"Fantastic." She prepared to hang up and then changed her mind. "Steven."

"Yes?"

"You didn't go back to sleep did you?"

I hesitated long enough that it was obvious I was trying to process the lie to truth benefit ratio, so I just told the truth. "No."

She laughed softly. "See you at 1:30."

Bucci's was an upscale Italian restaurant with a menu entirely in Italian. It was the kind of place where I would order by pointing at the menu to save myself the embarrassment of murdering the language in front of someone who speaks it fluently. Larry referred to Bucci's as a 'sure thing' when he went on dates. I had never been.

After my bed was half covered with clothes I put on and didn't like, I scolded myself for acting like a girl. I hung everything back up and settled on a pair of nice jeans and a long sleeve black button down. It was usually against my rules to wear anything with a collar on the weekend, but I wanted to make a decent first impression, though I wasn't sure why.

Traffic in the non-shopping district of downtown was light on Saturdays so I cut through it to get to the East side. The clock in my car read 1:10 when I pulled into the parking lot of Bucci's. I like being early. In my book, if you aren't ten minutes early, you're late. I think I got that from my father.

I waited in the covered entryway for Hala. Every few minutes, I would look at my left arm only to realize it was casted and then look at my right for my watch. At 1:21 I considered calling her to make sure she was going to be there. After a few minutes of deliberation I chose against it.

While I waited I tried to imagine what Hala looked like. I should have asked how I would know who she was, but I wasn't very good at thinking that far ahead. Based on her sexy and soft voice, I imagined a tall sexy brunette with large breasts, but I didn't figure I would get that lucky. I settled on the fact that she was probably a large, frumpy blonde.

At 1:29, a silver Mercedes S600 pulled into the parking lot. The person who stepped out of it was anything but a frumpy blonde. She was gorgeous. Thick black silky hair, dark skin, manicured fingernails, and a skirt decorated a perfectly shaped body. I said a small prayer hoping it was Hala. She pulled a pack of cigarettes out of her purse and lit one. She took a few drags, then stamped it out, replaced the pack in her hand with a stick of gum, and then pulled a small bottle of perfume out of her purse, spraying it into the air just around her. She didn't notice me until she had completed her ritual.

"Steven," she said from across the parking lot raising her hand. I wanted to correct her and say Steve, but I couldn't bring myself to do it.

I recognized the voice, but she also looked extremely familiar. I couldn't place where I had seen her until she approached me and took off her sunglasses. It was the nosey woman from the elevator in the American National Bank building.

"Hala?" I asked when she was within conversation range.

"Yes. Were you expecting someone else?" she replied.

"Well, to be honest, I wasn't expecting you."

She grinned. "Is that a bad thing?"

"Not entirely." I wanted to say something smoother, but chatting with beautiful women wasn't my strong suit.

I held the door open for her and she walked past me wafting the smell of cocoa butter into the air. I enjoyed a deep breath of it before following her inside, not in a creepy way, but in the way a person enjoys the smell of someone baking cookies.

She approached the host, whispered something in his ear, and we were immediately led to a corner booth near the back. I couldn't tell if she knew the host or was getting by just on her looks. The place was just as Larry had described it; a sure thing. Even during the day, the light inside was low. There were four main dining rooms, each with their own brick oven burning constantly to make the fresh bread they bring to your table. The interior was filled with dark wood, plants, black and white photos and vintage Italian product containers. I made a note to save up and bring April back.

I let Hala slide into her seat before I took mine. The deep brown leather cushion swallowed me as I sat down. My cast made a thud when I folded my arms on the table. Hala adjusted her blouse. Despite her wish to not be in the office on a Saturday, she was certainly dressed for it.

I started the conversation. No need to let her get the upper hand. "I think I have a few questions."

She raised her hand to stop me. "I'm sure you do, but no questions before wine. Do you like Cabernet?"

"Sure." I didn't even like wine. She already had the upper hand.

We made small talk about the weather while we waited for the mousey waiter to come take Hala's wine order. He swung by, she told him the name of a wine and a year and he disappeared. Moments later he returned with a bottle, an opener, a towel, and two small glasses. He cut the foil, used the corkscrew, popped the cork out, wrapped the towel around the bottle and poured a small amount in the two smaller glasses.

I followed Hala's lead as she swirled the deep red wine around inside the glass. It left streaks halfway up, and made the whole booth smell like wood barrels and dry flowers, or so she would later tell me. It smelled like old socks to me. I tipped my glass back when she did. I gulped mine down, while she chewed the wine a moment before swallowing. A simple nod from her and the waiter poured two glasses half full and placed them in front of us.

"We'll need a moment before we're ready to order," Hala told the waiter and he glided away. "Do you know what you want?"

"Actually, no. I was planning on pointing at something at random and praying it was good."

"Have you ever been here?"

"No ma'am," I replied.

"Please. Don't call me ma'am." She reached across the table and almost touched my hand, but backed off. "I'm not your mother. And how did you know where the place was if you hadn't been?"

"From a friend. He brings girls here on dates; well, he did, when he was single." Not that she needed to know that.

"Probably works well. Anyway, do you like veal?"

"Never had it."

"Then how about I order for you."

"Great. Then can I ask my questions?"

"Maybe."

Hala was a very in control woman. She had a quick answer for everything, even if it wasn't the answer I wanted. I had a feeling that when I asked my questions, I was only going to get the answers she wanted to give, and nothing else.

The waiter returned, Hala ordered two orders of veal, then folded her arms on the table to match mine. I couldn't help but notice that doing so lifted her breasts a little closer to her chin. The whole time I sat there, I felt like I was breaching my relationship contract with April.

"First off, what were you doing at the American National Bank the other day?" I asked.

"Business."

I wasn't going to let her generic answer stand. "What kind of business?"

"Well, that's what we are here to talk about today, now isn't it?"

"Is it? Were you counseling someone else at the same bank?"

"That's not what I do. It's actually quite the opposite."

"What are you, an assassin?" The question sounded better in my head than when I asked it.

The apparent absurdity of the question made her choke on the sip of wine she was working on when I asked it, though her reaction was slightly exaggerated. She dabbed her chin with her napkin while holding back laughter. "Not so much."

"So are we going to play twenty questions all day, or are you going to tell me what's going on?" While I enjoyed her company, her inability to give me a straight answer on anything was beginning to grate on my nerves.

"That depends on you. I need you to be honest with me, and then I can be open with you. That's how this has to work."

"How what works?" I picked up my wine and downed half of it. "And when have I not been honest with you?"

"Since we met actually," Hala said before taking a sip of her wine. "For example, when we first met, you said you didn't need a ride, that you had your car; you didn't. When I called, you said you were brushing your teeth; you were sleeping."

"That's it? Those are tiny white lies. No one really gives a...no one really cares about those lies. But sure, I didn't have my car, and yes I was sleeping. Better?"

She sat back in her chair. "It's a start. Anything else you want to get off your chest?"

"Like?"

"Oh, I don't know. Maybe about how you broke your arm?"

"You mean how I tried to kill myself?"

The fact that the words came out of my mouth left me feeling a little dirty. I didn't even know this woman, and I was telling her things I didn't even tell my girlfriend, best friend, or family. I hadn't admitted it to anyone, and now I was baring everything to a stranger. It was more shocking than it was uncomfortable. In a way, however; it was relieving.

She allowed me a moment to come to grips with my admission before speaking. "See, don't you feel better?"

The waiter appeared with our dishes before I had a chance to answer. He placed two hot plates in front of us, turned them so that the veal was the focal point of the plate, asked if we needed anything else, and left.

Hala carefully cut a piece of meat and gently placed it in her mouth with her fork. She chewed slowly and deliberately, as if she was analyzing every fiber of the meat. I took a bite of my food and saw why she took her time. It was pretty amazing veal, though I had no reference point for bad veal.

"Now that I've told you all my deep dark secrets, can we talk about why I'm here?" I asked. My guard was much lower after a bit of wine and food.

"You're here because you aren't happy with your life. I'm here to talk about your future. Let me ask you a question."

"Is it going to answer mine?"

"In time." Hala paused briefly. "Do you believe in the afterlife? Heaven, hell, and all that?"

"Oh."

"Oh what?"

I placed my napkin on the table. "Going to church isn't going to fix my problems. Thank you for your time," and I began to scoot out of the booth, though I really didn't want to leave.

"Sit down. I'm not from a church. If you would just listen and answer my questions this would probably go much smoother. "

I slid back into my seat. Something other than her looks was keeping me there. Curiosity was part of it. A desire to fix myself was also a contributing factor, regardless of how ridiculous it seemed.

"You're not from a church, you aren't an assassin, and you're not from a self-help group. Should I continue naming things you are not, or are you going to tell me what you are?"

"I run the local branch of an office responsible for verifying deaths and sorting out where people go when they die."

"You mean like a coroner?"

"Not where the body goes; where the soul goes."

I over exaggerated a snicker. She wanted me to tell the truth while she blew smoke up my ass. "You're sounding an awful lot like a church for not being church."

"Steven, I still don't think you're getting it." She rolled her eyes and sighed. "You know the guy with the skeleton face, black robe, scythe?"

"The grim reaper?" I replied wondering where she was going with the guessing game.

"Yes. I'm that guy, or girl. Well, I'm one of many. Can't be everywhere you know."

The thought that I was having lunch with a grim reaper was amusing. The fact that she seemed level headed and very convinced that she was a grim reaper was unsettling. I didn't believe her, but I thought I would give her a shot to prove it. Crazy or not, I didn't mind her company.

I reached out and touched her hand that was lying on the table. We locked our gazes. Mine was full of determination. Hers was confusion initially, then understanding and then the smile came. Instead of moving her hand, she placed her right hand on mine. Her touch was remarkably comforting. Then I watched as she tried poorly to hold back a gut laugh, until she couldn't any longer.

She laughed so hard that the other patrons around us began to notice. It put me in the uncomfortable position of being near the center of attention. I started sweating.

I leaned across the table. "What's so damn funny? Everyone is looking at us."

She composed herself long enough to answer through her laughter. "You were just trying to kill yourself weren't you?"

"No. And could you say that any louder? Jesus."

"Yes you were. " Hala paused to wipe the tears from her eyes. "I regret to inform you that it doesn't work like the cartoons or movies. Everything I touch doesn't die. Essentially I'm just a witness; I have a few other duties, but that's neither here nor there. I don't actually kill anyone." She fanned herself with her hands. "Thank you. I haven't laughed like that in a long time."

"I'm glad I could amuse you. And if it doesn't work like that, then how does it work? On top of that, how do I know you aren't just full of shit? I mean, this is all pretty unbelievable."

"Because I was sent to collect you when you threw yourself off that building, and since I wasn't there, you experienced a miracle."

"What miracle?"

"The part where you lived. You weren't supposed to. You should be dead and in hell already, but instead, you're having veal and wine with me. That should count as two miracles in my book."

"And..."

"And, unlike Mr. Roger Metzger that was in the room next to you at the hospital, you get another chance."

"You were there?"

"Of course; how do you think that doctor got those Fresh Start cards?"

Though I had been told to go to hell more times than I could remember, no one had ever said that's where I was supposed to be. Whether I believed in heaven or hell or not, it was a rough thing to hear. Hala seemed convinced that everything she told me was true. Her conviction helped me believe her. She had no reason to lie to me, as far as I could tell. I still wasn't fully convinced, but she did seem to know more than she should. The thought that she was a stalker was absurd. I wasn't a bad-looking guy, but she had the kind of beauty that bent the will of men.

My appetite had long since left, but I continued picking at my food like a sulking child. Hala finished her plate and slid it into the center of the table. I stared down at my plate and would occasionally look up to see her looking at me. She wasn't staring; she was watching. She was watching my reactions, waiting for me to come back with another round of questions or a smart ass comment.

It didn't come. I had nothing to say. A thousand questions rolled around in my head, but none of them seemed like real questions.

"I wasn't trying to upset you. It was simply the truth." She placed her hand on mine. "I know about your past, the things you've done. I think I can help keep you out of hell, but you're going to have to trust me. This is your *last* chance at redemption."

She said *last* the way a game show host asks if the contestant is sure of their answer. Whether it was a trick or not, something about the word last filled me with anxiety.

"This all sounds fine and dandy, and you're very convincing, but in all fairness, how am I supposed to take everything you say at face value? I don't think you're crazy, but I'm not big on faith."

She gave me a little smile that told me I was about to get the proof I was asking for.

"See that older man over there with his wife. The one in the khakis and white button down?"

"Yeah."

"Here in about..." she looked at the clock on the wall, "ten minutes he's going to have a heart attack."

"He's going to fucking die?" I asked in a loud whisper.

"Not here. He's going to go in surgery later. I'll get him then."

"That's fucked up."

"Why?"

I didn't have a why.

"Okay, people die, I get that but why him and why right now?"

"I don't know why him. I don't pick them, I just do my job."

It bothered me how she talked about death as if it was as serious as a hang nail. I didn't say anything more. I sat and quietly drank my wine and waited for the khakis guy to have a heart attack. As I watched the clock on my phone, Hala sat across from me quietly, hands folded on the table. Eight minutes passed.

"You might want to call 911 so I don't have to get him here."

"Haha."

"I'm serious."

Before I could respond with another 'haha', I glanced over, and the man's face was turning bright red and he was sweating. His wife started to panic. I started dialing 911.

Fortunately, Bucci's was a nice enough restaurant that at any given time there was usually at least one doctor dining there. On this particular Saturday there were two. I only knew that because both men arrived at the gentleman's table at approximately the same time and both were trying to reassure his wife that they were doctors and that they knew what they were doing.

The younger doctor chose words over action and asked everyone to step back and requested that someone call 911. My natural instinct was to not mention that I was already calling EMS. I didn't want the attention that comes with being involved. Hala's natural instinct was to point it out.

70

"We're calling them now," she said loud enough to make sure everyone knew.

Beads of sweat formed instantly on my forehead as I felt everyone turn their attention to us. As quickly as we were thrust into the limelight, we were out. Everyone's attention turned to the two doctors and the man lying on the floor. It didn't take long for the younger doctor to realize that he was of little help, as the older doctor had immediately sprung into action. Looking for something to do, he approached me and asked if I wanted him to speak to EMS. Without words I gratefully handed him my phone. He took it and returned to the center of the commotion.

When all the dust settled and the man was on his way to the hospital, I found myself planted in my seat staring into space.

"How partial are you to your job?" Hala asked, bringing me back to reality.

"Not very."

"Then put in your notice. You're coming to work for me."

"Doing what?"

"We'll get to that when you start. Don't worry, it pays good."

After that, Hala refused to talk about work, but she insisted on staying until the bottle of wine was empty. Against my better judgment I obliged. When the last sip was gone, Hala demanded that she take me home and that she would just have my car towed back to my house. Given my track record, I agreed.

We walked to her Mercedes quietly. I was trying to maintain composure. I wasn't drunk, but I wasn't far from it either. She unlocked the doors remotely, and I slid into the passenger seat. The cool tan leather felt good on the nape of my neck when I cocked my head back.

She asked me my address and she pecked it into her GPS with her fingernails. The car barely made a noise when it started. Only a slight rumble could be felt in the seat. Hala put her hand on the shifter to put it in reverse when she looked over at me.

"Not going to wear a seat belt?"

"If you haven't got me yet, I figure I'm in a pretty safe place."

Hala simply smirked and backed out.

Chapter 5

In the parking lot of my apartment, I was feeling somehow further away from sober. Conversation had been slim on the drive over and I wasn't sure if that was a good thing or a bad thing. April called during the drive, but I ignored it. I didn't want to explain that I just had lunch and drinks with an extremely beautiful and rich grim reaper who offered me a job doing God knows what shortly after I tried to kill myself, and to top it off, I found out I should be burning in hell. A lie would have to be carefully crafted. Again.

"What am I supposed to tell my current employer? If I tell them I'm going to work for...you they'll think I'm crazy. Assuming I'm interested, of course." I was more interested than I wanted to let on.

"Why would you tell them anything? But more importantly, what are you going to tell your girlfriend?" Hala said with a smile.

"I didn't tell you I had a girlfriend."

"You didn't need to. I could tell you felt guilty looking at my breasts all day."

I didn't have anything to come back with and Hala didn't seem upset. Lying to her didn't seem to get me anywhere, so I side-stepped the situation. "Yes, what will I tell my employer and girlfriend?"

"Tell them you found a data entry job on the internet with better pay and a solid retirement package. We operate out of the LDI Credit building downtown."

"The credit card company?"

"Yeah. The office is on the 11th floor. Be there two Mondays from now, 8 a.m. and call me, anytime, if you have any questions."

"I have a lot of questions."

"I guess you will just have to call me a lot." She smirked, "I would invite myself up for a drink, but I have some collecting to do, and you have to call your girlfriend back."

She left me standing in the parking lot as she sped off to go do death things. I wasn't the brightest, but I was fairly certain that she was hitting on me. I didn't mind at all.

Back in the comfort of my apartment, I called April back at her parents' house.

April answered after one ring. "Well, hello, stranger. Where have you been all day?"

"Well, dear, if you must know, I had a job interview." I figured that showing ambition might put her at ease.

"Really? I didn't know you were looking?" My plan worked. She was no longer bothered by my unaccounted for time, and was now curious to see what had come of my interview.

"I've been looking for a while; I just didn't say anything because I didn't know if anything would come of it. They contacted me early this morning and I went to the interview this afternoon."

"Why on a Saturday?"

"I don't know, maybe I'm taking someone else's spot and they don't want them to know that they're looking. Anyway, they offered me a job, and I think I'm going to take it. What do you think?" I wanted April to feel like she had a hand in the decision. She always felt better when I included her on things and I was still feeling bad for looking at Hala's breasts all afternoon.

April took a second to respond. I knew she was trying to formulate a series of questions so she could accurately gauge if I should take the position or not. She could already tell I was planning on taking it, just from the way I spoke, but she wanted it to feel like a long, thought out decision.

She was a calculating individual. Even her spontaneous moments were well planned out events, like the time she wanted to join the Mile High Club, so she planned a two-day vacation for us in New Mexico and intentionally bought tickets in the very back of the plane. We did our deed in the airplane bathroom, ate dinner that night, stayed in a seedy motel, and flew back the next morning. Her meticulous planning made leaving my comfort zone feel safe.

April cleared her throat and put on her serious voice. "First off, is the pay better?"

"They said it was, but I didn't get an exact number."

"And what company is this? Are they going to be around for a while?"

"It's LDI, the credit card company. I'm fairly certain they aren't going anywhere. I mean, it isn't LDI, but they are in the same building."

I could hear her scratching notes on a piece of paper.

She continued the interrogation. "Benefits?"

"A very sound retirement package and I think they even offer health."

"You know it turns me on when you talk about retirement. And with your recent track record, a little health insurance couldn't hurt. Last question. Why are you looking for a new job? Right now you get to see me every day, you sit next to Larry, the pay isn't bad, and you have some vacation time built up. Does this have anything to do with us?"

"I just need a change in my life. I've got to do something different. Yes, I'll miss seeing you every day, I might even miss Larry's dick jokes every morning, but this isn't to get away from either of you. I promise."

April was satisfied with my answers for the moment, allowing the conversation to change directions. We played the 'I miss you more' game for about two minutes before she said she had to take care of a few things before bed. She asked if I was going to be free Sunday after her flight got

76

in, to which I responded with the offer to cook dinner at her place while she unpacked.

I was harboring a mild case of guilt from not being completely honest with her, not to mention stress from figuring out how I would even begin to logically and convincingly describe the absurd nature of the job. The question was going to have to be raised with Hala about how honest I could be with people I was close to, but I didn't want to call her just yet. I began to wonder if lying was going to become a regular thing for me. It was that thought that continued floating to the top as I drifted off to sleep.

I spent Sunday morning and afternoon resisting the urge to call Hala. I wanted to talk to her again, but my guilt mechanism was firing on all cylinders. There was something inside me that wanted Hala to make me feel better about the decision. I would pick up the phone, walk to my room, sit on the bed, turn the phone on, then shut it off and take my place in front of the television. Next commercial break, I would stare at the phone and tell myself that I would call on the next break. Repeat, repeat, repeat, until it was time to get ready to go over to April's.

On my way to April's I stopped at a grocery store and picked up lasagna in a box, a pre-buttered loaf of garlic bread, and a bag of pre-mixed Caesar salad. I said I would cook. I didn't say it would be from scratch.

My arrival at April's apartment was perfectly timed. She was unloading her bags when I pulled up, and she left the big one for me. I gave her a welcome home kiss while we drug her bags over her threshold. I carried the largest bag to her room while she efficiently unpacked her makeup kit back into its rightful place in her bathroom.

April complimented me on not just getting pizza or Chinese food, to which I pinched her on the butt and told her she was welcome. I couldn't help but self-deprecate and tacked on a comment about how boxed lasagna wasn't much better, to which she playfully told me to shut up and get in the kitchen. I unboxed and threw the entrée in the oven while she unpacked. I asked her the usual questions regarding her parents, how they were, how the trip was, how the flight was, and if she needed any help. I received the typical responses of fine, good, okay, and no.

She emerged from her bedroom wearing a white T-shirt, probably one I left there, and a pair of tight grey sweat shorts that may as well have been panties. Her face was washed, exposing the softly freckled skin that was under her daily make up routine. A pony tail stuck out of the back of her head and bounced left and right as she hopped over to the couch. She stuck her hands out and waved them in, calling me to her. She was looking entirely too cute not to want something.

We snuggled up on the couch waiting for the bell on her oven to go off. As expected, she used that moment to begin the second round of her interrogation. I was impressed that she hadn't started in the parking lot.

"So," April began. "About this new job thing?"

"Yes, dear?"

"Tell me again why you were looking for a new job."

I placed my good hand just above her exposed knee. Over the next fifteen minutes, I explained how I needed to try something new, how I was happy with her, and how much better off I would be in a new job. After a while, I wasn't sure who I was trying to convince, her or me. Whoever I was convincing, it worked. April was on board. Unfortunately, that's when she began asking specifics.

"Who interviewed you?" she asked.

"Her name is Hala. I'm not really sure if she would be my boss, or if she just does hiring."

"A woman, huh? Is she cute?"

I should have expected that question. My first mistake came in the nanosecond it took me to calculate what I should say. April noticed my hesitation. I noticed her noticing my hesitation, made me smirk. That was my second mistake. The third mistake was when I actually spoke.

"No."

"Then why are you smiling?"

"I'm not." Ever since I was a child, when I got caught lying, I couldn't help but smile. It was my body's way of tattling on me. Stupid body. The longer the scene played out, the bigger my smile became.

"Jesus. She must be hot. You're ear to ear." April shook her head. "Is she hotter than me?"

"No." That response was already on deck, allowing me to spit it out in time.

"Alright, as long as there's no funny business," April said. "Where was your interview?"

Explaining that Hala and I shared a nice lunch and wine over veal at one of the most romantic restaurants in town was not going to help my situation at all. I had already been called out for lying, so I knew I wouldn't be able to get away with another. As a diversionary tactic I leaned in and kissed her.

She kissed back; only stronger. My tactic was especially transparent, but she was going to allow it. I moved down to her neck and nibbled on her ear as she lay back into the couch. I slid my hand down and grabbed the bottom of her T-shirt and started lifting just as the bell on the stove went off.

"Shit!" April exclaimed. "To be continued." She trotted off to the kitchen, removed the lasagna from the oven and placed it on the counter. She bounced back into the living room. "Where were we?" she said, lying back down on the couch.

Dinner was still mostly warm when we got to it. The interview wasn't brought up for the rest of the evening. Between the travel and the carbs, April was ready for bed early. She convinced me that I was too. I slept better that night than I had in months.

Monday morning we woke to her alarm, showered together, and I changed into the spare work clothes I kept in her closet. Like an old married couple, we shuffled around the apartment, brushing teeth, fixing our hair, looking for lost keys, and only speaking when necessary. It was comforting to be able to wake up with someone and not have to talk. We kissed as she shut the door behind her and we parted ways to our cars.

"Don't forget to put in your notice today," April yelled at me from across the parking lot.

"Thank you, dear." I gave her a thumbs up and a smile.

I followed her to work. On the drive in, I would pass her and as I did I would make a goofy face, then she would leapfrog me and make a kissy face. We played that game until we pulled into the parking garage.

Once on company property, we tried, poorly, to limit our interaction. Everyone knew we were dating, but we didn't want it to be an issue. Workplace relationships were generally on my no-no list, but when I met April, I knew I was going to have to make an exception. Also, having a six month dry spell before we met didn't do my resolve any favors. We parted ways on the eighth floor where I got off.

Larry was already hard at work, or at least he looked like he was working hard while surfing the internet. The morning stroll around the web was how he stayed up on current events. He justified his abuse of company time by claiming using the internet was saving trees, and that LaRose needed to do its part for the environment. It was either that or some other line of bullshit. It depended on the day.

"Morning, cracker," Larry said still facing his monitor.

"Cracker? I thought I was a honky."

"It's whatever. I'm open-minded. How was your weekend?"

"Good. I'm quitting," I said.

I wasn't facing Larry, but I heard him stop then turn his chair to face my back. It took all I had not to crack a smile.

After realizing I wasn't going to turn to face him he asked the question.

"Quitting what?"

"This place. I got another job offer over the weekend and I'm going to take it."

"Where? Doing what? Giving handjobs down at the pier?"

"You know the LDI building downtown?" I asked rhetorically. "It's there. It's a data entry job, but the benefits are good. And we don't have a pier. We're landlocked, fucker."

"So you're leaving me, just like that."

I turned to face him and I put my hand on his shoulder. "It's not you, it's me," I responded.

"That's what they all say."

We traded a few more insults before he started the interrogation. He asked what exactly I'd be doing, to which I responded data entry and then played dumb. Next he asked why and I told him the same story I told April. They talked on occasion, so I wanted consistency. From the questions he was asking, I was starting to wonder if he and April had gotten together to compare notes. He even asked about who interviewed me. For

Larry, I went into more detail about Hala's beauty, but I still left out where we interviewed. Had I told him, he would have never believed I didn't sleep with Hala.

"When are you going to tell Fat Ron's Shitter?"

Larry was referring to our immediate supervisor Ron Shipper, whom everyone but his 'pets' referred to as Fat Ron's Shitter. He was late forties, 5'10" and about as big around. His enormous head was bald on top, with a halo of unkempt salt and pepper hair, and abnormally small ears upon which rested a pair of thick black framed glasses.

Ron was an intelligent asshole, which made things worse. I can handle a really smart person, I can handle an asshole, but it's extremely frustrating to deal with an asshole who unfortunately is almost always right. The name calling was adolescent at best, but that's how offices work. Ron was fond of saying he had an open door policy, though that usually meant you were free to enter his office and be belittled at your convenience. We often speculated that his wife was the subservient mail-order type, or didn't exist at all.

Telling Ron I was quitting was going to be a bittersweet event. The thought of quitting was much better than the reality of it. I imagined myself walking into his office coolly, giving him the bird, and walking out to the applause of my coworkers. I knew it would likely be nothing like that.

"I'll tell him after lunch."

The morning went faster than I wanted. I had barely gotten through my emails and two cups of coffee before it was time for lunch. Due to the amount of employees at LaRose Financial, everyone had staggered breaks and lunches to keep traffic in the halls and the cafeteria to a minimum. Unfortunately, that meant I was eating lunch three hours after I arrived at work, and only thirty minutes after my first break. Lunch was half an hour. The best part was that I got to see April for the last ten minutes of my lunch before having to jump in an elevator and rush back to my desk.

I joined the herd heading down to the second floor. The smell of cafeteria food greeted everyone as we walked off the elevators. Monday was usually 'home-style' cooking. That amounted to meatloaf or fried chicken, mashed potatoes or macaroni and cheese, and your choice of green beans, corn, or mixed veggies. I was a meatloaf, potatoes and green beans kind of guy.

I slid my tray behind Larry's as we walked the food line and talked shit back and forth. I made fun of him for getting fried chicken, like I always did on Monday. He folded his napkin into a triangle and told me I dropped my hood.

We took a table near the south wall, which was primarily windows. It turned out to be an overcast day, making the window wall a popular spot. On bright days, one would think I worked with vampires. It was my favorite spot because it was good for people watching, especially around lunchtime.

When eating was involved, conversation between Larry and I was slim to non-existent. At best we would comment on the state of the food; good or bad. By the time we finished eating, April arrived with her tray of fried chicken, macaroni, and corn.

"You going to make fun of her for getting fried chicken?" Larry asked pointing to April's tray.

"What's wrong with fried chicken?" April asked before sitting down.

"Nothing." I replied. "Larry is just being sensitive."

"Larry," April cocked her head to the side. "Why are you being sensitive?"

"Because this fucker's leaving us." He pouted.

"I already told both of you, I'm not leaving you, I'm leaving this place. Better benefits. Obviously I need health insurance," I said, raising my cast in the air.

April placed her hand on Larry's shoulder. "It will be okay. We will get through this." She turned her attention to me. "How did Ron take it?"

Larry piped in. "You mean Fat Ron Shitter?"

April gave him a glare, informing him that she didn't approve of name calling.

"He hasn't told him yet," Larry said.

"Thanks, tattle tale. I will. I was going to do it after lunch." I looked back at Larry. "Fucker."

"Boys," April looked back and forth between Larry and I. "Do I need to separate you two? Just make sure you do it sooner rather than later."

I was able to turn the conversation away from me after that by promising I would and asking Larry about his relationship. That was always good for a few laughs. Sometimes I thought he made up fictitious situations just to have something funny to say.

The timer I carried with me to time my breaks and lunches went off before Larry could finish his story about how his girlfriend's cat interrupted their sex the night before by walking under them during an awkward position. I patted April's hand, gave her a wink and Larry and I left for the elevator.

Back at my desk, I took a few moments to muster up the courage to quit. My stomach was a little queasy and my palms were sweaty. I looked at Larry before I got up from my desk and he gave me the reassuring nod I needed. He would mess with me about it later, but he knew it was better for me.

I took my time weaving through the other departments before I made it to Ron's office. The blinds were shut, but the door was cracked.

According to his policy, if the door was open even a little, it was safe to enter. I knocked first.

"Enter." Ron's voice boomed out, getting the attention of those that sat near him. It immediately made me uncomfortable.

I eased the door open to see Ron sitting behind his desk, staring at his double monitor set up. His thick fingers were banging away at the keys. He didn't bother to look at me, so I approached the desk and sat down in the chair on my left. A few seconds passed and he was still hacking away at his keyboard.

"Should I come back?"

Ron stopped typing turned his eyes towards me, shook his head 'no' and returned to whatever it was he was doing. While I waited, I looked around his office and faked interest in the things on the walls while I waited for him to speak to me.

He finished typing and opened his mouth as if he was going to speak, then he shut it and began proof reading what he had just written. It took long enough that I ran out of things to look at, so I stared at the floor. After a few corrections, he was pleased with his writing and he cleared his throat, letting me know I could look up.

"What can I do for you, uh, Steven?" My name wasn't amongst his most used so it took him a few seconds to remember who I was.

"Well, I actually needed to put in my two weeks' notice."

The words came out easier than I had expected, but then came the awkward moment of silence while he processed what I said. Perhaps it was my imagination, but Ron's face turned a little more red than usual. His expression remained calm while he considered his next move.

"Okay," he said before he dug through his desk and pulled out a small packet of papers. "Please fill out this exit interview sheet, and I will have security walk you out when you are done."

"You're letting me go now?" I asked looking down at the forms in front of me.

"Look, Steven, it's nothing personal. I'm sure you are a fine person, but I don't want you milking the company clock. When someone decides to leave, they've already left. I'd rather spend two weeks training someone to do your job than spend two weeks watching you surf the web and steal pens."

"I don't steal pens."

"If not pens, it would be something else." He pushed his glasses up and straightened his posture. "If you'll excuse me, I'll let you finish filling these forms out while I get security."

He left his chair and opened the blinds so he could see inside his office while he was out of it. He closed the door behind him and walked to the first desk near his office to use the phone. It was Allison Pettigrew's. She was about his same age, loved office gossip, and was part of Ron's elite group. The mere thought of her made my stomach churn. I could see the look of excitement on her face as he explained that he needed a security escort for a former employee.

I grabbed a pen from his pen cup and waved it at him, so he wouldn't think I was stealing his stationary. The exit interview forms asked for my pertinent information, my feelings about the company, and reason for departure. Much like I wanted my informing Ron to go differently, I desperately wanted to put a slew of insulting remarks from the top of the page to the bottom, but that just wasn't my style.

I filled out each line completely. I answered every question positively and simply entered 'new opportunity' as my reason for leaving. Upon completion, I waved the pen at Ron again and replaced it in the cup where I found it. I carried the forms out of his office where Ron stood with Silas, one of the security officers for the building. Silas was an older ex-military guy, who was nice enough, but always meant business. He was the only guard in the building allowed to carry a gun instead of just an asp.

Both Ron and Silas stood, arms folded and weight shifted to one side as if it was a huge inconvenience that I took so long filling out my forms. Had I known it was a big deal, I would have taken longer.

"What about my things?"

"You may come back after normal operating hours and have an escort bring you up to get your things," Ron said.

"But my keys are at my desk."

"Rules are rules," the security guard added.

In silence, I was escorted to the stairwell and walked all the way down to the first floor. My former coworkers couldn't help but stare. The water coolers were going to be abuzz with wild rumors about why I was being escorted out. I hoped Larry would be smart and set people straight. The reality was that he was going to tell everyone I got busted looking at porn on the internet. That's what friends are for, I suppose.

"Why couldn't we take the elevator?" I asked Silas.

"Security reasons. There are no cameras in the elevator and if you decided to get froggy, I like to have room to play."

I didn't ask any more questions.

My escort left me when the automatic front door opened. I stepped out into the cool, wet air and took in a deep breath. I had a few hours to kill before I could get my things, so I found the nearest tavern that opened early and sat down to enjoy a soda.

A solid hour passed before my phone started dancing on the table in front of me. That was apparently how long it took for the news to travel back to Larry or April. I checked the caller ID. Larry must have found out first.

"Hello," I answered.

"That mother fucker," Larry responded. "I can't believe he had you escorted out. What a dick move."

"Yeah, it's whatever. I wouldn't worry about it. But he wouldn't let me get my keys. Can you swing them by Bollocks Pub when you get off?"

"Starting early, are we?"

"I'm having a soda, for now." My phone beeped. "Hey, April's calling on the other line, can you bring them?"

"Yeah, but I might be keeping them. I'm buying your first round." Larry hung up without giving me a chance to respond.

I changed lines. "Hello."

"I can't believe Fat Ron Shitter fired you." April was obviously worked up.

"Hey, now. I thought you didn't approve of name calling." I was trying to keep the situation light-hearted.

"That was before he fired my man. It's on now."

"It's okay. I was quitting anyway. Larry's going to bring me my keys when he gets off. Care to join us?"

"Where are you?"

"Bollock's Pub."

"Of course I can join you, but I might be keeping your keys. I'm buying the first round," April commanded.

I didn't have the heart to tell her that Larry already called dibs on the first round. I would let them argue it out when they arrived.

"Okay. Don't stew on this the rest of the day. Seriously, it's no big deal."

"I'll try."

"Good. Well I'll see you in a few." We exchanged goodbyes and then hung up. I ordered another soda and a glass of water. Hydration was going to be key in surviving the evening.

April and Larry showed up together. They played paper-rock-scissors to determine who was going to buy my first drink and April lost. She did however pull the 'I'm sleeping with him' card, and Larry had to concede. I was glad; she would get me something easy to start with. Larry would have gone for something that involved tequila.

April ordered me a gin and tonic, an orange-colored cocktail for her, and brought Larry back a wine cooler and said that some guy at the bar bought it for him. It was that kind of kidding that made me glad she was my girlfriend.

Over the next few hours, we traded tales about work time pranks, discussed everything that was wrong with every place we had ever worked, made sex jokes of all kinds and had one of the best times I could recall in years. The drinks flowed freely as did the conversation. It was just what I needed.

Around ten, I suggested it was time for everyone to leave, since they had to work in the morning. April offered to take me home and whispered an enticing proposition in my ear. I was happy to go home with her.

"But you're just as drunk as I am," I argued.

"I've had virgin drinks all night. I'm as sober as I was when I walked in the door."

"God, you're good."

"Yeah," she said. "I know."

"What about you?" I asked Larry.

"My girl is coming to get me in about ten minutes. I hope. You two go on," he said.

We took him up on his offer and headed for the door. Later I would only remember getting into Aprl's car and wanting the heater on and windows down.

The next thing I remembered was waking up face down on April's bed to the sound of her alarm going off.

"Good morning, Sunshine," she mumbled while brushing her teeth. She was already showered and dressed.

I rolled onto my back and looked at her through squinted eyes. My head was pounding, there was drool on the side of my face, and I could smell my breath. My cast and a pair of April's fuzzy socks were the only pieces of clothing I had on. April noticed me looking at the socks.

"Your feet were cold on my legs, and I couldn't find yours," she replied. "There's some ibuprofen and water on the night stand. You'll need it."

"God, you're good."

"Yeah. I know."

After a quick shower, April took me to work with her so I could get my car. I gave her a kiss in the parking lot before she entered the elevator. It felt nice being able to kiss her on company property. Despite the hangover, I felt like a new man. I had some time off, I had a great woman, a good friend, and a new opportunity.

I hopped in my car and headed home. As soon as I arrived, I opened up my cell phone and called Hala. She answered on the second ring.

"Hello, Steven. I'm shocked it's taken you this long to call. Last time I saw you, you looked like you had a million questions."

"I've got just one question today. What would you say if I said my workday schedule found itself empty?"

"I would say I'll see you next Monday for orientation then," she replied.

"Great."

Chapter 6

The days leading up to orientation dragged on forever. Part of it was the building anxiety of having to start a new job. More than once I spent hours on the couch wondering if I had made the right decision. I didn't know Hala, I had no real reason to believe that she was telling me the truth and I was about to lie to my girlfriend and my best friend. That new man feeling I'd had just a few days prior was now a fond memory.

I tried to keep myself busy by cleaning my apartment, but you can only clean eight hundred square feet so much. The television was no help as usual. The only decent distraction was when April came over on Friday. I made her an actual home cooked meal, if chili counts as home cooked.

Sunday night I laid out all of my clothes for Monday morning. I went with black shoes, slacks, a deep blue shirt, and a grey and blue tie. I sent April a picture message for her approval, and she sent me back a picture of her thumb pointed up.

With my house in order, clothes laid out, alarm set, and the coffee pot all set up, I changed into a pair of black gym shorts and climbed into bed at 9:07. I wanted to be well rested. If Hala was telling the truth, I was going to be in for an interesting Monday.

At 10:13 I turned the alarm clock around, thinking it may have been the light keeping me up. At 11:44, I turned it back around to check the time. I finally took a couple of nighttime cold pills at 12:17, and 12:53 was the last time I looked at the clock until 5:53 when I woke up; seven minutes before my alarm was set to go off. Frustrated, I rolled out of bed and into the shower.

I had to leave the left sleeve of my shirt unbuttoned to get my cast though it while I dressed. I did my best to roll the sleeve over the cast. The coffee pot started at 6:00, so it was ready by the time I finished dressing myself. I enjoyed one cup of coffee before shutting the pot off and dumping it down the sink. I didn't want to have to pee during orientation, so I kept my fluid intake to a minimum.

Before I left, I called April, she bid me good luck and asked me to call her on lunch. We made kissing noises over the phone before hanging up. I locked up and headed for my car.

Like in the movies, I half expected the car not to start, but it did, just like every other morning. I gave the steering wheel a pat, like it did something special, turned on the radio quietly, backed out, and headed to work.

I found the entrance to the parking garage under the LDI building with little trouble. I went three floors down before I found a place to squeeze in my car. I had to walk back up those three floors to get to an elevator that opened into the lobby. Just before the elevator were two reserved parking spots. One read 'Andrew Tandy' and the other read 'Hala Adams'.

96

It hadn't dawned on me before that moment that Hala might be that high up the ladder. Had I known, I might have dressed nicer and drank less when we went out for lunch.

Enough people were waiting to ride the elevator that I had to wait for it to go up, drop off its passengers, and come back down. By the time I got on, a line had formed behind me, and I had to ride the elevator full. I took my place at the back so as not to draw attention to myself. Not that there was any reason I would. I began humming inside my head in time with the Muzak rendition of 'Imagine' that played over the elevator's sound system.

I wondered how many of the people in the elevator did what I was going to be doing. There couldn't possibly be that many, could there? I thought. The doors opened and we filed out of the elevator before I could ask myself too many questions.

I stepped out into the lobby on the south side. It was impressive to say the least. The north, east and west walls were glass until the fourth floor. In the center of the chamber was a pool with a gigantic golden statue of Atlas holding the Earth and water flowed from the globe and into the pool. Eight onyx columns shot from the floor up to the ceiling. Large planter boxes held various trees and plants in two semi circles around the fountain.

Near the north side of the chamber was a reception and security desk. Not having received clear instructions from Hala about where to go,

I decided to start there. I waded upstream through a small crowd that knew where they were going and approached the young woman seated inbetween two security guards.

She waited until I had fully approached the desk before speaking. "Welcome to LDI. How may I help you?" she asked.

"I'm here for orientation." I wasn't sure how specific I could be about the position. "At Hala Adams' request."

"Very well. Have a seat" she said motioning to a set of black leather couches facing the reception desk.

I took my seat at the one on the left, as it gave me the best view to watch people scurry about to their destinations. The receptionist picked up her phone, punched in a few numbers, spoke briefly, then hung up. She returned to her duties without so much as a 'Someone will be right down' or a ' it will just be a few moments'. After sitting for twenty minutes I began getting apprehensive. The lobby was nearly empty, except the two security guards, the receptionist, and one elderly woman pushing a cleaning cart around, picking up the mess from the morning stampede.

I heard one of the elevators arrive at the ground floor, and with a 'bing', the doors opened. A single person exited the elevator. He was a black man nearly seven feet tall, and that included the slight forward bend in his posture. His thin frame was swallowed in his faded black suit. Long, bony hands exited the cuffs of his jacket, while monstrously large feet stuck out from his just too short pants.

98

He was a man probably in his late sixties or early seventies. The skin of his face clung loosely to his skull, creating deep pockets and folds. His hair was almost completely white, standing out especially well against his dark complexion. He had sad puppy dog eye sockets, but the eyes themselves were sharp and aware.

The long walk to me was labored. His knees were the source of his discomfort. His legs bowed slightly inward when he walked. His shoes barely left the floor as he walked, making a scuffing noise with each step.

I stood to greet him, and before he was within reach, he thrust his hand out to shake mine. Given his impressive wingspan, he was about ten feet away when he started the reach. I leaned forward to bridge the gap. His left hand rose to wipe the corners of his mouth before he spoke.

"Good morning," he said in a slow deep voice. "I'm Calvin, and you must be Steven."

"Nice to meet you, Calvin, and you can call me Steve."

"Alright, Steve it is." He released my hand, wiped the corners of his mouth again and pointed to the elevator. "Shall we?"

"Certainly."

Something about Calvin made me feel like I was talking to my late grandpa. It was more than age, it had more to do with the rock solid hand shake, the slow methodical way of speaking, and the casual yet respectful way he approached everyone. I was willing to bet that Calvin had already summed me up within fifteen seconds of the handshake..

"Thanks, darling," he said waiving one hand to the receptionist who genuinely smiled back at him.

I followed him to the elevator. I stayed behind him so he could dictate the pace. It was a quiet walk except for the scraping of his soles across the floor.

Calvin waited for me to enter the elevator. Upon entering, I scooted my way to the back corner. He entered and pressed the '11' button. It lit up and a few seconds later the door closed and we were on our way.

"So," Calvin started, "Hala told me you tried to kill yourself."

Calvin stared straight ahead. There was no malice in his voice, no disapproving tone, nor was there any judgment. He was simply making conversation. My initial reaction was to be offended, but it faded quickly. He looked back and noticed the look on my face.

"Oh, I am sorry. I didn't mean to offend. When you are as old as I am and have worked here for as long as I have, you tend to forget that most people don't deal with death every day."

"No offense taken," I said, "just caught a little off guard. And yes, I did, I guess."

There was something cathartic about being able to speak plainly to a complete stranger about my most troubling times.

"Nasty business, suicide is. I thought about it a couple of times, but I guess I was always too chicken to go through with it. Of course I'm so old now," he wiped the corners of his mouth again, "if I want to die, all I have to do is wait."

We shared a well-timed and scripted laugh that ended when the doors opened to the eleventh floor. The doors opened and I followed Calvin out. Based on the lobby, and the general nature of what I understood the business was, I expected something more lavish. I didn't expect fountains on every floor, but maybe some gold here and there, expensive works of art, possibly marble floors.

I was greeted with a long hallway with grey and blue Berber floors, fluorescent lights, and khaki painted walls. The only gold pieces I could see were the cheap gold painted sconces about every twenty feet down the length of the hall. Each one was placed in between a door and a glass panel. Each of these doors must have led to separate offices.

I followed the shuffle of Calvin's feet to the last door on the left. The blinds were drawn shut over the glass panel, making it impossible to see who or what was inside. Calvin knocked on the door.

"Come on in," a woman's voice said from inside the room.

Calvin opened the door and waited for me to enter ahead of him. I stepped through the door and into a spacious and well decorated office. There were two desks; one on the left and one on the right of the door. Behind the door on the left sat a woman in her mid to late forties. She stood to greet me.

She was almost six feet tall and extremely thin. A full sleeve tattoo covered her left arm. The right arm appeared clean Her bright red hair was just slightly brighter than any shade found in nature. She had short bangs in the front and it dropped just below her shoulders at the back.

"Judy, I'd like you to meet Steve. He's the new sorter," Calvin explained.

She thrust her thin hand out to me. "Pleased to meet you, I'm Judy Bosworth. I'm the Human Resources Manager for our little organization. Have a seat."

We shook hands and I took a seat in front of her desk. Calvin sat beside me. Judy was the last to sit. I placed my arms on her desk, and my cast made a thud. Judy had noticed it immediately, but the noise piqued her curiosity.

"How did you hurt your arm?" she asked.

"I fell off a building," I said. It was the truth, of sorts.

"Fell?" Calvin gave me a disapproving look.

"Well, I jumped off, actually."

Judy shrugged her shoulders. "How was it?"

"Was what?"

"Trying to kill yourself?" she asked while digging into the top drawer on the left side of her desk.

It appeared that everyone in the office treated death like most people treated a broken washing machine or a stubbed toe. It was a minor inconvenience. They weren't cold or callous about it, just very business. It was something I would have to get used to.

"It was okay I guess. Until the sudden stop, that is." I decided to try and make light of it. "I could have ended up with a broken everything. Instead, I have this." I waved my cast in the air.

"Someone must be watching out for you," Judy said, still rifling through her desk. She finally found what she was looking for and placed a packet of papers in front of me. She began searching another drawer and pulled out an ink pad. "Sorry, we haven't hired anyone in a while. Not a lot of turnover around here."

"That's good," I replied. "So, what's all this?"

"Most of those papers are general forms you need to fill out, for taxes and whatnot. There's an equal opportunity employment notice, a right to work notice, a 401k information kit, and an enrollment form for the Fulltime Fitness; it's a gym down on 3rd and Benson. We pay one hundred percent of your fees, so it doesn't hurt to join even if you don't use it."

"I use the steam room," Calvin added out of the blue.

"Good deal." I didn't know how to respond, but I felt like I should.

Judy continued on. "You'll need this," she handed me the ink pad, "when you get to the last sheet. Just mash your palm down in the ink and stamp it in the center of the sheet, then fill out the info at the top."

"Is this a criminal background check?" I got nervous. Hala said she knew what I had done, but she never mentioned doing a background check. Having already left my other job, I went into panic mode and began sweating immediately.

"It's a background check of sorts," Judy said.

Calvin placed his large hand on my shoulder. "Don't worry. It's not a criminal thing. It's seeing who you've been before if this isn't your first time through the system."

"You mean, like past lives?"

Judy answered. "Yes. Your palm and finger prints are much more than most people think. It's like the grooves in a record. In those grooves is information on who you were, how many times you've been through, how you did in each of those lives. It's fairly general, but there's a ton of information there."

"So how do you read it?" I looked down at both of my palms. I considered each groove, each wrinkle, every fold. I wondered what it was going to say about me.

"We don't. There's a home office we send the prints to, they send a report back," Judy stated.

"Palm readers can do it, but it's extremely limited. They are descendants of the ones who used to read them manually. That art has been watered down through the centuries, making their information...less than reliable," Calvin said before wiping the corners of his mouth. Based on his tone I had the feeling he had gone to a palm reader before and was given bad information.

"Where's the home office?" The idea of multiple offices handling the afterlife intrigued me.

"Only Hala knows that. There are a number of secrets in this business, and we keep them well. Let me put it this way; we taught Apple how to keep a secret." Judy was amused by her analogy and chuckled to herself. "But, I've rattled on enough. If you don't get started, you're going to spend your whole first day filling our HR forms."

She seated me at the desk on the other side of the office. I began filling out forms, signing, initialing, and dating. Calvin took a seat on the edge of Judy's desk. They leaned in and spoke to each other in low voices. I couldn't hear what they were saying, but something told me it had nothing to do with me. I learned in prison that every time someone is whispering around you, it rarely actually involves you.

Twenty minutes later I made it to the last page of the packet. I had one stack of paper far off to my right, face down, of forms I had completed. Another stack to my left contained information for me to take home and read over. Directly in front of me was a white sheet of what felt like construction paper. At the top one blank read 'Name' and another said 'Opportunity'.

"I get the 'name' part, but what do I put in the 'opportunity' field?" I asked.

Judy stopped what she was saying to Calvin and they both looked at me. "Oh, you don't fill that out. The home office will fill that in when they find out who you are. It's how many chances you've had."

"Why does that matter?"

Calvin spoke up. "Hala will explain that to you later. Just press your hand on the ink pad and press it in the center of the page."

I flipped open the cover on the pad and pressed my hand into the ink. It was uncomfortably hot. I flipped my hand over to look at the palm. The ink that transferred to my skin was gold. Not golden, it was gold. I pressed my hand hard on the paper and pulled it back. I had to hold the paper down with my cast to remove my hand from it.

The gold faded to white and disappeared. I ran my hand over the sheet, and could feel where my palm had been, but couldn't see the mark I had made. I flipped my hand back over and my palm was still gold.

"Ummm."

"Oh, sorry. I forgot to warn you. It does that," Judy said looking at my hand.

"Which part of 'it does that' were you supposed to warn me about? The hot part, the disappearing part, or the part where your hand stays gold?"

"All of those really. Calvin, do you mind taking him to the break room to get some milk before you see Hala?"

"Not at all, my dear." He changed his attention to me. "Let's go.

"Nice to meet you again, Steve," she said rising from her chair.

I made my way to her to shake her hand, but after I thrust my hand out I pulled it back, remembering that it was still gold. I settled for a wave. "Likewise."

In his gentlemanly fashion, Calvin opened the door. He waited for me to exit, then took the lead back down the hallway to the elevator and to the seventh floor. The elevator doors opened into a small waiting area and a hallway that ran left and right. To the left were more offices, to the right was a set of double doors that led into the cafeteria.

The cafeteria was fairly standard. A buffet line led down one side of the room. Square brown Formica tables and hard back chairs populated the right. Along the wall opposite the entrance were floor length windows peering out into a small park behind the building. Immediately to the right of the entrance rested a row of vending machines.

Other than Calvin and I, the only people in the cafeteria were a handful of workers in hair nets, khakis, and blue T-shirts cleaning up from the breakfast crowd. Calvin shuffled over to one of the vending machines and pulled some change from deep within his pocket. He counted out a dollar and plunked it in the machine. He made his selection and a container of milk fell to the bottom of the machine. Calvin placed his right hand on his upper thigh to support himself as he tried to bend down.

"Here, let me get that," I said, shooting in between him and the machine.

"Thanks," he said. "It's not the years, it's the mileage, you know."

"Put yourself through the ringer?"

He chuckled. "You could say that. I'm sixty-seven, but I've lived enough life for a man twice my age."

"So no complaints?"

"Oh," he began before wiping the corners of his mouth, "I've got a couple, but I'll save 'em for my maker. Now take that milk to the restroom and wash your hands with it."

"Wash my hand with milk?"

"I know, I know. It's a little bizarre, but it's the only thing that will get that gunk off your hands."

"Can I use soap afterwards?"

"Please do. I'm going to sit my old bones down over here and wait."

I trucked off to one of the restrooms just outside the cafeteria, milk in hand. I placed my milk on one of the urinal heads and took a leak. Much to my dismay, I looked down and noticed that I had turned part of my penis gold.

"Shit," I said to no one in particular. I carefully shook off, flushed, and closed my pants. I didn't want to get busted washing my privates with milk my first day, so I decided it would have to wait. I grabbed up my milk bottle, walked over to the sink, popped the cap off and poured it into my hand. The ink mixed with the milk and rolled off into the basin in a gooey golden mixture that resembled pale honey. Satisfied, I soaped, rinsed, and dried my hands. Sure enough, the gold ink was gone.

I returned to find Calvin sitting at one of the cafeteria tables with his head back, snoring quietly. He looked so peaceful that I would have felt bad nudging him awake, so I left the cafeteria, and re-entered, closing the door behind me hard enough to stir him, but soft enough it wasn't obvious. I even pretended to look elsewhere when I entered to save him from any possible embarrassment.

"Did it come off?" he asked, straightening his posture.

I put my palm up so he could see. "Yes, sir."

"Good, good." Calvin pressed off the table next to him to stand himself back up. "Let's go see Hala."

Back to the elevator we went. When the doors closed, Calvin pressed twenty-one on the number pad. It was the last number on the panel. The ride was short and quiet. I thought Calvin might still be shaking his nap off.

The doors opened into another waiting area. This time it was manned by a receptionist. She was an older woman, probably near Calvin's age. She was seated, but it was clear that she wasn't much taller standing up. Her hair was curled then combed out, creating a fluffy white pillow around her head. The paleness of her hair and skin was offset by the rouge liberally applied to her cheeks. I imagined her doing cross stitch and baking pies in her spare time.

"Good morning, Calvin," she said, fluffing her hair.

"And good morning to you, Beatrice. How are you on this lovely day?"

Beatrice blushed. "Oh, Calvin, just call me Bea."

"As you wish," Calvin replied. "Is she in?"

"Yes, though she's with Mr. Tandy. It may be a moment."

Beatrice pointed to the cushy leather chairs against the wall on either side of the elevator and told us to have a seat. I took my seat but Calvin stayed by her desk to chat. I tried not to overhear what was being said, and based on Bea's giggling, I was glad I succeeded in hearing nothing.

After only a minute or two, the large oak door leading to Hala's office opened. From that door emerged a man that couldn't be much over thirty. He wore a grey suit that was obviously quite expensive, but he wore it poorly.

"You waiting for me?" he asked looking at me.

"No sir," I said starting to rise to greet him.

"Cool." He didn't shake my hand, he didn't acknowledge Beatrice or Calvin. He headed directly for his office and shut the door. I lowered back into my chair.

That was my introduction to Andrew Tandy, the president of LDI financial services. I wasn't particularly impressed. I expected more professionalism from someone of his stature, maybe even suave. Andrew was neither. He was more like a frat boy that couldn't let go of the good

110

old days, just with a ton of money. I was glad I would be working for Hala and not him.

While I sat and passed judgment on Andrew, Hala had come out of her office and was standing beside me but I hadn't yet noticed her presence. Calvin and Beatrice stopped talking and that was what caught my attention. I turned to look at Hala's office and was shocked to see her standing there. I jolted in my chair, which drew chuckles from the observers.

"Good morning, Steve. Has Calvin been taking good care of you this morning?" Hala asked.

I stood up to shake her hand. "Absolutely. How are you today, Hala?"

"Splendid." She shook my hand. She looked into my eyes for what seemed like an unnatural amount of time; however, I couldn't bring myself to look away. She gave me the same mysterious smile she had given the last time we met.

"Calvin, I'll bring him down when I'm done. Make sure his desk is ready."

"Will do." Calvin turned to address Beatrice, "Bea, always a pleasure. Steve, we'll see you in a bit." He wiped the corners of his mouth and forced himself off the edge of Beatrice's desk. His shoes scraped along the floor on his way to the elevator.

Hala stuck her hand out towards her office door. I bowed my head slightly and followed her directions.

Chapter 7

The interior of her office was more impressive than the lobby. It was larger than my entire apartment and better furnished. The wall opposite the door was made entirely of glass. LDI wasn't the tallest building in town, but it was the tallest in the area, affording Hala a spectacular view over the city. Her massive desk backed up to the center of the glass, over twenty feet from the entrance.

The wall to my left was primarily a large bookcase floor to ceiling, and packed full. Most of the books were antiques, or at least looked that way and many were complete sets, with common binding and similarly faded color. On either side of the bookshelf were two plain wooden doors with matching gold handles. Both doors were closed.

Directly to my right was a kitchen twice the size of the one in my apartment. The counters were cut from large slabs of black granite as was the matching island. Further down was a sitting area with a full couch and loveseat facing a sixty inch flat panel television.

"This is your office? It looks more like an apartment," I asked in shock.

Hala smirked. "I know, it's a bit much. Have a seat."

"Where?"

"Anywhere. Just get comfortable."

I meandered around her office and tried imagining what it would be like to have something so lavish. Hala loosely tailed me around the room, waiting for me to ask questions. I couldn't wrap my mind around it and resigned to taking a seat on the couch. I sunk into the couch, and as badly as I wanted to lean back and enjoy it, I scooted forward to the edge and straightened my posture.

"Are you always this tense? Relax. Sit back. We've got plenty to discuss."

"Sorry. First day jitters I suppose."

"Nothing to worry about," she reassured me. "What do you think so far?"

"In a word; impressive. I mean, I haven't actually learned anything about my job yet, but everyone has been really nice."

Hala smiled. "I didn't want to just push you into it. There's going to be a lot of information to take in while you learn, and I believe in easing into it."

She asked me how Calvin had treated me, to which I responded positively. He seemed like the kind of guy you could talk to all day, and it would never get boring. We talked about the gold ink and how she's responsible for getting it because it's only made one place in the world, and she has to fly to Africa every few years to get it. I asked what it was made of, and she said she didn't know, but assured me it was safe for my skin. That made me feel better since my manhood was still gold.

"How does this business operate without being noticed? Is Andrew in on it? Does he know what we do?" It felt odd saying 'we', as I had only been part of that 'we' for about four hours.

"We are a division of LDI for tax purposes. I have approximately forty employees between all of our subdivisions that are listed as LDI employees, but none of us have anything to do with the other employees in this building. I put Andy in place years ago, under the stipulation that he doesn't ask any questions. It works out quite well, because he doesn't want to ask any questions. He wants a paycheck. Long story short, he doesn't know, doesn't care, and we all work for LDI. That being said, be careful who you talk to in the building about our work."

"What if someone asks me what I do?"

"Tell them you work for me. That should suffice. If nothing else, lie. Although, you've always been a bad liar. On second thought, tell them you do data entry for Hala's group."

I found myself offended by the fact that she called me a bad liar. Lying wasn't something to be proud of, but it always stings a little when someone says you are bad at something, even when you aren't supposed to be good at it. I was also ashamed that during the course of three conversations, she had already passed that judgment upon me.

"What do you mean, always?" I asked.

"Well, at least once in every conversation we've had, you've tried to lie to me, and I've known it was a lie every time. Don't worry; being a bad liar isn't what I would consider a character flaw." Hala smiled again. "You know, how rude of me. I haven't given you the tour of my office."

I went along with it and followed her as she showed me her kitchen, though I had already seen it. She walked me to her book case and explained that she had collected books for years and that she had read nearly every book on the shelf. I wouldn't have believed her, but she wasn't saying it in a bragging fashion, it was just fact. Hala pointed out various pieces of art around her office, and why they were important to her.

She opened the door on the left of her bookshelf. It opened to a large restroom. The plain look of this restroom led me to believe this wasn't her personal restroom. I was correct. She closed that door, and opened the one on the other end of the bookshelves.

The second door led to a fully furnished bedroom. A king size four post bed sat with the headboard along the far wall, draped in a deep red down comforter. The comforter was in shambles, exposing white linens. It appeared that the bed was recently used. A little voice in my head assumed it had to do with Andrew, and that voice was a little jealous. I pushed that thought to the side, telling myself that Hala wasn't that kind of girl. Of course I didn't even know what kind of girl she was.

To the right was an all glass wall, carrying over from the office. Armoires sat on either side of the entrance. In the far left corner was a spiral staircase, and along the left-hand wall was another door, that no doubt led to her private bath.

"Do you live here?"

"Sometimes it feels like it, but no. I live out in the country and when I'm stuck here late, I just sleep here. Like last night for instance."

"Oh," I said. That little voice was relieved.

"You didn't think it was...oh my..." she smirked. "I suppose I should make my bed more often. It does look bad when a gentleman leaves my office and my room is a mess. I assure you, I'm anything but interested in Andy."

I didn't think that I had implied all of that from my 'oh', and was embarrassed that my thoughts were that transparent. I was a poor liar and a poor thought hider. I wondered what else I would be bad at by the end of the day. Back peddling didn't seem like an option, so I just went with it.

"A little tidying up wouldn't hurt."

"Noted," she replied, composing herself again. "I haven't shown you the best part." She trotted off to the spiral staircase like a child showing off her favorite toy.

She took off her heels and led the way up the stairs. I did my best not to look at her perfectly sculpted backside as she ascended. It proved to be a more difficult task than I expected. I decided to stop staring about five steps from the top.

At the top was a small landing and a plain metal door. The door felt out-of-place compared to the rest of her office. When she opened the door, it was clear why it didn't match.

The wind whistled through the crack as she worked the door open, filling the stairwell with fresh air from outside. Sunlight poured in behind with the wind, lighting up the stairwell. My eyes hadn't expected sunlight and immediately started watering.

I followed her out to the roof wiping my eyes and squinting. A light breeze swirled around us, wafting Hala's coconut smell towards me. A six-foot tall concrete wall divided her side of the roof from Andrew's. Hala's half had modest furnishings. She had four white beach chairs that were in laid back positions around a small table and a big red umbrella that rose out of the center of the table.

"This is nice," I said walking close to the edge. The closer I got, the less my legs wanted to continue. I found myself about four feet from the edge, standing still.

"It's my little piece of heaven," Hala said leaning over the edge. "When work gets to be too much, it's my refuge."

I walked back towards the table and chairs. "I can see why. It's quiet up here."

"Scared of the edge now?" she asked. It was uncanny how Hala always knew what I was thinking.

"I suppose so."

"Come here." She held out her hand. "If you were going to die, I would know about it. You've got nothing to worry about."

I couldn't argue with her logic. I didn't take her hand, but I eased my way to the edge. My palms got sweaty and I could feel my pulse in my jaw, but I was there. Standing next to Hala I could smell her again, which helped ease my tensions. I closed my eyes and leaned my head over the edge. I took a deep breath and opened my eyes.

We were closer to the ground than when I had tried to kill myself, but still high enough that a fall would be fatal. The thought briefly passed through my mind that I could hop over and finish the job. It wasn't that I was suicidal at that moment, but once you try, the thought never truly leaves.

"Can I ask a question?" I kept my gaze over the edge.

"Sure."

"What if I fell?"

"You mean what if you jumped?"

I didn't respond. She knew what I meant.

"You would die," she said looking down.

I backed away from the edge slightly.

"You're not going to though. I would know. I get notified when someone is going to die, plain and simple. If you were going to attempt suicide and fail, I wouldn't get notified; if you were going to succeed, I would get notified. I haven't been notified, so you aren't going to jump."

"There are exceptions aren't there? I mean other than my last...thing."

She turned to face me. "Jump and find out."

That was my cue to change subjects. My ego was telling me that I was the only exception, though I had a feeling I wasn't alone.

"While I could stand up here all day, I'm assuming you'll be expecting me to do some work in exchange for a paycheck."

"Right you are. Go have a seat and I'll go over the basics of what you'll be doing, then we'll get you back to Calvin."

I approached the chairs and put one in an upright position. Hala did the same and we took seats on opposite sides of the table. That was where she took on her first non-mysterious role since we had met. She finally opened up about what I would be doing.

She explained that my basic job duty would be to go through the files of people who were going to die. I would evaluate each person's file, enter the data into the system, and based on their overall performance in life, the system would tell me if the person was hell bound, going to heaven, or had to try again. She said my official title was Sorter. Regardless of being heaven or hell bound, Hala would receive those files so she or one of her other Collectors could go collect the souls. This usually happened anywhere from one to six months after a sorter processed the file. Basically Collectors just had to witness the death, say a few prayers and document it. All who got another chance went to Calvin. Calvin was a Recycler.

Calvin's job was to hand out all the files for sorting and to take all the files that qualified for another chance and relocate the soul. Based on how many chances they have had, how good or bad their score was, and to the extent of his jurisdiction, he would assign a place for that soul to come back to. Once he figured out the next destination for the soul, he would pass the folder on to the Hala for collection. She said he could explain it better, and resigned to let him do so.

She also informed me that the department was going through a transition. Until recently, all of the data was kept in hard copy only, and now they had thousands of years of information to enter into the database so that the offices around the globe could communicate better. She assured me it wasn't going to be as boring as it sounded. I believed her.

She checked her watch and noticing it was almost noon, she asked if I would care to join her and Calvin for lunch. I accepted the invitation. We took the elevators down to the parking garage where we met Calvin and we all piled into Hala's car. I squeezed myself into the backseat behind Hala, so Calvin would have plenty of room for his legs. Hala asked if I had a preference for lunch, and having none, she took us to a tiny Mediterranean diner not far from the office.

The host knew Hala and Calvin by name and inquired as to who their guest was. It was another situation where I didn't want to be noticed. Hala introduced me as Calvin's newest team member, Steven. She told me the host's name as we shook hands, but I couldn't pronounce it, let alone

120

remember it. The lunch rush hadn't quite hit downtown, but we were the last to get seated without a wait.

Hala ordered a fattoush salad, hummus with steak for Calvin, and a chicken schwarma sandwich for me. She guaranteed I would like it. I had never met anyone quite like her in my life. She knew exactly what she wanted, never doubted anything, and was always right. While I wrestled with the thought if it was a turn on, or overbearing, April called. I went to put my phone on silent, but Hala waved me on and told me to go ahead and answer.

"Hello."

"Whatsup, babe?" April asked.

"Oh, just eating lunch. My bosses took me to this little Mediterranean place. How's work going?"

"My drive in was lonely, my breaks have been lonely, and my lunch is lonely. I miss you."

I was never good about talking on the phone in front of people and I certainly didn't want to get mushy with my new bosses sitting beside me. "I miss you too," I said a little quieter than normal.

April picked up on it. "Are they right there?"

"Yeah. Sorry."

"So what if I started talking dirty?"

"You wouldn't..."

April proceeded to mention a few acts that she knew were on my list of favorites. While it was enjoyable, I started sweating and feeling uncomfortable. Content that she had tortured me enough, she bid me farewell, told me to call her later, and hung up.

"Everything okay on the home front?" Hala asked.

"Oh, yeah. Just checking in," I said wanting the conversation to go somewhere other than my personal relationships.

I think Calvin sensed my reluctance.

"What do you think so far, Steve?" He threw a wink on the end of his question. Either that or he just twitched. I couldn't tell.

"So far so good. Just a little anxious to get started, you know."

Calvin nodded. "I understand. I remember my first day. Well, parts of it anyway. It seems like it was just yesterday, but it must have been about twenty years ago."

"Twenty three," Hala reminded him.

"Is that so?" Calvin shook his head side to side. "I can't believe Beverly has been gone that long." He wiped his mouth.

"Not to be rude, but who is Beverly?"

"My wife," Calvin said. "She passed from a heart attack, God bless her. After I buried her, I tried to drink myself into oblivion, until I met Hala, that is."

"You've known each other for that long? Not to be rude, again, but how old are you Hala?"

"A woman never tells her true age. I haven't lied to you yet, and I don't want to start now."

Calvin interrupted. "Regardless, Hala helped me sober up and get back to living. And back when I started we didn't have computers to do all the work for us. We didn't even have calculators. I bet there are a lot of people in heaven glad that I'm good at math."

"And you had to walk uphill both ways in the snow to get to work didn't you?" Hala asked patting him on the back.

"Well, one way," Calvin replied.

Our lunches arrived, turning our attention to the food. As suspected, Hala was right; my sandwich was good. Conversation slowed while we ate, which was okay for me. After the food was gone, we didn't waste much time getting back to the office. Hala wanted me to at least look at a file before the end of the day.

On the way back, Hala asked Calvin who I would be training with. Calvin rattled off a few people's names, mentally and verbally going through his roster before he reluctantly chose Bruce. I could tell he wasn't excited about the decision, which concerned me.

"Why Bruce?" Hala asked, obviously confused by Calvin's choice.

"He knows the most. He may not be the most personable, but it will be good for Steve to learn from him."

"Not the most personable?" Hala followed up.

"Okay," Calvin turned in his seat so he could see me. "He's a bit abrasive, but he knows what he's doing. If he gives you any guff, just ignore him."

I didn't have anything to respond with. It sounded like I was going to be set up with an asshole. I immediately missed sitting next to Larry and questioned whether I had made the right decision. I think Hala noticed my silent concern.

"I wouldn't worry about him, Steven. He's all bark. Calvin is right though. He's been with the company for a while and knows his stuff. Besides, if you're a quick learner, you won't have to deal with him very long."

I looked at her through the rear view mirror and gave her an appreciative smile that she reciprocated. We listened to Calvin try to get steak pieces out of his teeth with his tongue for the remainder of the ride.

We returned to the parking garage. Hala kept the car running and informed us that she had somewhere to be and that she would be back to check on me by the end of the day. Calvin and I climbed out of her car, and she was gone before we reached the elevators.

"You ready to get started?" Calvin asked as we approached the eleventh floor.

"Absolutely."

The truth was that I was ready to take a nap. It was customary that if I didn't get started early, all my motivation for the day was gone. So far, all I had managed was having a few conversations, turn my penis gold, and eat lunch. It wasn't the most productive day I've ever had.

We were late enough getting back from lunch that there was little demand for the elevator. A middle-aged white woman hopped on at the sixth floor. She greeted us with a nod, but said nothing, making me think she was not involved in our aspect of the business. She got back off at the eighth.

"How do you know who we can talk to and who we can't around here?" I asked as we stepped of the elevator.

"As far as Collectors go, you won't ever know them, they work for us, but don't work in the office. They generally don't even know where the office is. Most of them are part timers anyway. They hold down regular jobs, and only do a couple of collections a year. Hala does the bulk. I'm the only Recycler, and you'll be working with a small group that you will get to know. Everyone else works for Andrew's side."

About halfway to Judy's office, Calvin opened a door on the right. It was an office I had passed by earlier in the day. They certainly did a good job of blending in. We walked in an office space about the size of Hala's, but instead of fine art, books, a television, and a kitchen, this room was packed with ten spacious cubicles. While it wasn't nearly as impressive as everything else I had witnessed, each workspace was three to four times larger than my former desk at LaRose.

Each cubicle was approximately six feet tall and they were arranged around the edges of the room. The center of the room was filled with an oblong conference table easily accessible by each of the workers. The surface of the table was hidden under banker's boxes full of manila folders.

When we entered, only the forefront workers noticed us, until Calvin called everyone's attention. Once again, I found myself the center of attention. As often as this was happening, I guessed I was going to have to get used to it. I wasn't yet.

He wiped his mouth before speaking. "Everyone. Everyone. Can I have your attention, please?" There was more wind in his sails than he had let on all day.

Eight heads turned my way. Starting on my left, the first desk was empty. The second desk was occupied by a short thin man in his late forties or early fifties with deep black hair, and a mustache that could have been a star in an 80's police show. I would later find out that this was Bruce Fellows.

To Bruce's right was Tao Nguyen, an elderly Vietnamese woman whose English was better than she let on and whose egg rolls, it turned out, were the highlight of every pot luck dinner. Next to her in the corner was Matthew Beringer. Matthew was in his early forties. He looked like the typical family man. Docker pants, a pale green polo shirt, obviously purchased by his wife, and a buzzed homemade haircut. He had given up on chasing women so long ago that he no longer cared to dress himself, and was perfectly content that way.

To his right was an empty desk. The next two desks were populated by Heather McGreevy, Irish by marriage only, and Linda Forscythe. Heather was tall, blonde, petite, late thirties, and completely in love with herself. Linda was the almost the exact opposite, short, pudgy, short red hair, but not the sexy type. It was a strong possibility that Matthew and Linda used the same barber. Her only similarity to Heather was that she was also completely in love with Heather. No one openly questioned if that love was friendly or otherwise.

The next corner desk was occupied by Judah. He was early thirties and was absurdly Jewish. Not religiously Jewish, but he was Jewish like Americans claim to be Irish. He had curly black hair, a large nose, and was smarter than anyone else there, except Hala. He was also an enormous smart ass, which wasn't surprising, considering his chubby frame; he probably used it as a defense mechanism. I guessed he had lost a number of fights. A small flag tacked to the back wall of his cubicle read 'Dradel This!' and had the Star of David in the background. I could tell he was going to be entertaining.

Next to Judah was Sue Cauldon. Sue was mid-forties, brunette, and tall. She was the quiet type. I sensed that she didn't like people. She didn't hate them, but rather chose to stick to herself. I appreciated that.

Last in line was Phyllis Gonzales. Phyllis was the youngest in the room. At best, she was late twenties. She had an athletic frame and was no taller than 5'5". She had her straight black hair pulled back in a pony tail that may have been a bit too tight. All business. I imagined there was a silent war between her and Heather for prettiest girl of the bunch.

After Calvin explained that I would be the newest Sorter, he took me around and introduced me individually to each person, starting with Phyllis and working counter-clockwise. By the time I got to Bruce, his was the only name I could remember other than Judah.

Everyone else stood up to greet me. When we approached Bruce he simply turned in his chair, gave me a weak hand shake, and said his name. There was no 'welcome' or 'glad to have you' like the others had greeted me with. He quickly turned back around in his chair after the greeting. Calvin had to tap Bruce on the shoulder to let him know that he would be training me. The news was not well received.

"Bruce," Calvin said, "I'm going to have Steve train with you."

"Okay," Bruce said looking at his monitor.

"Alright then. You two have fun. Steve this will be your new desk for now," Calvin said patting the back of the chair on his left.

"Sounds good," I tried my best to sound excited, though I already carried a great disdain for my new cubicle neighbor.

Chapter 8

"What have you learned about the job so far?" Bruce asked.

"Not much. I know that we enter data from a folder to determine who goes to heaven or hell and who tries again. Then Calvin takes the folder and either sends it to Hala so she or one of her Collectors can collect or he recycles them. I'm not really sure what that entails though."

"You don't need to. For now, you will be entering data from the legacy folders behind us into the system," he pointed to the boxes on the table behind us, "these are folders for souls that have already been handled, so there is no risk of you screwing something up."

Bruce stood up and walked to the table in the center of the room and grabbed a folder from the box closest to him. He returned to his desk and placed the folder in front of his keyboard and opened it. Inside the folder was a stack of yellowed papers approximately half an inch thick.

"Once you have your computer powered up, you will open the database. It's the icon on your desktop that has the three arrows called 'Compass'." Bruce made quote marks in the air before pointing to the icon in the upper left hand corner of his screen.

Since Bruce already had Compass open, he closed it so I could see how to open a desktop icon. I couldn't tell if he genuinely thought I didn't know how to operate a computer or if he was just being a dick. It was probably both. He double clicked the icon and sat quietly while the database loaded.

The icon he was talking about contained a three-part block arrow. The first arrow pointed up and was white, the second arrow stemmed from the white arrow and wrapped around the right side, behind the white arrow, and back to the front, stopping just shy of the left side of the arrow. The last arrow stemmed from the bottom of the white arrow. It was similar to the white portion, except it pointed down, was slightly longer and was red. The imagery felt self-explanatory.

"Once it's open, click directly on the 'Legacy' tab." He made quote marks in the air again. "Do not open any other tab until you know what you are doing. Understood?"

"Yeah, got it," I replied. I wasn't generally a confrontational person, but I could tell that Bruce was going to bring it out of me. I could make it through the day. *After all*, I thought, *the day is half over*.

He began explaining every facet of the Legacy entry screen. From the first sheet in every folder, you gathered the collected soul's most recent first, middle and last name. In that folder's case, the name was Walter Glenn Pickens. Also on the front page was their overall life score before their death, with a maximum value of 1,000,000, at least that's as high as the system went. I guess it didn't matter after that point. This score was determined where the soul was headed after collection. Walter was a lucky one, clocking in at 784,000.

130

Bruce explained that 750,000 to 1,000,000 sent you to heaven. A score of 350,000 to 749,999 meant you tried again, assuming you still had chances left. Anything below that was hell bound. Just hearing him say 'hell bound' made me uncomfortable. I made a note to ask Judy or Hala about my folder next time I saw them. I wanted to know how bad my score was. Hala already said I was hell bound, but since she thought I still had a chance, I assumed I must have been borderline. I made sure not to drift too far off in my own thoughts for fear of Bruce's scolding.

The second page was for all those who had been recycled before. It listed each previous name and score. Bruce explained that even though the names and score were listed, each time a soul was recycled, it got a new folder. If they didn't, some folders would be a few feet thick. That was the reason for the database and the entry of Legacy files in the system. More and more people were being recycled, and just the sheer amount of paperwork stacking up at the offices around the globe was becoming a security risk.

From page three to the end was a complete list of every deed Walter had done in his life. The first hundred pages or so contained what Bruce referred to as common deeds. These were either sins or acts that Walter did in his life that moved his score up or down.

Each deed was given an eight digit code and assigned point value. For example using the word 'shit' was a code 10483601. Using it in a non-malicious way could get you minus one point; like referring to dog shit.

Telling someone to eat shit and meaning it was good for a minus three, depending on the intent. On the flip side, holding the door for someone was a code 10033678 and was good for plus two points. You couldn't hold the door open for someone more intently, so its value was fixed. Perhaps I should have held more doors open.

While entering the codes and points into the system, it wasn't necessary to know what each code meant, but Bruce was kind enough to show me where the decoder was in hard copy and the digital copy on the server. He suggested I read through it on my free time, because the company didn't pay us to be curious.

It was nearing the end of the day and Bruce was clearly tired of talking to me. He instructed me to sit at my desk and review Walter's folder, but not to get into the last section until tomorrow. Him telling me to stay out of it, of course, meant that it was the first thing I was going to do when he wasn't looking.

Four o'clock hit, and everyone started packing up their belongings to head home for the day. I pretended not to notice, reading through the first part of the folder. Bruce also seemed to not notice it was quitting time. He sat entering data on the folder he was working on before I paired up with him. One by one my other new coworkers came by to tell me goodbye. Judah made it a point to ask if I was ready to quit yet while making an obvious nod towards Bruce.

"No, I think I'll come back tomorrow."

"Brave man," Judah said slapping me on the back.

I returned my attention to the folder, watching Bruce out of the corner of my eye. He continued working away. Within minutes, it was just the two of us.

"You can go home now," Bruce said.

"Oh, okay." I acted surprised. "I was just wrapped up in this folder here."

"Unwrap and go home. There's nothing more for you to do today."

I left the office unsatisfied. The drive home was quiet. There was too much on my mind to turn the radio on or hold a meaningful conversation with anyone, so I waited until I was home to call April.

"How was your day?" April asked before saying hello.

"Dandy. How was yours?"

"Pretty average. You're the one who should have a lot to talk about."

"I know. Sorry. My day went downhill after lunch."

"What's wrong? Don't like the new job?"

"It's not that. The job itself is good. I just got sat next to a douche bag, and that's who's training me. The worst part is that he knows what he's talking about, so he's a smart douche bag."

"That's the worst," April sympathized with me. She had always been a good listener and knew exactly what to say to make me feel better.

"It will be alright," I said, consoling myself. "Enough work though. What does your week look like?"

"Oh, I forgot to tell you. My folks are in town this week, and they'll be staying at my apartment until Thursday. Don't worry; you don't have to meet them just yet."

April's parents only lived about five hours away, but they didn't get out much, which just made it inconvenient to set up our first meet. They sounded nice enough from everything she told me, but I wasn't in a rush to meet them. We had been dating for about six months, but I felt it wouldn't reach weird status as long as I met them within the first year. Meeting my girlfriend's parents meant having to retell my life story, which was something I wasn't exactly fond of doing.

"I will if you want me to."

"You can meet mine after I meet yours."

"You really are the greatest." I blew a kiss into the phone.

"That being said, I will let you buy me a bunch of drinks on Friday. I'm going to need them."

"Deal. Should I invite Larry, or is this a private affair?"

"Invite only," she joked, "but I think Larry can make the list. I might invite some of my friends. It'll be fun."

We finalized plans and hung up. I placed the phone down and it rang immediately. It was Larry.

"What's up?" I answered.

"Nothin, man. How was work?"

"It was alright. Nothing too crazy." Except the whole heaven, hell and reincarnation thing, I thought.

"Any honeys?" Whenever Larry tried to sound urban or hip, it sounded more forced than a white rapper.

"Honeys?" I knew what Larry was getting at, but I tried to never get directly to the point with Larry. It was more entertaining to get him to explain himself all the time.

"Yeah. Senoritas, hotties, big breasted maidens, so forth and so on," he replied with enthusiasm.

"Maidens? I didn't get a job in King Arthur's court. And if you must know, there are a few that aren't too shabby." I fed him a morsel.

"Not too shabby? So...work hot?"

"Is that all you think about?"

"Mostly."

"Don't you have a girlfriend?"

"Mostly."

"Meaning that she isn't in the room."

He paused to double-check his surroundings. "Yeah. She's in the shower."

I changed subjects to get him off track.

"Did they find my replacement yet?"

"Not yet, but they are interviewing. There's this one chick I hope they hire. She has an ass like...really, that's cool, they have full dental, huh?"

"She's out of the shower?"

"Yeah. I'll talk to you later. I have some business to attend to."

Before I could say goodbye, he was gone. I sent him a text message about getting together that Friday night. He responded two hours later in the affirmative. It occurred to me that he did that so I would think he had some crazy marathon sex with his girlfriend.

I spoke to April again just before bed. She wished me luck for my second day and assured me it wouldn't be too bad. I believed her. I always believed her.

I laid down to go to sleep around 9:30 p.m. The thought crossed my mind to pray before I went to sleep, but I didn't know how to, nor did I know what to pray for. The notion faded quickly. I made a mental note to check to see if it helped a person's score.

My alarm was set for 6 a.m., but when my eyes opened at 4:17, I knew there was no going back to sleep. I was wide awake, my cast was itchy, and my mind was already up and running. I began trying to think of everything I had ever done that could change my score.

I tried to start at my teenage years. How many times did I engage in premarital sex? Was drinking underage bad? Some countries don't have a drinking age. Was it a regional thing? I used to cuss a lot. I tried to run the numbers on an average of twenty cuss words a day at a worst case of three points a piece, twenty-one thousand, nine hundred a year. Take that times seventeen years was three hundred and seventy-two thousand, give or take a few hundred. Shit. My number crunching turned into a depressing venture, so I abandoned it before I fell into another slump.

I wrapped my cast in a bag, took a shower, and got dressed. By 4:56, I was ready for work, coffee was brewed and I was already one cup deep. No one else I knew was up at that hour, so I did the one thing I could do. I went to work.

The traffic was barely noticeable at five in the morning. When I arrived, the parking garage was nealy vacant. Despite having my choice of parking stalls, I didn't park exceptionally close to the elevators. At LaRose, even though there were no assigned parking stalls, everyone had their normal spot, and I didn't want to piss anyone off on my second day.

The lobby was creepy empty. Even the security guards were gone from the front desk. I made my way to the elevator and headed up to my office. The lights were already on. I peered in the window to see who was in the office before entering. No one was immediately visible, so I entered.

Still sitting on top of my desk was Walter's folder. I sat down and powered on my computer. I arranged a few things on my desk before I opened the folder. The faint sound of shoes scraping across carpet caught my attention. I turned around to find Calvin approaching me.

"Good morning," I said standing up. I turned around, hiding the folder on my desk, like a child hiding a cookie he just got caught stealing.

"Morning," Calvin replied. "What are you doing here so early?"

"Couldn't sleep. Just thought I'd come in and get acclimated."

"I understand. I couldn't sleep when I started here either. I'd lay awake at night, contemplating everything I had ever done wrong in my life." He took a sip from the coffee cup in his hand, then wiped the corners of his mouth. "Now, I can't sleep because I have to get up and pee a hundred times a night. Either way, I guess I just wasn't meant to be a sleeper."

"How long did it take you to stop counting up your mistakes?"

Calvin took a seat in Bruce's chair. It was a labored effort. "Oh, going on about twenty some years now. I'll let you know when I stop. Eventually you will worry about it less and less, though."

"Good to know."

"So what were you working on?" he said leaning over to see the file on my desk.

"Just one of the Legacy folders. To be completely honest with you, Bruce told me not to look at the back section until he said so, but I'm here to sneak a peek."

Calvin shook his head in disapproval. I felt stupid about coming clean, until I realized his disapproval wasn't at me.

"Well, don't let me stop you, open it up." Calvin sat back in Bruce's chair.

I placed my right hand on top of the folder. "You sure?"

"Pretty sure. You're probably going to be disappointed though. It's not nearly as exciting as you might think."

I flipped open the front cover and flipped carefully through the pages Bruce and I had gone through. After the last sheet of Walter's deeds, was a section about twenty pages thick, paper clipped together.

I removed the paperclip as if I was unwrapping a birthday present and carefully placed it to the side. It had left an indention on the first couple pages, so I could return it to the exact location it came from before Bruce arrived. Pages three and four resembled printed sheets of college ruled notebook paper. Each line had a page number column, a section column, and a score column.

Page three was completely full with a few scores written in black and many of them written in red. Page four was mostly full, but the majority of the scores were in black with only a couple of reds. I looked at Calvin for the okay to continue. He nodded in the affirmative.

I laid sheets three and four face down on top of the rest of the paper work. Sheet five was labeled 'Page 1' in the upper left hand corner and contained a bold heading across the top of the page 'Unique Deeds'. The remainder of the page broke down into three distinct sections. Each section contained one or two paragraphs of text. I glanced at Calvin again before reading on.

Walter Glenn Pickens, July 8, 1951, 16 years old - Urinated on his dog, Arthur, for the destroying his Crime Tales issue #11. -8

Walter Glenn Pickens, September 14, 1951, 17 years old - Returned property to Davis General Store that his friends stole the previous day. +7

Page after page was filled with unique deeds. Some were good, some were bad, some were just plain weird. I read a few random deeds throughout Walter's life. For the most part, he seemed like a genuinely good guy. It was pleasing to know that he went to heaven.

"Who keeps track of all this stuff?" I asked Calvin.

"The home office collects all this data. They send us the files with all deeds recorded, we just figure scores."

"Why don't they figure it there, if they keep track of all of it?"

"Our people our problems, I guess. Perhaps it's a separation of church and state thing. I do know they couldn't do my job from there, they don't know this place like I do."

"Where's the home office?"

"You'll have to ask Hala that one." Calvin patted me on the shoulder. He then used my shoulder to help himself up. "I don't even know where it's at. Now put all this back together before Bruce gets here. He's usually the first."

I did as Calvin instructed. One by one, I placed the pages back in the exact order they were in, returned the paper clip and closed the folder up.

"What now?"

"Come into my office. I would like to show you a little about what I do." He wiped the corners of his mouth and smiled. "I'm not going to be around forever, you know."

I double checked to make sure Walter's file looked exactly like it did before I left work the previous night. Satisfied, I headed to Calvin's office which was separated from the main bullpen by a wall with a plain red wood door, which was almost always open, and a small two by two window. In the window was a set of bone white blinds. All the blades were turned to allow more light in.

Despite my delay, I caught up with Calvin before he could work his way around his desk. He carefully lowered himself into his chair. It was an older style office chair. The cushions were covered with brown leather, which had worn out and turned tan on the arms and the seat. The back still looked brand new. I discovered why when Calvin sat down. He immediately leaned forward and rested his arms on his desk, which was also starting to show signs of wear.

He had been in that position so long that the office had grown around him. The carpet faded where his heels had scuffed paths from the door to his seat. Dust had settled on all the places he never touched, like the tops of his two desk lamps, and on the bookshelves that covered the wall behind him.

The tri-state area map behind him appeared to be the most used thing in his office. The wooden tray at the bottom had dark spots where he would hang his left hand while he swept the map with his right. Handwritten notes were chicken scratched around the edges with arrows pointing to various locations.

On each side of his desk were stacks of folders that he would gather from the bullpen as they were completed. The stack on his left was the stack that still needed recycling, while the stack on the right he had already determined new locations for and were waiting for Hala to retrieve.

Calvin allowed me ample time to look around before asking me if I had any questions. I wasn't sure why, but I asked why he didn't have any pictures of his family up. It wasn't a question I would normally ask, but it struck me odd that someone his age wouldn't even have a picture of a grandchild or wife up.

He explained that his wife had passed about twenty years prior. They had no chldren. He said that because she was the kind of person that would have recycled everyone into only the finest situations and areas, he found it hard not to do the same while her picture was staring at him.

By the time he had finished his story, I could hear someone else in the office, I turned around to see Bruce placing his things on his desk. Calvin and I watched as he leaned over to take a peek at the folder on my desk. He was probably making sure I didn't work ahead, as he had strictly forbidden it.

"Better get out there. Remember to ask him the same questions you asked me when he shows you the unique deeds section."

I returned to my desk. "Good morning, Bruce. How are you?

Chapter 9

My second day was spent with Bruce explaining in painstaking detail how to figure the unique deeds section of the folder. He impressed upon me that while we had to consider each unique scenario, it was not our place to judge. He repeated that line between ten and fifteen times before the end of the day.

In the legacy files, the scores had already been figured, so all I had to do was enter the data into the system. On new files, I had to take each deed, determine whether it was a positive deed or negative. From there, I would find an approximate common deed in the database. Based on the point value of the similar common deed, I would adjust the final score up and down depending on the intent of the deed, number of victims or beneficiaries, and find a final score for the deed.

For practice, Bruce took Walter's folder and covered up every score for twenty-seven pages with white tape. He then had me start with the first one and try to figure the score. Though I appreciated the practice, I was certain it was more to keep me out of his hair than to improve my understanding.

Figuring Walter's file kept me busy for Tuesday and Wednesday. By the time I finished on Wednesday, I only had twenty minutes of work left. Instead of getting Bruce to go over my scoring, I chose to browse through the Compass program to fill the time. No need ruining two good days by talking to Bruce.

Communication with the rest of the world was equally slim on Wednesday. April was busy with her parents, and Larry had a date night with his girlfriend. I spent Wednesday evening in my underwear, watching reality television. While watching, I couldn't help but tally each person's score as the show progressed. It was in direct violation of Bruce's rule of no judging, but it sure made watching more bearable.

I was in bed early each night, but my sleep hadn't improved much since Monday. Thursday I went in early again. Just like before, Calvin was there before me.

We discussed how I was doing on Walter's file, and he gave me a few hints on how to find common deeds that were close to the unique deeds. He even went so far as to double-check a few of my answers and helped me adjust them before Bruce came in. I think he wanted to make me look good to knock Bruce down a peg.

As it came time for the others to get to work, Calvin promised we would start getting into how his job worked the next time I was in early. I questioned if he was taching anyone else his job and when he said no, I asked why, especially since there were others with much more seniority.

He answered with a half-joking, "You're the only one here."

I left Calvin's office, making a loop around the cubicles to see if I could remember the names of my coworkers. Most of them had identifying objects on their desks. It made it easier to remember them if I could associate them with some object on their desk.

Bruce was easy enough to identify. Tao was the only Asian in the office, and I had known a number of Tao's before, making her name easy enough to remember. I had to return to Calvin's office to ask who the guy who sat next to Tao was and who the two girls were next to him. He said Matthew was the ordinary guy, Heather was the pretty one, and Linda was the Danny Divito to Heather's Arnold Schwarzenegger. It seemed like an odd reference coming from him, but I didn't question it.

I remembered Judah. Judah and Jew sounded similar enough, though I felt a little racist for even thinking that thought. Sue reminded me of myself. Her desk was empty except for her work. Pictures of friends decorated the entirety of Phyllis' desk. I remembered her name, partially because she was the prettiest girl in the office, save Hala. It's a shameless thing, but I always remember the pretty ones.

Content that I knew everyone's names, I greeted them as they filed in. It wasn't that I really wanted to be best friends with any of them; I just didn't want to be the weird new guy that doesn't talk to anyone.

Bruce was the first one in again, and though it pained me, I greeted him. "Morning, Bruce."

"Good morning," he replied in his generally cold manner of speaking. He sat his things down on his desk and took his seat.

146

The thought crossed my mind to ask him how his evening was, but I imagined he would inform me that it was none of my business. I pretended to continue working on Walter's file as Heather and Linda rolled in.

"Good morning, Heather; Linda."

"Good morning." Linda responded first. "How are you today? Liking the job?"

"Morning," Heather said.

"I'm good, and yeah, the job is interesting. I've still got a lot to learn, though." I caught Bruce grin out of the corner of my eye.

It was ten minutes before Matthew arrived. He had a wet spot on the shoulder of his shirt.

"Morning, Matthew. How are you?"

"Tired and covered in spit up, but other than that, I'm doing well."

"Just have a baby?"

"Yeah, well, my wife did. Twins. It's fun, but it might be the death of me. So, if you see my file come through here, be kind, will you?"

"Will do."

Matthew headed off to his desk. By the time I turned my chair back around, Tao, Judah, Phyllis and Sue were all walking in together. Phyllis was packing light. She had a *People* magazine and a sports shake. Tao was carrying a tan canvas shopping bag filled with what I assumed was her lunch. Sue had her purse and a lunch. Sue usually ate lunch at her desk. I think it was to avoid the crowds in the lunch room.

Judah brought up the rear. He wasn't the kind of guy that took the time to pack his lunch. He also didn't appear to be the kind of guy that ironed his clothes before work. A laptop bag was slung over his shoulder and both hands were carrying tall coffees from the cafeteria.

"Morning, morning, morning, and good morning," I said as the group passed by. My greeting was met by a 'morning', 'good morning', a nod, and an 'ugh'.

"Long night, Judah?" I asked.

Judah leaned down and bumped me with his elbow and gave me a wink. "I'll let you know when it ends." I got the impression that he exaggerated the rowdiness of his lifestyle a bit, but he was nice enough it didn't detract from the pleasantness of his existence.

Everyone settled in for the day's work. I gave it about ten minutes before I let Bruce know I was ready to go over Walter's folder. He made me wait until he could finish what he was doing before he would review my work. I asked if I could start on another file while I waited, but was informed that it wouldn't be wise to work ahead until I was sure I knew what I was doing.

I sat patiently humming a tune that I made up as I went along. My humming quickly inspired Bruce to stop what he was doing to look over my scoring. He took a deep breath in and closed the folder that sat in front of him. Without leaving his chair, he leaned over and grabbed Walter's folder from my desk.

Bruce went section by section, removing the white tape and comparing my scoring to the scoring already in place. His irritation showed that I had more correct than he expected. At Calvin's suggestion I intentionally got a few wrong, and Bruce was excited to circle them with his red pen.

Through all the pages, Bruce found eight errors. He placed the folder back on my desk, opening it to the first page with a mistake.

"There are eight mistakes in here. Get them right and we can move on."

Bruce calmly reopened the folder he was working on. Even though I knew the correct answers to all the mistakes, I tried not to make it look too easy. I spent the next five minutes correcting my scoring. I spent the following fifty-five minutes pretending to correct my scoring.

"Done, boss," I said leaning over and placing the folder on his desk.

"I'm not your boss," he said opening the folder.

"It's just a figure of speech. I didn't mean to offend."

"You didn't offend me, I was merely correcting you."

"I'm sorry. Done, Bruce."

"That's better."

I watched as he double checked my corrections.

"Not bad." Bruce put the folder back on my desk. "So, I imagine you think you're ready for a 'live' folder." He made quote marks in the air when he said 'live'.

"Only if you think I am." I was stunned that I received a 'not bad' from Bruce. I expected him to tell me how ignorant I was.

"I don't. That being said, if you can do five more legacy files like that, we will try you out on one."

"Sounds like a plan. Where's the next folder?"

Bruce grabbed a stack of five folders from the table and placed them on my desk. He told me to work independently, but he wanted to check all five of them before putting them in the complete pile.

The rest of the work day went swimmingly. I began working on a file for a sweet little old lady named Beverly Hemmingway. Her record was nearly perfect. Of the one hundred and seven times she cussed in her life, none were malicious. She tithed, gave to charity, and was happily married for sixty-four years.

I couldn't get into the unique deed section of her folder before the end of the day.

I was the last to leave my desk. Bruce wrapped things up earlier than normal and was the first one gone. The others were walking out as I was putting Beverly's folder away. Besides Calvin, who seemed to never leave, Phyllis was the last of my coworkers to vacate the office. As soon as the door shut behind her, it reopened and Hala entered.

150

She was wearing her typical style of clothing; a black skirt, a blouse open a little further than appropriate, and black heels that made her almost as tall as I was. I assumed she was looking for Calvin so I gave her a nod.

Hala stopped at my desk. "What do you think so far?"

"It's good."

"Just good?" She took a seat on the edge of my desk.

"Well, you know. It has its better moments."

"Meaning that there are some not so good moments?"

She was leading me and I knew it, but my defense wasn't there to object. Hala wanted to see if I would complain about Bruce. She wanted to know what I was like after I was finally comfortable somewhere.

"I'm not saying that." I stood up and leaned on my desk, but on the other side of my chair. I needed a safety barrier from Hala. "How's the death business going?"

"Oh, you know, it has its better moments."

Hala propped herself up and started to walk towards Calvin's office. I watched for a few seconds, but before she reached his door I stopped her.

"Anything come back on my history yet?"

Hala looked back over her shoulder. "Not yet. Worried?"

"A bit. You said I was hell bound. Do you remember my score?"

"I don't. I sent your file on to the home office over a month ago. It's got to get there and get back. It can take some time. Don't worry, we'll figure something out."

"I sure hope so."

Hala disappeared into Calvin's office and the door shut. I finished gathering my things and left. On the drive home, I kept going over what Hala said. She knew for weeks that I was going to try to commit suicide. Moreover, if she knew that far in advance, why didn't she collect me? Hala wasn't the kind to make mistakes.

April called around 6 p.m. and took my mind off things. Her parents had just left and she was ready to vent. Her mother was the Betty Crocker type and invaded her kitchen for the entire week. Her father was a couch potato who was incapable of picking up after himself or letting go of the remote. According to her, she had been held prisoner in her own house for the last week and couldn't wait for Friday.

She wasn't usually the kind of person to complain, so I let her have at it. It took her about thirty minutes to calm down. Afterwards she wanted to hear about my day. I tried to keep it vague. I hadn't been a sorter long enough to know how to lie about it very well.

"It was just a regular day. Bruce told me that something I did was 'not bad', so I guess I'm getting things right."

"Good job. So if I say 'not bad' after sex, that's a good thing?"

"It beats the usual 'that's it?'." I snickered at my self-deprecating remark.

"Good point. I'll try to be more encouraging from now on."

"Thanks, you're a doll. Are we still on for Friday?"

She huffed. "After the week I've had, you bet your ass." Her cussing felt like she was doing it just because she hadn't been able to while her parents were there.

"Alright. Maybe afterwards I can earn a 'not bad' from you."

"I'm sure you'll manage."

We made small talk back and forth for another half hour before saying goodbye. I called Larry to make sure he was still game for Friday. His phone went to voicemail, so I left him an unnecessarily long message. I knew his phone wouldn't let him erase his messages until he listened to the whole thing.

I had slept so poorly the rest of the week that I immediately drifted off when my head hit the pillow. The snooze button felt my wrath Friday morning. When I finally arrived at work, I had to park four floors underground, squeezed between a poorly parked SUV and poorly parked station wagon. I was the last to get to my desk, but was still on time.

Beverly's file was still sitting on my desk waiting for me to enter her unique deeds into the system. I was so anxious for the weekend to arrive that not only did I get through Beverly's folder, I got through Jacob Dempson, Samuel Patrice, and Michelle Hart before the end of the day.

Jacob and Samuel were recycled, but Michelle went to heaven. Nothing spectacular stood out about any of their folders.

I barely spoke to anyone the entire day. It was probably the best day Bruce had the entire week. As soon as quitting time came around, I was out the door and in my car in under ten minutes.

April called me before I could leave the parking garage. We confirmed plans and I forwarded them on to Larry via text message. His response was simple and to the point.

Yes, Mother.

Larry did have a way with words. I was actually excited to see him. I was feeling nostalgic about his daily berating, which was much more entertaining than Bruce's. It helped that I could dish some back with Larry.

A quick shower and a change of clothes and I was on my way to pick up April. When I arrived at her house she was nearly ready. She applied a quick layer of lipstick, and we headed off to the bar.

We were the first to arrive. We found a large table near the back of the bar, behind a set of pool tables. Within minutes of our arrival, two of April's friends arrived; Jennifer and her boyfriend Clint. Jennifer was okay, Clint was a bit of a douche bag. He was into cage fighting in a ridiculous way. It was obvious from his eighty dollar branded T-shirt and his neck tattoo, though I doubt he had ever been in a real fight himself. Luckily, Larry showed up shortly after them. His girlfriend wasn't a fan of bars that didn't have a dance floor, so she had gone out dancing with her friends.

154

"Glad you could join us." April jabbed at Larry before I had a chance.

"Sorry, I was busy banging Steve's mom." Larry was quick to retort.

It was best to disarm Larry early, so I chimed in. "Yeah, she called just before you got here and said you need to come back and finish the job. Having problems keeping up with a retiree?"

"Oh stop," April scolded. She proceeded to make introductions for Larry's sake.

After everyone stood, shook hands and sat back down, the waitress came by and took our drink orders. The girls ordered cosmos, Clint ordered a mojito, I ordered a Boulevard Wheat, and Larry started the evening with a Jack and Coke.

Initially, April talked to her friends and I talked to Larry. Then I would talk to April and her friends would talk amongst themselves and Larry would sit back and scan the room for good-looking women. It wasn't until the second round that everyone loosened up and mingled.

As the conversations rotated around the table, I took some time to sit back and just listen. Clint and Larry began talking about gambling, April and Jennifer were talking about lip gloss. I wasn't particularly interested in either topic.

Inevitably, someone brought up work. My ears perked up in the hopes that no one would ask me what I do for a living. It started off with Clint asking Larry what he did.

"I work at LaRose with April. Different department though. Steve used to work there until he got fired," Larry replied to Clint's question before thinking his answer through.

"Thanks, dude."

Whenever someone talks about another person getting fired, everyone wants to hear the story, whether it's a good story or not. I think it's because we hear what the other person did and think 'Well, I don't do that, so I won't get fired'. I was no better. I always wanted to hear the grim details. That particular situation, however, I wished no one would ask.

It was Jennifer who dashed my hopes. "Why did you get fired, if I may ask?"

"Yeah, it's fine." It wasn't. "I took a position somewhere else and they fired me when I put in my two-week notice. It was no big deal."

Clint decided he would try to console me. "That's fucked up, man."

Jennifer was determined to dig until she found something of interest in my story. "How long ago was this?"

"A couple of weeks ago."

"Well, where are you working now?" Clint asked, helping Jennifer dig.

"I started this week at the LDI building downtown."

"Oh, you work for LDI?" Jennifer responded gleefully. "I've got a cousin that works there. Do you know Hugo Ortiz?"

"No, I don't work directly for LDI. I work for an independent group on the seventh floor."

"Holy shit, you're one of Hala's people aren't you?" Jennifer had a look of shock on her face.

I was certain I did too.

"Yes, she's my boss, but not my direct supervisor. How do you know Hala?" I was hoping to turn the conversation back towards Jennifer.

"Hugo told me that there's a division at LDI that doesn't have anything to do with LDI. He said that no one really knows what you guys do and that you aren't allowed to fraternize with the other employees there. You're like the CIA of LDI."

"I assure you it's not quite that cloak and dagger."

"Well, what do you do?" asked Clint, butting his nose into the conversation I was trying to avoid.

At that point, April's ears perked up. Larry had even stopped scouting for breasts and was now leaning in intently listening to the conversation. I knew that pausing too long would immediately make everyone think I was lying, regardless of what I told them.

"Well, I'd tell you but then I'd have to kill you, I'm sorry."

All eyes on me. Fuck.

The awkward moment of silence was followed by an awkward moment of laughter. April started it, and it spread. Man, she was a life saver.

"Seriously," April interjected, "he just does data entry."

I wiped imaginary beads of sweat from my forehead and proceeded to enjoy my evening. After a few rounds I was even enjoying Clint's company. A few rounds later, it seemed like half the bar was signing my cast. Our group was the last to walk out of the bar.

Instead of taking a cab directly home, we piled in one cab and took it to Grits 'n Eggs, a shitty little dive that served breakfast twenty-four hours a day. It may not have been the cleanest place in town, but everyone knew it was the best place to satisfy a drunken pancake craving at 3 a.m.

With our bellies full and senses returning, we all parted ways in separate cabs. April and I took our cab back to my place. The ride back was quiet. Perhaps I was just being paranoid, but I couldn't help but think that something was bothering April. About five times in as many miles we had the same conversation.

"What's wrong?" I would ask.

"Nothing. I'm just tired."

"Okay. You sure?"

"Yes."

Every girlfriend I had ever had was notorious for using that tactic. It's impossible to argue that someone isn't tired. Then, if you press the

158

issue, you're annoying them and then that becomes what is wrong. Machiavelli didn't have shit on women.

We arrived at home and engaged in the typical frolics that follow an evening on the town. I didn't wake up until 11:15 a.m. on Saturday. When I woke, the bed was empty and had been in that state so long, April's side had gone cold.

I rolled out of bed to discover that I had dodged a hangover, prompting me to give a sophomoric fist pump in the air. I looked in the bathroom, but April wasn't there. The events of the previous evening ran through my head, while I tried to remember if I had done anything stupid. Nothing out of the ordinary came to mind.

I called out her name as I walked into the living room, and she was still nowhere to be found. The kitchen was visible from my bedroom door, and unless she had stuffed herself in a cabinet, she wasn't there either. My cell phone was sticking out of the back pocket of the jeans I left on the living room floor the night before. I picked it up to dial April's number, but before I could finish dialing she walked through the front door carrying a large brown grocery bag.

"Good morning, sunshine," she said looking over the grocery bag. "How are we feeling?"

"Fine, except I thought you abandoned me."

"Well, I did, but only to get groceries for lunch and dinner. You really need something more than Hamburger Helper in you cabinets."

"Why? Stroganoff is the best thing to ever happen to the cardboard box."

"Be that as it may, I'm cooking two meals today and you are going to eat both of them and like it."

"Mac and cheese and burritos?"

"No," she said placing the bag on the counter. She began pulling items out of the bag. "For lunch, we are going to have reubens, with Greek salad."

"Exotic."

"Shush," she scolded. "Then for dinner, we are going to have stuffed pork loin with homemade mashed potatoes and asparagus."

She crumpled the empty bag and threw it away. Lying on my counter was a fresh loaf of rye bread, assorted fresh vegetables, a bottle of thousand island dressing, a pork loin from the butcher's around the corner, a bag of potatoes, and a half-gallon of orange juice. Orange juice was my favorite.

"What's the occasion?"

"No occasion, necessarily."

"Necessarily?"

"Take a shower, silly. A girl can't just be nice to her guy after a good night out?"

"I suppose she can," I replied, still mildly suspicious.

I did as she asked and took a shower. I returned from the bedroom dressed in my usual Saturday attire; jeans, Chucks, and my Winnipeg Jets shirt. I realized that I was overdressed when I saw that she had changed into her black and white panties that reminded me of prison garb in a late night cable movie and one of my white T-shirts.

As promised, ruebens were prepared and sitting on the coffee table. Greek salad sat in a separate dish, and in front of each plate was a full glass of orange juice. She sat, legs crossed on her spot on the couch.

"Lunch is served."

While the situation piqued my suspicions, it was too tempting to really worry about. I was a certain fat little bear and she had just set out a pot of honey. Not only did she have a meal laid out, was sitting quietly in her panties, but she had the opening scene to Blazing Saddles paused on the DVD player. I smelled a set up. I didn't care.

Ninety three minutes later, I cleared the plates and the coffee table. She had been so kind already, I refused to let her get up to do anything but use the restroom. When I returned I made her accept a back rub from me. Not surprisingly, she didn't protest. I was trying to soften her up to get information. My plan failed as we ended up in the bedroom.

Not quite ninety-three minutes later, we emerged from the room and returned to the couch. Our clothes stayed in the room.

"Alright. Today has been too good. What's the catch?" I asked.

"Why does there have to be a catch?"

"It's already ridiculous that I have a girlfriend as good as you, and now you're being even nicer than normal. Are you going to have me killed?"

"Okay, you've got me. I was fattening you up for the kill," she replied running her thumb across her throat. "In all seriousness, though, I do have an ulterior motive, but I wanted to save it for dinner. Can you trust me until then?"

I squinted like I was leery of her motives. "I suppose I could let it go for a bit. We should start cooking soon though."

We lounged about for another thirty minutes before mustering up the motivation to cook. By we, I mean she cooked. Every time I would ask if there was something I could do, she would kick me out of the kitchen.

"Aren't there any sports on?" she asked, pushing me out.

"Yeah, but you're in here wearing nothing but a 'Kiss the Cook' apron. How the hell am I supposed to watch TV?"

"Find a way, or I'm putting my clothes back on."

It went that way for an hour and a half. When the egg timer went off, she put everything on plates and put them in the oven on warm and demanded that we put on nice clothes for dinner.

I had to go to my back up suit, as my good suit was recently ruined due to an unforeseen suicide attempt failure. Though, I suppose it would have been more ruined if it had succeeded.

Something happened when I put on my suit. I began feeling a subtle depression creeping up. At first I didn't know what it was, but subconsciously, my brain had already realized that, had my suicide attempt succeeded, the suit I had on would have been the one I was buried in.

I imagined myself lying in a casket, cold and still. My skin like wax, eyes shut, my hair trimmed and combed, rouge on my cheeks. Then I imagined my family crying over me. My thoughts jumped to what April would be doing at that moment if I had been dead and buried. Would she be cooking for someone she deserved? Would she be locked in her room, crying herself to sleep? I continued getting dressed as those questions bounced around my head.

I had just finished tying my tie when she emerged from the bathroom. All of the horrible thoughts I was having disappeared in an instant. The light from the bathroom behind her amplified just how shapely she was. Her long red dress hugged every feature from the top of her breasts to just below her knees.

She had curled her hair and done her makeup. The dark eyeliner around her eyes made them more brilliant than usual. Long, dangling diamond earrings draped down beside her long neck, accentuating the curve where it met her bare shoulders.

I made a swirling motion with my hand and she did a turn. I approached her, kissed her, and put my arm out for her to take. She fed her arm through mine and I led her to the table. Like a gentleman should, I pulled out her chair and helped push it in. I went to the oven and removed the plates carefully. I brought hers to the table first, as I only had one arm I could use safely.

I returned to the oven and carried my plate to the table. I returned to the kitchen and opened a bottle of wine. When I got back to the table, I poured about an ounce into her glass so she could swirl it around and sample it, as if I knew what she was doing. She gave me the nod, so I filled both of our glasses and took my seat.

"See," she said, "you can be a gentleman."

"Shhh. Don't tell anyone. And I just have to say, you look amazing."

"Thanks. You're not too bad yourself."

"Yeah, nothing says sexy like a cast." I sipped my wine while I formulated the appropriate way to ask her what was with all the spoiling and fancy dress. "Soooo, are you going to tell me what this is all about, or-"

"Fine, jeez pushy." She took a gulp of her wine. "We've been together for a few months now..."

"About seven."

"Right, and I didn't know if you would be keen to the idea of maybe, well you see, I know things haven't been real easy on you lately, and, well, my lease is coming up in a month, and I really like you, I think I love you, and..."she trailed off.

164

"And..." I heard the word love, and it immediately made sense. I think I loved her too. It was an odd sensation. I knew I really liked her and we were good together and I had feelings for her, but I had been so focused on my issues that I hadn't taken the time to really examine them. I felt stupid that someone had to say they loved me before I realized I might love them. I found myself rattling on in my head while she hesitated.

"And I know it's early, but what do you think about moving in together. You don't have to answer now, just think about it."

"Yes."

"Yes, like yes or yes like you'll think about it?"

"Yes, like I would love that." I used the word love to try it out, but I didn't want to full-out say 'I love you' yet. It would have felt cheap to say 'I love you', when she was the one that brought it up first.

She popped up from the table to run over and kiss me, as best she could in heels. She collided with me with such force that we almost toppled over. April planted a few more kisses on my face before getting back up. As fast as she had attacked me, she returned to her seat. She straightened her hair and posture before speaking.

"I mean, cool. That's good."

"Yeah. It will be. Now let's eat."

It took about an hour to finish our dinner, mostly due to all the talking. By the time our meal was done, we had a date lined out for her to move in, how we were going to split bills, how we would manage time for ourselves.

I had thought that the subject of moving in together would make me nervous, but with April, it didn't seem to bother me in the slightest. She was about as close to the perfect woman as I had ever seen.

Then I realized I had a problem on my hands. I wasn't going to be able to keep my job a secret from April much longer. I had heard stories of people leading double lives before and it always sounded way to difficult and stressful for me.

I had to devise a plan. I needed to talk to my coworkers. First, I needed to talk to Hala to find out how bad my score was. Some of the other Sorters were married or had girlfriends, so I needed to get their advice on the subject. If all else failed, I would have to resort to the truth.

April and I finished our discussion about moving in together and then finished the evening in the bedroom. We spent Sunday relaxing, watching television, and eating leftovers. April left around 6 p.m., still glowing.

I called Larry to tell him the good news. I also wanted to see if he approved. Having the approval of your best friend can make a world of difference on delicate decisions.

"Congrats." he said calmly. "Can I have your balls, since you won't be needing them anymore?"

"What the hell? I thought you liked April."

166

"I do. That doesn't mean you should move in together."

"I know. We're moving in together because I like her." I was careful to avoid using the word 'love', to avoid any further backlash from Larry.

"That's great and all, but look at my situation. Tonya and I moved in together about a year ago. Now I have bath beads, tampons, hand towels, all kinds of unnecessary shit in my house. I have to ask permission to go out. The toilet seat is always down. Do you see where I'm going with this?"

"That you're the happiest I've ever seen you?"

"Oh, yeah, I'm just fucking with you. I think it's great. You need someone to keep your ass in line."

"Thanks."

I called April and informed her of Larry's approval. Not surprisingly, she had called Jennifer to get her opinion. She told me that she received a similar rash of shit from Jennifer before receiving her blessing. With best friend approvals out of the way, we discussed telling our parents and decided it would be best to wait. We spent another ten minutes on the phone before bidding each other goodnight.

It took me about five minutes to drift off to sleep, but it wasn't meant to last.

Chapter 10

"Stop! Don't shoot!" I screamed, sitting straight up in bed with my arms crossed in front of me like a shield.

The gunman was already gone. The gunman never existed.

As I tried to catch my breath, I looked over at the alarm clock. 4:17 a.m. glowed in red numerals. I turned the face of the clock down to hide its light as I pulled the sheet back up to my neck and laid down.

There was no possible way I was going back to sleep and I knew it. Instead of trying to sleep, I tried to remember my dream before getting up. The initial shock of waking up had shaken loose some parts of the nightmare. I remembered that I was back on top of the American National Bank building, only I wasn't trying to kill myself, I was trying to save myself from something. The gunman wasn't a man at all, it was a woman.

She looked like April in the face, but she was dressed like Hala. Larry was there, but he was sitting on a bucket counting cash. Everything else was fuzzy. I decided it best not to worry too much about it and get ready for work. I had a lot of information to gather.

Calvin was going to be my first stop. He had promised to show me how his job worked the next time I was in early. It also helped that he was always the first one there in the mornings.

As expected, Calvin was there before I was. I knocked on the trim of his office door to notify him of my presence.

"Come on in. I was expecting to see you."

"I've got to ask. What time do you get up in the morning?"

"Three. I'm usually in bed by nine. Men need six hours of sleep, women need seven. Children and bums need eight."

"I'll have to remember that."

"So, what brings you in this early? A strong desire to do good? Or is it something more sinister?" He wiped the corners of his mouth.

"Sinister I suppose. Nightmares to be exact."

"They do happen. Anything exciting?"

"No. Standard fare really."

"Darn. I was hoping for a good story."

"Hate to disappoint."

"I'll live...for a bit longer anyway."

"Good to hear."

"Let me guess. You're here to hear a story?"

I took a seat. "You did promise to show me how your job works."

"I did?"

"Afraid so."

"Alright. Let's get down to business. After all, I don't have enough time left to waste any."

He grabbed a folder that was supped to be recycled that he had already set aside for this occasion and went to work. He started by explaining how the map behind him worked. Each state, each county, city, or neighborhood carried values consistent with the number of hell bound, heaven bound, and recycled individuals.

Typically, a neighborhood that consistently had more people going to hell would have a lower value than one full of heaven bound souls. That value wasn't the only factor in determining each areas overall scoring. Other things like economic conditions, education, crime rate, population, number of churches, and community resources all factored in.

When a person's soul was set to be recycled, Calvin would review their scoring, the number of chances they had used up and take where they had been placed previously into account before determining where that soul would be placed. On their file, he would write a coordinate based on that location. After collection, that file would be sent to the home office. Generally within sixty to ninety days, that soul would be recycled to that area as a pregnancy.

From there, that soul's file would start over. Clean slate. The downside was that each time a soul was recycled Calvin had to make the conditions a little less favorable. He didn't have to, but that was the approved practice. If that soul had been recycled in his area more than three times before, he had to ship the file to the neighboring office to the East. All folders moved East.

"Why do you have to make it harder?" I asked.

"It's like a paper airplane," he said wiping the corners of his mouth and taking a deep breath before starting the next part of his speech. "You fold it, you fly it, but it doesn't fly right. What do you do? You unfold it, refold it, and throw it again. Maybe it flies straight, maybe it doesn't. If it doesn't, you repeat the process. Eventually, the paper gets worn to the point it can't be used. We are not much different."

"So, you're comparing the human soul to a paper airplane?"

He smiled, buying time to catch his breath. "Basically yes. I used to have this great analogy about darned socks, but you youngsters just don't get the reference. Want to hear it?"

I looked at the clock on the wall. "I'd love to, but it looks like it's about time for me to get to work. Next time?"

"Deal."

I took my seat and powered up my computer. I noticed a stack of folders on my desk that weren't there on Friday. I flipped through the first couple and realized they hadn't been scored yet.

I leaned back in my chair and yelled towards Calvin's office, "What are these folders?"

"Live folders."

"Bruce said I wasn't quite ready."

"You're never ready until you do it. I'll deal with Bruce."

"If you say so."

"I do."

I turned back to the folders. I sat the top one directly in front of me and the remaining four in my 'In' box. It felt good that Calvin thought I was ready to actually do the job they hired me for. It also felt good that I was circumventing Bruce's temporary authority. Take that, Bruce.

The folder in front of me was for Jacob Mancine. I immediately knew something was wrong when I felt how thin the folder was.

Jacob was only going to be twenty when he died. Not a lot of history for a twenty year old. That alone was enough to dampen my spirits. It didn't stop there.

His basic deeds included, but weren't limited to drugs, drugs, theft, assault, more drugs and arson. He was a bit of a potty mouth and by all counts, just an asshole in general. Still, I couldn't help but feel bad. If not for him, for his parents. No parent wants to outlive their child.

The crew started arriving when I was about halfway through his basic deeds. I took time to greet them as they poured in and for the most part, they responded kindly. The exception being Judah who looked a little too ragged to be at work. Most likely it was a late night out on the town. I let him quietly shuffle past me. Bruce was oddly the last to enter. Had he been more friendly, I might have been inclined to ask if he had a rough night. As the situation stood, I honestly didn't want to engage in any more conversation than necessary.

172

I greeted him as I had done with everyone else. Surprisingly, he said good morning as he walked by. As he spoke he took the time to glance over and see what I was working on. He immediately knew I wasn't working on a Legacy folder.

I had expected a tongue lashing. Bruce walked on by, sat his things down, and powered up his computer. For the first time since I started, he looked content. I figured content was the closest he ever came to happy.

I tried to extend a proverbial olive branch. "You seem happy this morning. Did you have a good weekend?"

"Not particularly, no."

"So why the smirk?"

He scoffed. "Because you finally did something right."

At first I thought he was pleased that I was working ahead. I soon realized I was wrong.

"You didn't listen to me, so you obviously don't need me, so I obviously don't have to train you anymore. Today just might be a great day."

His overuse of the word 'obviously' sickened me. I suppose I had it coming, but it still pissed me off. I was also a little embarrassed.

I returned to Jacob's folder to take my mind off of how angry I was. It offered little consolation. Every score I entered into the system took Jacob closer and closer to being recycled. By the time I finished his basic deeds, he was well within the recycle zone. His unique deeds section wasn't very thick. For his sake, I hoped he saved a burning bus full of orphans and nuns from driving over a cliff and landing on a church.

His unique deeds were about as far from my hopeful scenario as possible. There were only a few to enter, and none of them were good. The last was the one that sent Jacob over the threshold. It also hadn't happened yet.

I knew it hadn't happened yet because he was going to get methed up, run a red light, killing a woman in another car. That woman's name was April Klein.

My hands trembled as I entered the points. Perhaps it was a different April Klein, I thought; I prayed. I quickly looked through the stack on my desk to see whose folders I had.

Joseph Martin, Richard O'Hara, Bethany Jenkins were the first three in the stack. I squinted my eyes as I pulled the last folder off the stack, my body reacting like a child about to receive a shot. I slowly opened my eyes and looked around to see if anyone was watching. The only person not engrossed in their work was Judah, who was desperately trying to stay awake by doing a series of standing stretches.

I looked down, and sure enough it was April Klein. My heart sank and I felt nauseous. I ripped open the front cover hoping desperately that it wasn't my April. I scanned through her basic information, confirming my worst fear. It was my April.

My legs felt weak as I stood up to head to the restroom. Beads of sweat formed on my forehead and I felt out of breath. I felt like a punched out boxer; I wanted to fight, but had no strength. I finally reached the restroom and locked myself in a stall to gather myself.

I took a seat and put my face in my hands. A myriad of half complete thoughts overwhelmed me. It wasn't fair was the first thing that solidly came to mind. Things had just started turning around, April was moving in, I liked my new job, and I was supposed to be finding a way to not go to hell. I raised my hand to punch the stall door, but instead clenched my fist until my nails dug into my palm. The pain helped me contain the outburst. I couldn't let anyone know what was going on.

If only I had picked a different day, a different building, or a different method I would be dead and none of this would be my concern. Unfortunately, I was too scared to jump off a building again and it wouldn't do anyone any good. I had no choice but to calm myself enough to focus on the big picture.

There were three questions I had: Was there any way I could save April? Was it ethical for me to look at my girlfriend's folder? Lastly, how could I avoid hell? The first question I would have to figure out on my own, as I felt I couldn't bring it up to anyone without endangering April. The last I needed help solving, but it was going to have to wait. The second would require some digging, but was not my primary concern.

After a few minutes in the restroom, I returned to my desk, rubbing my stomach, trying to pretend I had some gut troubles. I was about as good a thespian as I was a liar. My act was only made believable by the fact that I was still sweating and I was certain my face was flush. It was a wasted effort, as no one was particularly interested in my restroom breaks.

Jacob's folder sat on my desk, still open to the last unique deed. I must have read it six times before entering it in the system. Seeing his status change from recycle to hell bound offered me a small degree of guilty satisfaction.

I briefly considered not turning his folder in, but I thought that if anything, it would save his life and not April's. The last thing I wanted was to do him any favors. I needed information.

Once complete, I entered Calvin's office and sat down.

His back was to me. His old hands slid cross the map looking for a zone. He tapped the map twice and turned to write the zone down. That's when he noticed me.

"Everything alright?" he asked.

"I guess," I said. "I just had my first hell bound folder."

Calvin smiled. "I was wondering when you would be in here for that. I gave you Jacob's folder on purpose."

"Why?" I immediately became suspicious.

"You may have noticed he was a repeat offender." Calvin wiped the corners of his mouth. "He was one of my first. Well, he was my first as Melissa Coates, but that was a whole life time ago. I had a feeling he was headed that way, and you needed to get a tough one out of your system."

"Is that the only reason?"

He cocked his head slightly to the side. "Yes. Is there something about Jacob and you I don't know? You aren't related are you?"

"No, no. I was just wondering." I wanted to press him for more information, but I didn't want to put him on guard.

"Alright then. Are you okay with the fact that you are, in a way, sending a person to hell?"

"Hell yeah, I mean, yeah. I didn't make him act like an ass."

"Fair enough. You took that better than I expected. I'm proud of you."

The thought crossed my mind to say, 'it's easy when the guy is going to kill your girlfriend', but I opted against it. Instead I asked how I would get ahold of Hala if I needed to. Calvin informed me that they were going to have a meeting later that day and he would send her my way when it was done, if she had time. I had her cell phone, but I didn't think we were at the point in our personal or working relationship where I could just give her a call. Besides, I didn't want to interrupt her witnessing someone's death. It seemed unprofessional.

I returned to my desk as my coworkers were heading for lunch. When the room was nearly clear, I slid April's folder into my top desk drawer and locked it . I wasn't ready to process it.

Judah came by on his way out and invited me to lunch with him, Phyllis, and Matthew. I felt like being alone, but it seemed like a good opportunity to get some information before I spoke with Hala.

Judah and I caught up with Phyllis and Matthew just outside of the building. Matthew was hurriedly smoking a cigarette. Phyllis was busy scolding him about it. Judah and I joined the group and we quietly walked to a nearby sandwich shop. We engaged in light chatter about the weather, but nothing substantial.

After sitting down with our meals, Judah started in with the questions.

"Alright, Steve, what's your story?"

Phyllis slapped him in the arm. "Way to ease into a conversation. I'm sure he doesn't want to give us his life story over one lunch."

I soon realized I was going to have to give to get. "No, it's fine. Not a whole lot to tell really. Lived here most of my life, except a short stint I did in prison after I got all my friends killed in a car accident. Only child, both parents still alive. I graduated college behind bars, bounced around on a few jobs, had a few girlfriends, then I broke my arm, met Hala and now I'm sitting here with you, enjoying a delicious Cuban Chicken sandwich."

"Jesus," Judah responded. "You've lived here your whole life?"

It was a clever cover-up to extinguish the awkwardness that everyone was feeling. I had become used to telling people about the accident. It was like going to confession for Catholics, only instead of a priest, I confessed to strangers.

It seemed that others weren't as comfortable hearing it. Fortunately, I worked with a group of people who read about all manners of horrible events and thus, they were reasonably desensitized. Their looks of shock quickly dissipated. The only sound coming from our table was that of Matthew crunching on a mouthful of chips.

"Pretty much," I added to break the silence.

"I'm really sorry," Phyllis added.

"No, I don't mind living here." I smiled, but she didn't get the joke, at least, not at first.

"I mean about, oh..."

"It's fine. It was a long time ago. As I've learned after my short time here, we all make mistakes. Some more than others, I suppose, but that's life."

"I put my cousin's eye out with a stick when I was seventeen," Judah confessed, assuming it would make me feel better. It started a chain reaction.

Matthew was mid-chew when he spoke for the first time since we arrived. "I stole a bald eagle feather from the zoo when I was twenty."

"I, ummm," Phyllis wanted desperately to claim some wicked deed she had done so she could be included, but being so young, her resume was on the slim side. "I once made out with two guys in the same day."

Phyllis caught three blank stares.

"What does that measure on the deed scale, Phyllis?" Judah asked.

"Does it even register?" Matthew added.

"Yes. It's a three, if you must know," Phyllis responded defiantly.

I tried to back her up. "What's putting an eye out worth, or eagle theft for that matter?"

"Well, it was accidental, so, a seven. But if I had meant to, it's at least a twenty." Judah had obviously done his research.

Matthew was mid chew again when he answered "Four, but only because it went against local law; it's not against universal law to take a bird's feather or anything," he said and then he quickly returned to eating.

Phyllis was satisfied with my defense. She gave me an appreciative look and tried to change the subject. Unfortunately, what I hadn't calculated was that I was going to get asked about my accident.

Judah was the bravest one. "If you don't mind me asking, what was your deal worth?"

"I haven't seen my file yet. I don't know. Though I imagine it's not good."

"They had mine in on my second day," Matthew added.

Phyllis and Judah had theirs on day number two as well. While it was irritating that I hadn't gotten to see my folder yet, it did help me end that particular portion of the conversation.

"Can I ask a work question?" I asked to the group, rhetorically. "Do your girlfriends, wives, or boyfriends know what you do?"

"Sure." Matthew was the first to answer. "She knows I go to work every day. She knows I do data entry and she knows where I work. As for what I do specifically, no."

"My boyfriend thinks it's great," Judah added with a lisp and bending his hand at the wrist. "Seriously though, I don't tell the women in my life what I do. They can't be trusted." He shot Phyllis a suspicious glance.

"Oh, shut up, Judah. You haven't had a date in months, and no, we aren't allowed to talk about it. It goes against your record in a big, bad way."

"So lying is acceptable?"

Judah put his hand on my shoulder. "It's not lying, it's being vague. Lying would be telling someone you are a race car driver to get in their pants; being vague is saying you have a boring desk job to avoid getting sent to hell."

"Fair enough. Vague it is then."

The remainder of lunch was spent comparing our sandwiches and the varying degrees of tastiness of each. I had to force myself to finish my sandwich. Because of my nerves I felt full after the first bite, but I didn't want to let on that anything was wrong. I kept looking for a window to try and get any more information to help April, but I didn't want to be the guy that only talks about work. In my experience, only talking about work was a great way to get people to stop talking to you.

I offered to throw everyone's trash away, though my offer was unanimously refused due to my broken arm. I reassured my co-workers that it was just a fracture and that it's not going to get any worse by tossing out a bit of trash. They grumbled as I stacked all the trays and dumped them. Matthew stepped out to smoke while the rest of us refilled our drinks. We met up with him just outside the door and walked back to the office.

When we arrived, Hala was already waiting for me at my desk. In fact, she was sitting in my chair, fiddling with the lock on my drawer, turning the key that I left in it to the left and right. A lump formed in my throat.

"Calvin said you wanted to talk to me," she said with a grin.

"Yeah. I just had a few questions."

"Shall we go somewhere more private?"

Her offer sounded more personal than professional, but that was how most things she said sounded. I agreed. Bruce gave me a 'go to hell' look on my way out the door. I graciously returned it.

By more private, Hala apparently meant her office. We proceeded to take the elevator up to her floor. Beatrice was manning the reception desk and having a bit of a heated discussion with Andrew. Andrew was slightly more presentable than the first time I met him. His hair was combed at least.

He didn't notice us step out of the elevator, which is probably why he was still talking to Beatrice the way he was.

"Look, Bea," he had both of his hands on her desk in an obvious yet poorly executed attempt at intimidating her,"I need to speak with Hala now. I know she's in there, she just had a meeting with that black guy."

Hala stopped me just outside the elevator by putting her arm across my chest. The smile on her face told me that we were about to witness something noteworthy.

"Listen here, Andy," Beatrice started, "first off, remove your hands from my desk. You don't seem like the type to wash after you use the restroom. Secondly, you don't call me Bea, my name is Beatrice. Thirdly, *that black guy* has a name and it's Calvin. He's a wonderful man, perhaps you should take a lesson from him. And lastly, Andy, if you want to speak to Hala, you can make an appointment like everyone else, or you can turn around."

As entertaining as it was, I immediately felt uncomfortable. Andrew turned around to see Hala and I standing there staring at him. He looked at Hala, then me, then back at Hala.

Hala spoke first, "Is there a problem Andy?"

"Andrew."

"My apologies. Is there a problem Andrew?"

"I just needed to discuss a few things with you, but it appears you're busy," he glanced over at me. "I guess I'll make an appointment."

· "Please do. It's a terribly busy time for me and my group."

Hala led me into her office, leaving Andrew and Beatrice to hash out their differences. She closed the door behind me. Even though I had been in it before, her office was still just as impressive as the first time.

"Shall we head to the patio? It's a beautiful day out," Hala suggested.

"We shall," I replied. "I mean, yes." I never used the word shall. Despite my current situation with April, I was still a guy and prone to acting like an idiot in front of the fairer sex. I found it got worse for me around Hala.

"Great. I'll grab us a couple of drinks and we'll head up. Beer okay?"

"Am I allowed to have beer on the clock?"

"When you're with me, you're allowed to have anything I offer." She smirked. "I'm the boss, remember?"

"Fair enough." I made a conscious decision to not read too much into her previous statement.

She grabbed a few bottles from her fridge and led the way to the balcony. With each step, I became a little more anxious. I knew what information I wanted, but I wasn't sure how to get it discreetly. I wanted to know about my folder, but I was actually more interested in what I could do for April.

We stepped out onto her roof patio. She was right. It was a beautiful day out. It was nice when I went to lunch, but it was even better from that height. She pointed to a chair and told me to take a seat. She grabbed a chair near mine, turned it to face me, and took a seat.

"What's on your mind?" she asked handing me both beers.

I opened one and handed it back to her. "Quite a bit actually." I opened my beer.

"Had your first hell bound today didn't you?"

"I did, but that doesn't bother me so much."

"Really?" she didn't seem convinced.

"Well, it did a little, but that's not why I wanted to talk to you."

"Then what is it?"

"It's about my file."

"What about it?"

"I haven't seen it yet. Everyone else said they saw there's on their second day." I didn't want to rat anyone out, so I stuck with the 'everyone'. "When you offered me the job, you said I was hell bound, but I need to know how bad it is."

For the first time Hala didn't seem to have an answer right away. She stalled by taking a few drinks of her beer. She carefully placed the bottle on the ground while she searched for words.

"Do you trust me?" she asked placing her hand on my leg.

I looked down at her hand, and wondered where the conversation was going. "Sure."

"Sure or yes?" she asked removing her hand.

"Yes."

"Then I'm going to tell you what's going on with your folder, but please don't ask why. I promise I will tell you when the time is right, but now isn't that time."

"Deal."

"Your folder is back at the home office being modified. The last deed in your folder never happened, so it needs corrected."

"Okay, what's the big deal? You messed up and I didn't die. Doesn't that happen every now and again?"

Hala stared at the floor. "I didn't mess up. I intentionally didn't collect you."

I could tell she struggled not only to tell me that she did it intentionally, but she also appeared to want to tell me more. I was confused and elated at the same time. I didn't understand why a woman I had never met, who watches people die every day, failed to do her job when

186

it was my turn. On the other hand, I realized that there might be some hope for April.

Without trying, a bit of the information I was looking for had landed in my lap. It took effort to hold back my grin. It was much easier when I looked at Hala and noticed her eyes were misting up. She wasn't crying, but it wouldn't have taken much to push her over that edge.

I opted to stay quiet instead of asking if she was okay. If she was okay, she wouldn't be on the verge of crying. We sat in silence for a few minutes while she collected herself. I tried not to look directly at her during the wait. I didn't want to make her more uneasy; that and even on the verge of tears, she was dangerously beautiful. I did my best, only making intermittent glances when I took a drink.

A deep inhale and long exhale let me know she was better. I took another sip and looked at her down the length of my empty bottle. I caught her doing the same to me.

"How about I go down and get another round for us?" I offered.

"I think I could use another," she said, making one last sniffle.

I placed my hand gently on her shoulder as I walked past, to signify that things would be alright. She was quick to bring her hand up and put it on top of mine. Her fingers were warm and soft. At that point I wondered who was comforting who.

After a few seconds, I walked away, letting my hand slide off her shoulder. Her hand stayed up on her shoulder. I could still feel her touch halfway down the stairs.

I returned to the roof with our drinks. Hala was standing, looking over the edge of the roof.

"What was it like?" she asked without looking.

"What?" I replied as I approached the ledge.

"Jumping."

I became a little worried about her mental state at that point and decided to lighten the mood. "A lot better than the landing, that's for sure."

She turned her head to look at me. "Seriously. Don't worry, I'm not thinking about doing it."

"Then why do you ask?"

"Curiosity, I guess."

"It was sort of nice, I suppose; knowing that you didn't have to worry anymore. That one brief moment of pain would end a lifetime of it. Of course, in retrospect, it was selfish, stupid, cowardly, and a number of other words that aren't pleasant."

"Would you ever try it again?"

"I could say no, but you never know what you're going to do." I took a drink and swirled my bottle. "If I were to do it again, you would have to collect me, huh?"

"Probably," she said staring out over the city.

188

"Well, at least it would be someone I know."

She didn't respond. I didn't expect her to. We stood there leaning against the ledge, watching over the city, letting the cool breeze blow away the thoughts of death and suicide, heaven and hell, and collecting and counting. It was the most normal moment I had shared with Hala since we met.

"Do you mind, staying up here for a bit?" she asked.

"Not at all."

Chapter 11

The next couple of weeks at work were fairly normal, considering my occupation. After my afternoon with Hala, I took some time to reflect upon what we had talked about, and how I could use the information to not only save April, but keep myself out of hell. Knowing that there might be hope was enough to help me sleep a few hours a night.

I spent most evenings either at April's planning the details of the move or at my place brooding in solitude. When I wasn't doing either of those things I was digging through my closets, finding anything I could to give to charity. *It couldn't hurt*, I though. I even convinced April to give some of her clothing away. I figured as a back up plan, if I couldn't save her I would try everything I could to help her score, though I doubted that she was in any trouble in that department.

The nights spent at my house, I would wake up from a nightmare and within an hour, I would find myself sitting at Calvin's desk. I think we both liked the company. Nights I spent at April's I would wake up after about four hours of sleep and lay motionless by her side until the alarm sounded.

Some days, Calvin would have an extra cup of coffee setting on his desk waiting for me. When I asked him about it, he would simply state that he had a feeling I would be in. More than work, we discussed life lessons he had learned. He had a story for almost everything. Unfortunately, his memory wasn't as sharp as it once was, and every now and again he would pause for an uncomfortably long time, trying to recall a name or a place, then decide it was gone forever. Such moments were usually followed by him cursing his age and then moving on without the particulars. It was as amusing as it was sad. I wished I had known him when he was younger.

April and I continued making plans for her to move in, as if I knew nothing. Her folder lay in my desk drawer, untouched. The urge to peek at her past deeds was overwhelming at times, but in the end, I felt it was an obscene invasion of privacy. I knew I would have to do something about it, but each day I would convince myself that tomorrow would be better. A lot of tomorrows came and went; none of them were quite right.

Since that day on the rooftop, I had barely seen or heard from Hala. She called my desk the day after to tell me thank you and to let me know that the home office received my folder. She said it would be a couple more weeks before it would be corrected and sent back. Beyond that, I heard nothing. Calvin would mention her on occasion, saying how busy she was.

Larry was nearly as scarce, but that's how he was. When things were going well, he was relatively quiet; when things were blowing up, he was by your side one hundred percent. He called me to make sure I still wanted to have April move in, and when I confirmed, he stated he was glad and then changed the subject to the new girl they hired in my place and how big her breasts were.

Despite my quiet dilemma, things were going well. Hala had admitted that she didn't collect me on purpose, which meant that the things in our folders weren't set in concrete. I wasn't sure how, but I knew there had to be a way to save April. I was going to find out soon what was in my folder, so that I could devise a plan to save myself. Bruce had taken a standpoint of non-interaction with me, which was more than acceptable. I was getting more comfortable with my job and my other coworkers. We had even made it a habit to go out to lunch once a week. I used that time to gather as much information as possible without making it obvious. Unfortunately, nothing I found out helped me with April.

During my first few weeks, I sent twenty people to heaven, seven to hell, and eleven to Calvin's office for recycling. They were numbers I was comfortable with. On top of live files, I entered a number of Legacy files. For the most part, none of them stood out, except one.

I came across Margaret Wilson. Margaret was on her forty-third attempt, giving me plenty of past names to search on the internet. It was a good way to spend break time. The only interesting person she had been was Joachim Murat, King of Naples from 1808 to 1815. As I read through Joachim's biography on Wikipedia, I skipped over most of the names, because either I didn't care or they were French and I couldn't pronounce them. I did find out that he was executed by firing squad. Included in the biography were some of his last words.

"I have braved death too often to fear it," he said before telling the soldiers to aim for his heart and avoid the face.

I wondered if he really knew how many times he had faced it and if I would feel the same once I figured out my past.

Her other lives weren't nearly as interesting, and this most recent was no better. As Margaret, she lived a good clean life and was on her way up. I was happy for her, but it did nothing to take my mind off of things. Bad people were usually more entertaining.

On the following Thursday I woke up in the middle of a nightmare involving zombies and headed into work. April stayed at her apartment that entire week because it was the last week of her lease and she wanted to soak it all in, so Thursday was the third day that week I had spent with Calvin.

I knocked on the door before entering Calvin's office. He told me to enter, but there was something different about his voice; something sad. The cup of coffee he usually set out for me wasn't there. I didn't think much of it, until Calvin stopped what he was doing to turn around and acknowledge my presence.

Calvin looked like shit. There wasn't any one thing in particular, he just looked about ten years older than usual, which was saying a lot. Despite his dark skin tone, he looked pale. His shoulders were hanging lower than normal. His eyebrows seemed to droop almost over his eyes. The bags under his eyes hung low, making him look like a basset hound.

"What's going on, boss?" I asked cheerily, hoping that would pep him up.

He attempted to gather himself before speaking. Out of habit, he wiped the corners of his mouth. "It's nothing important."

"Bullshit." I didn't intend on it sounding as harsh as it came out.

"Hey, now, son," he said shaking his bony finger at me.

"Just calling it like I see it."

"You're right. It is bull crap." He took in a few deep breaths. "My folder came up."

"Shit."

I was still struggling with the possibility of April's death. I tried to wrap my mind around how Calvin must have felt knowing his time was coming. I didn't want to say 'I'm sorry' because it didn't do the situation justice. We both stared at Calvin's desk, waiting for one of us to come up with the appropriate thing to say next.

"Is there nothing you can do?" I asked. I felt guilty that a small part deep inside me became excited. I imagined that he would tell me the secret to avoiding collection in an attempt to save himself. It was a foolish misjudgment of character.

"Not really much to do," he said. "Even if I did manage to put it off, I wouldn't want to put Hala through that, and it would catch up to me eventually."

"What do you mean put Hala through that?"

Calvin was about as bad of a liar as I was. "Nothing, I just meant that, oh, I don't know, it's nothing."

"So what if someone accidentally forgot to process your folder?"

"It would be really, really bad for that person," he replied, looking at me like he knew what I was thinking. "That's a surefire way to tank your own score. Besides, it was Bruce who got my folder. No way around that guy. At least he had the courtesy to tell me before he left yesterday."

"Can I ask which-"

"Heaven."

"Congrats, how long?"

"Same as all the others. One to six months, but one can't know for sure."

I decided to go for a long shot.

"What if you were to move out of district before you were collected?"

"A new file would just show up at the new office, Hala would receive notification here to destroy the file here and someone else would collect me. Running doesn't help."

Shit. Escape was the only back up plan I had in case I couldn't save April. It appeared that option wasn't an option at all.

Calvin changed topics and returned to one of our topics from a previous work session; ethnic hardship. When reassigning someone, Calvin liked to take someone's ethnic background and potential ethnicity into consideration. He insisted that it wasn't a racist concept, just a reality.

The truth was that depending on the zone to which someone was assigned, they would be subject to certain factors. His first example was a young black man living in what Calvin referred to as the black ghetto. Suppose he grew up decent enough, but had a problem with stealing that prevented him from going to heaven, but didn't exactly send him to hell. Recycling him near the same area, but in a predominately white neighborhood would certainly impact his quality of life. The idea was to make each subsequent attempt at life a little harder each time.

He furthered his examples by talking about a well to do white business man who cheated his way to the top, lied, and committed adultery. Despite his terrible behavior, he tithed and gave to charity. Again, someone who wasn't good enough for heaven, but not bad enough for hell. Recycling him in an area where his Mexican maid was likely to live would affect his ability to make the same mistakes twice.

I was admittedly out of my comfort zone discussing race. As a white male, it was generally frowned upon for me to make any assumptions about other races and creeds. Anyone who knew me knew I didn't care, but I didn't want to say the wrong thing in front of Calvin. He noticed my uneasiness and told me to quit being a sissy about it.

He gave me a few more examples before the others started showing up for work. Bruce was the first to arrive. After placing his things down, he came by Calvin's office. I gathered by the way he stood in the doorway that he wanted to talk to Calvin in private.

"Good morning, Bruce," I said, expecting a glare in return.

"Good morning, Steve," he said gleefully.

I looked back at Calvin who was as shocked as I was.

"Morning, Bruce." Calvin wiped the corners of his mouth, "What can I do for you? Steve, we'll talk later."

I returned to my desk and Calvin's door shut behind me. It stayed shut for another two hours. In that time I had already finished one file from the previous day and was halfway through another one. I checked my desk to make sure that April's folder was still in it and untouched. It was. Finally the door opened and Calvin came out for a short time, but I was certain it was for a restroom break. He wasn't known for his strong bladder.

It wasn't until lunch time that Bruce came out of the office. Normally I would avoid conversation with Bruce at all costs, but my curiosity was getting to me. I thought I would start simple and see if he gave me anything.

"How's it going in there?"

"Good," he said, grabbing his keys out of the desk and heading for the door.

Damn. Nothing.

Calvin was shortly behind him, so I didn't get a chance to ask what they were talking about, not that he owed me an explanation. I went to lunch with my curiosity unsatisfied. Were they talking about Bruce taking Calvin's spot? Did they know I was holding a folder? About a thousand different possibilities rolled through my head before I gave up trying to imagine what they were talking about and called April at her desk.

"LaRose financial, this is April, how may I help you?"

"You could hurry up and move in with me so I have a warm body to sleep next to every night."

"Well, Mr. Mysterycaller, I'm afraid I already have a boyfriend I'm moving in with."

"He sounds like a chump. You should move in with me."

"But I haven't even told you about him," she said, holding back a chuckle.

"Fair enough, tell me about him."

"He's a nice enough guy. Rather handsome when he chooses to clean up. Hung like a..."

"Like a what?"

"Oh, I probably shouldn't say."

"No, it's okay, you can."

"Nope," she clamped shut. "I'm not telling."

"Damn. Fine. How's work going?" I asked.

She sighed. "I'm a debt collector. Other than the last thirty seconds, everyone I have talked to hates me."

"Remember, honey, they don't hate you. They hate paying their bills."

"You're right. Fuck them."

"Wow."

"Sorry," she apologized with minimal sincerity. "How's your work going?"

It was one of those times where I wished I had a normal job and could share what I do with my loved ones and talk about the problems of the day. I knew that for the rest of my life, I wasn't going to be able to have a normal conversation about my profession. I desperately wanted to tell her about Calvin. Necessity being the mother of invention, I created a suitable lie, or at least a partial lie.

"I found out this morning that my boss only has one to six months to live; cancer I think."

"Hala?" she asked in a surprised tone. "She's so young."

"No, Calvin. The old black guy."

"Oh," she replied flatly.

"Oh?"

"Well, he's no spring chicken."

"No, but that still sucks."

"I know, I'm sorry. That wasn't very nice of me."

"It's okay."

"We'll talk more about it tonight, I've got another call coming in. I love you."

Before I could respond, she was gone. I returned to work without eating. My curiosities and concerns were starting to weigh heavy on me. Bruce and Calvin spent the rest of the day in his office. Before the end of the day, I had sent two people to hell and honestly didn't feel bad about it. I was too consumed by my own worries to worry about others.

Typically, I would call April when I got off work, but I had worked myself into such a bad mood that I decided not to call her. If she wanted to talk, she could call me. It was selfish and childish and I knew it. After a few minutes on the drive home, my phone rang, and sure enough, it was April.

"Hello."

"Awfully professional way to answer the phone for your girlfriend, don't you think?"

"I suppose."

"Something on your mind?"

"I'm sorry. It was just a long day at work."

"Want me to come over?"

"No, that's okay."

I actually did want her to come over, but she only had a few days left in her apartment. Besides, it wasn't like I could tell her what was vexing me.

"Are you sure? I could come over, maybe make some dinner, maybe make some something else..." she trailed off.

"As great as that sounds, I think I'm just going to go home, shut the blinds, shut out the lights and stew."

"If you insist. If you need anything, let me know."

"I will."

I was true to my word. I walked in my door and turned the lights on long enough to sit my things down and throw blankets over the curtains to help block out any light. The only visible light source was the timer on the microwave. I exchanged my work clothes for a pair of gym shorts.

I laid down on my couch face down and within minutes I was sound asleep. My week of early mornings with Calvin had finally caught up with me. I could have slept the whole night through, but instead I was ripped from my slumber by a rapping on my door.

One eye squinted so I could see the time on the microwave from my couch. It was 8:43. My first thought was that the visitor would go away. Had it been April she would have called first. Larry never made random visits. The knocking stopped, but was followed by my cell phone ringing.

My bloodshot eyes rolled back in my head. Apparently whoever it was knew I was home and wasn't leaving until I answered. Instead of going for my phone I went straight for the door. The ringing stopped as I unlocked the door. I opened the door to find Hala standing in front of me with tears in her eyes.

"Holy shit, are you okay?" It may not have been the most sensitive way to ask, but it was all I had.

She shook her head no while staring at the floor.

"Well, come in." I put my good arm around her and ushered her in my apartment. I looked down the hallway to make sure no one saw her come in. I had a reputation to worry about, and more importantly a girlfriend. "What's going on?"

It bothered me when the people I considered strong and independent were at their weakest. Each time I witnessed it, it made me think there was no hope for people like me who constantly stood on emotionally shaky ground.

Hala took a seat on my couch. She was dressed more casually than I had ever seen her. She was wearing jeans and a white V-neck T-shirt. Her dark hair was frazzled and her makeup was running down her soaked face. I felt terrible for thinking she looked good even at her worst. Regardless of the situation, I'm a man, and that's just how we are.

"Do you want something to drink?" I continued asking questions, thinking she might answer one of them. She nodded her head yes.

It appeared I wasn't going to get anywhere vocally, so I grabbed a bottle of beer and a bottle of water out of the fridge. I almost grabbed the leftover milk from when I had to get the gold ink of my privates, but realized it was way past its expiration date. I shoved it back behind a flat 2 liter of soda.

I placed both bottles on the coffee table in front of her. Without hesitation, she grabbed the beer. I took a seat within arm's reach of her and watched, waiting for her to speak. The beer was half gone before she seemed to acknowledge my existence.

"Thank you," she said regaining her composure.

"No problem. Care to talk about it?"

"Not tonight," she struggled to say whatever it was she wanted to say.

"Then when?"

"How about dinner, tomorrow night?"

I found myself in quite the predicament. I had April, loved April, and was on the verge of having her move in with me, assuming I could keep her alive. In front of me was Hala who was as tempting as a woman can be, obviously in distress, and oddly interested in me. On top of that, she had information I needed to save the girl I loved.

From a relationship standpoint, I knew that dinner with Hala was a bad idea. From an eternal resting place of my soul and the possible length of my girlfriend's life, it wasn't such a bad idea. Weighing the options was proving difficult.

Hala weighed them for me. "It will be worth your time."

"But I-"

"Tell your girlfriend you have to stay late at work. Or you could tell her the truth. It's up to you."

The problem was that I didn't really know what the truth was. I didn't know if it was a work related dinner or something else. It certainly felt like something else. While I considered the offer, my phone rang.

It was the one call I didn't want at that moment.

"I have to take this." I grabbed my phone and headed for the bedroom.

"What's up, babe?" I asked.

"Just wondering how my darling is doing," April answered.

"Fine, I just woke up about ten minutes ago."

"Great. Then open your door. I have a surprise for you."

I began sweating. On a night when I said I wanted alone time, my girlfriend was going to walk into my apartment and find me not alone; and not only with company, but with my attractive boss to boot.

There was no choice and no time to fabricate a lie. "Okay."

It felt much like jumping off the American National Bank building all over again. Nothing left to do, but to do it. I walked out of my room looking over at Hala sitting on my couch.

204

She returned my blank stare with a confused look that deepened as I approached the door. I unlocked the deadbolt then the door lock. A deep breath in gave me the courage to pull the door open.

Standing in the hallway was April. She was wearing a long grey coat, unbuttoned and held slightly open, revealing a few thin strips of black lace and white bows covering just enough of her skin to be considered as underwear. Shiny black pointed heels made her about four inches taller than normal. Her hair and make-up were done. In her left hand was a six-pack of beer.

I stood, jaw open, in my doorway. My eyes traveled from her hair to her feet and back again. For a brief second, I forgot about the woman sitting on my couch.

While I forgot, April noticed.

Her coat clamped shut.

"What the fuck?" she managed to spit out.

"I-"

Hala had worked her way to the door before I could finished stumbling over my words.

"You must be April," Hala stated extending her hand.

April was still holding the beer in one hand and her coat closed with the other. Whether that was the reason she didn't extend her hand or not, it was obvious she wasn't going to shake hands. Hala dropped her arm back by her side.

While embarrassed and angry, April managed to keep her cool. "And you would be...?"

"I'm sorry. I'm Hala, Steven's boss. I know this must look terribly inappropriate, and I'm afraid that's my fault." She paused, waiting for April to say something, but it didn't come. "I just came by to talk to Steven about a position that we have opening up."

"And, it couldn't wait until morning?" April looked inquisitively at me.

I had nothing.

"I'm afraid not. I don't know what Steven has told you about his immediate supervisor, but he will be leaving us, and I need someone to take his place. I find these discussions are best held outside of work, so as not to alert the other employees."

"I see," April replied, clearly not satisfied.

"Babe, why don't you come in?"

April entered and gave a look around the apartment. The look on her face said that she was looking for signs of a struggle. Seeing none, she took a seat on the couch where Hala had been.

April waved her hand at the love seat near my couch. "Hala, come, have a seat."

"Thank you," Hala accepted.

It was like watching two seasoned warriors exchanging glances before battle. Neither one wavered in the slightest. April knew that

206

nothing had happened, but it was her duty as my girlfriend to defend her position. Hala was difficult to read. She simply appeared to enjoy the struggle.

I stood by the open door, watching the posturing. I needed to support April. At the same time, I needed to not push Hala away.

"Can I get anyone anything to drink?"

"I'm fine," Hala replied while still looking at April.

"Sure, honey. I'll take a beer. Thanks," my better half responded, still sizing up Hala. She handed me the six-pack.

I took the beer to the fridge and opened two; one for April and one for myself. I took two quick drinks from mine before approaching the living room. It helped build courage. I handed April her drink and leaned on the arm of the couch between the two.

"So," April said leaning forward on the couch, "tell me about yourself. Steve speaks so little about his job and coworkers, I sometimes wonder if he really has a job." She added on a fake chuckle at the end of her request.

Hala was up for the challenge. "Not much to tell I'm afraid. I'm married to my job and that affords me little time for much else. What about you?"

"Me?" April hadn't expected Hala to take the offensive. "Where to begin...I work at LaRose Financial; that's where I met Steve. I have a degree in accounting and human resources. I like reading crime novels, Mexican food, and chocolate ice cream."

"I'm a Rocky Road girl myself."

I started to feel left out, so I butted in, "I like mint chocolate chip."

"That's gross," April responded, curling up her nose.

"Yeah, Steven, that is gross," Hala added making the same face as April.

Apparently the women in my life had a better time bonding when they could disagree with me on the same issue. Just the simple act of picking on me seemed to lift the tension in the room.

Hala reached across the table and grabbed the beer she hadn't finished. April sat back on the couch and grabbed my hand, pulling me down next to her. This act sufficiently demonstrated her ownership of the room.

"Well, April, it was nice meeting you, but I don't want to interrupt your evening any longer, so I'm going to go."

"Oh, you don't have to go," April said in a way that actually sounded like she meant it, though I knew different.

"No, no, I must. I have a meeting very early in the morning. But I must ask, do you mind if I borrow Steven tomorrow night so we can finish our discussion?"

April wanted to say no, but she knew she had to say yes, so as not to look like an untrusting possessive girlfriend. Saving face was part of establishing her domain.

"Of course. Just have him home by nine. I've got plans for him," she said, patting my leg.

"Will do. Steven, I'll come by your desk and get you around four."

"Okay." I stood and walked her to the door.

I waved goodbye as she walked out and I shut the door with my cast. When I turned around, April tossed me her coat.

"You're in trouble," she said approaching me with a vicious look in her eyes.

Chapter 12

The alarm went off and April rolled over and slapped the snooze button. I rolled to face her and gave her a kiss on the cheek. My mouth tasted like I had eaten from a cat box, so I was careful not to breath when I did it. We laid in bed awake until the next alarm went off.

We showered together and got dressed with relatively few words exchanged. It wasn't until we kissed and parted ways to go to our separate vehicles until she said anything about the night before.

"Nothing happened with her, right?"

"What?"

"With Hala, I mean."

"No. She seriously showed up ten minutes before you arrived. Besides she's my boss, and more importantly...I love you."

"You sure?"

"Yes."

"Then have fun tonight."

"Okay. I love you."

"I love you too."

April kissed me and headed for her car. I watched her until she pulled away before getting into mine.

I turned the radio on to drown out my thoughts on the way to work. At work, it was harder to ignore them. At least half a dozen times between my arrival and lunch, I put my hand in my desk and touched April's folder with the intention of looking at it. No matter how hard I tried, I couldn't bring myself to follow through.

Calvin took the day off, which was the first day he had off since I started. I was reasonably certain he wasn't dead yet, because I would have heard about it. Bruce was happier than usual, but everyone else was their normal selves, which made me believe they didn't know about Calvin's situation yet.

From the very first file of the day, I knew it was going to be a long one. By lunch I had already sent two people to hell. It was the first time I had a married couple come through together. I took solace knowing that they would at least be together for eternity.

April called me the moment I stepped out of the building for lunch. We didn't talk about much. It was more of a courtesy check-in than a conversation. After getting off the phone with her, Larry called. Apparently, April talked to him.

"So, big dog. Got some lady problems?" Larry said before I could say hello.

"No. Out of curiosity, have you been talking to April?"

"Just briefly."

"And?"

211

"And nothing. She just asked if you had mentioned your boss or a promotion or anything like that."

"And?"

"And, like a good friend I said that the only thing we had talked about recently was how excited you were to have her move in."

"Good man."

"Yeah, I know," Larry responded confidently. "So, really, what's going on?"

"Nothing. Hala stopped by last night in tears and ten minutes later April shows up in lingerie with a six-pack. It was downright fucking uncomfortable."

"Sounds sexy. Get a little doubles action?"

"Jesus! Really? No." I tried to sound disgusted. "I'm lucky I didn't get stabbed."

"But the thought crossed your mind."

"That's not even remotely the point."

Larry chuckled. "Well, I'm bored. Just stay the course and keep me informed, you know, in case I have to cover for you or whatever. Just don't fuck this up with April. She's a good lady."

"I didn't plan on it and you shouldn't have to cover for me. There's nothing going on between me and Ha- I'll call you back."

I hung up the phone. Standing behind me in line, waiting to tell the sandwich artist her order, was Hala. I wasn't sure she if she had been

212

behind me the whole walk from the office or if she had just arrived. When I noticed her she was looking up at the menu as if she didn't know what she wanted.

The shit eating grin on her face gave away that she had been listening to me for longer than I had hoped. My most pressing concern was which part of the conversation was making her smile. Could she hear Larry on the other end? Had she been listening since I talked to April?

"Oh, hey, Steven," Hala greeted, fighting the urge to laugh. She acted like she knew a secret no one else knew and it was killing her not to comment on it. "Funny meeting you here."

"Funny, indeed. Busy day?"

"A couple of collections this morning. Nothing I can't handle."

The tears of the previous night were replaced by her usual confidence. It was probably a façade, but most powerful business women, let alone Death, don't run around crying in sandwich shops.

"Good deal." I turned to the young lady taking my order, "I'll have a smoked turkey on wheat, mayo, pepper jack, and pickles." I returned my attention to Hala. "How long have you been behind me?"

"Since about 4th street."

As I tried to recall what I was talking about around 4th street, she ordered a meatball sandwich on white with provolone and red onions. We slid down the line, three people away from the register.

"It was just before you got off the phone with April."

"Thanks."

"No problem. You buying? I'll get dinner."

"Sure. I suppose it's the least I could do."

She was good. She knew it would make me feel more masculine buying her meal. She was stroking my subconscious ego. It's the ego that knows it's a ploy, but likes it regardless. Sadly, she wasn't even trying to hide it and I wasn't pretending to not like it.

Hala patted me on the back, "And hey, it's not my concern if there's nothing going on between you and Ha."

"That's good." I didn't have anything witty to retort with.

I waved my hand at the two of us to indicate our meals were together and handed the cashier my debit card. He ran the card and handed me two drink cups and our sandwiches in one bag. Hala's amusement was apparent.

She took the cups from my good hand and took them to the fountain. "Raspberry tea?"

"Sure."

She filled the drinks while I found a booth. I placed the bag down, slid into the booth and dispersed the sandwiches. Hala joined me when the drinks were full.

We sat quietly sipping our drinks and eating; both of us wanting to bring up the previous evening. I decided to nut up and be the first for once.

214

"So, about last night...can I ask what that was all about?"

"You can ask whatever you want."

"Okay, what was that all about?"

"You don't know?"

"If I knew would I be asking?"

"Yes." She paused. "You're kind of slow aren't you?"

"I must be."

"Calvin."

"Not the promotion thing, I mean the tears."

"Those two things are related."

"In what way? You're Death. I didn't think collecting people would make you cry. Surely you've collected people you've known before."

"Normally it doesn't and I have more than I care to remember, but Calvin is a little different."

"In what way?"

"Tonight."

"Tonight?"

"Yes, tonight. I really don't want to have this conversation here. Let's just enjoy our sandwiches and company and I'll tell you tonight."

"You drive a hard bargain, but okay."

As agreed upon, we enjoyed our sandwiches and each other's company. We filled the time in between bites with talk about the weather, local news events (not that I ever watched the news) and how good our lunch was. It was another one of those moments where we seemed like two completely normal people having a completely normal lunch. For all the world knew, she didn't just get done collecting two souls and I wasn't going to go back to work to send people to heaven or hell.

Despite the appearance of a normal conversation, in the back of my mind, I was constantly thinking of ways to get information from Hala about how to save April and get my folder. I'm sure Hala had her own agenda as well. I had a feeling I knew what it was, but I refused to admit it to myself.

I finished my sandwich before her and took the liberty of refilling our drinks. When I returned to the table, she was wrapping up her trash.

"You coming back to the office?" I asked, scooping up our collective garbage.

"No, I've got one more today and it's a ways out. I'm going to have to haul ass to get back by four. If I'm late, you better wait for me."

"Maybe I will, maybe I won't."

"You'll wait," she said, leaning in and kissing me on the cheek.

I looked around to make sure April wasn't standing behind me, or anyone I worked with for that matter.

"It was just a friendly kiss on the cheek. Quit worrying."

"I wasn't."

"Liar. It's okay. I've got to go. I'll see you later."

I had to leave as well, but I stopped by the restroom to give her a head start. It wasn't that I didn't want to talk to her, but I needed a few moments to gather myself. Admittedly, I enjoyed her advances. That being said, I knew they were inappropriate, given my situation. The evening was going to require a delicate balance of restraint and pursuit.

Certain that I had given her ample time, I washed my hands a headed back to work. Halfway back I felt one rain drop on the top of my head, then one on my hand, then three, then the skies broke out into a full on downpour. I ducked and dodged under every awning I could on the way back to work in a futile effort to keep dry. When I entered the lobby at the LDI building, I almost slipped and busted my ass. A few people tried to act like they didn't notice me doing the arm waving balance maneuver. Their restrained snickers turned into restrained belly laughs when the gentleman behind me walked through the doors, slipped and tossed his soda in the air on his way to the floor.

I turned to assist only to realize it was Judah.

"Holy shit. Are you okay?" I asked, extending my right arm.

"Well, my ass hurts a little and my pride hurts a lot, but I will live. Thanks."

He tugged on my good arm and I pulled him to his feet.

One of the security guards noticed the incident and found his way over to make sure Judah wasn't hurt, or more likely going to sue. Judah assured him he was fine, and the guard got on his walkie-talkie and called for someone to bring a mop and a wet floor sign.

Judah and I walked slowly to the elevator. I think he wanted everyone who witnessed his fall to ride up without us. By the time we reached the elevators, we had to wait for one to come back down.

"You've been spending some time with Calvin lately," he said "Do you think he's acting kind of strange?"

Since I didn't have a lie prepared, I dodged first. "What do you mean?"

"It's just that whenever I talk to him, he seems distracted." The elevator door opening caused him to pause. He took a moment to make sure the elevator was empty and that no one was in ear shot. "You don't think he got my folder do you?"

"Oh. No. Surely if he had it, he would tell you, or whoever worked it. Right?"

"Maybe. I mean, it's the courteous thing to do, though I think it's actually against company policy to let someone know that their time is coming." He pressed the door close button as soon as we entered the elevator. He obviously didn't want anyone else in on the conversation.

"Really?"

"I think Hala thinks that if someone finds out it's their time, they are more likely to beg and plead and try to wheel and deal. It really ruins the experience."

"For who?"

"I don't know. Her I guess. I mean, we get to see our folder when we start, but from then on, you're not supposed to see it. It's kind of cheating the system as it is."

Relief came when I realized he wasn't going to ask me anything I was going to have to answer with a lie. "I suppose you're right." Feeling more comfortable, I took the opportunity to dig for information. "Have you ever gotten the folder of someone you know?"

"Fortunately, not yet. Though I'm not really sure how I would handle that. Unless it was someone I knew and didn't like."

"Know of anyone it has happened to?"

"I heard it happened to Bruce, but that was before I got here. I think it was his mother or something."

"Is that why he's a-"

"Dick? Probably. From what I heard, he used to be a pretty regular guy."

"So he went ahead and processed it?"

"I don't know." Judah paused and smiled. "Maybe you should ask him."

"No thanks. I'd rather break my other arm."

We parted ways when the elevator opened. Judah wanted to go to the restroom to wash the soda out of his shirt. I returned to my desk and to April's folder.

I had expected the rest of the afternoon to go slowly, but I was only half way through Jacob Schnell's folder when Bruce stood up to gather his things and go home. He took longer than usual, probably trying to make sure I was on my way out. I looked over at him and gave him the 'have a good evening' nod, and continued with my work.

I received a number of 'have a good weekend's and 'see you Monday's and before I knew it, I was alone. I finally stopped working on Jacob's folder when I felt my cell phone vibrating in my pocket. The screen read 'Hot Pants'.

"Hello, dear," I answered.

"Hello, you, dear," April responded.

"How's it going? How was your day?"

"Good. Well, as good as it can be, considering what I do."

"I completely understand." I had a feeling something was on her mind. "Everything okay?"

She huffed. "Yes, just suffering from feminine insecurity."

"About tonight?"

"Yes."

"Don't worry about it. She's coming to get me, then we're going to eat and talk about work. Remember, she's not the one I'm having move in with me."

"Are you sure you still want to go through with that?"

"April, I love you, now quit worrying."

"Promise?"

"Promise."

"Okay. Perhaps when you're done you can come by my place for some after dinner entertainment."

"I think I could manage that."

She made me promise that she had nothing to worry about one more time before she would hang up. I obliged and re-opened Jacob's folder to kill time until Hala arrived. I was a page in when I felt a fingernail run quickly down the nape of my neck. Initially, I thought it was a bug, which is why I jumped up out of my chair.

"Jesus!"

"Nope, just me," Hala said, watching me regain my composure.

"Sorry. I thought something was going to bite me."

"Don't worry. I don't bite, unless you like that sort of thing."

The comment made me feel uncomfortable, aroused, and shocked all at once. Her recent increase in aggression was concerning me. Part of me thought it was just harmless flirting, while another, lower part, felt that her advances were intentional, calculated and a direct attack at my willpower.

"Well..." I shrugged my shoulders.

"Are you ready?"

"Sure thing."

I gathered my things and we headed to the parking garage. She demanded that she drive and I didn't argue. She drove about twenty minutes to McNally's, a tavern on the outskirts of the downtown area. We parked behind the building and walked around to the front in pouring rain.

The bar was dark and smelled of years of cigar smoke infused into the hard wood; it was a scent that even overpowered the smells coming from the kitchen. Once our eyes adjusted to the low light, we found our way to a high-backed booth in an empty corner. We sat on opposite sides of the table. We avoided discussion and eye contact of any sort until the waitress came by.

She was exactly what one would expect from a waitress at a bar for professional drunks. Faded sneakers, tapered jeans, an oversized T-shirt from a band no one ever heard of, cinched to her expanded waist by a nail pouch she used to hold tickets and money. Her breasts were large and sagging, probably from rearing three or more children, and her face had become hard and creased, resembling the wood that covered the walls and floors of the establishment she had clearly spent too much time in. Her voice was the product of years of smoke inhalation, though she didn't have the mouth of a smoker, nor the fingers. The skin on her hands was much softer and smoother that the rest of her, hinting that when she wasn't working, she did enjoy the occasional manicure or massage. There was class hiding somewhere in there that had never reached its full potential.

222

With our drink orders down, she disappeared behind the bar, giving us a few moments of privacy.

"So, what was the other night all about?" I asked.

"More than you would think."

"So enlighten me."

"Let's wait until our drinks arrive. It's going to take a while."

On cue, our waitress returned with two beers in icy mugs with an inch of head each. When she placed them down, I noticed her check out Hala's ring finger and mine. Seeing they were empty, she gave me a grin and a wink. I smiled back.

Hala moved the ashtray in front of her and lit a cigarette with shaky fingers. The deep red nails on her hand sparkled with the flame of the lighter. She aimed her first long exhale over her right shoulder and above our heads. I followed her puff with a drink.

"To explain the other night, I need you to know a few things about your past, and mine."

"So my folder came in?"

She acted like I didn't ask the question. "First though, I want to talk about work."

Hala was good at dangling the proverbial carrot in front of my face. I knew that pressuring her wasn't going to change the order in which she planned on telling me, so I had to be patient and indulge her.

"What about it?"

223

"We need a Recycler."

"What about Bruce?" I cringed at the thought, "Hasn't he been there forever? Or Matthew?"

"Bruce isn't exactly a people person, Matthew doesn't care, and I happen to know that you have been spending time with Calvin, learning what he does. On top of that, there can't be a conflict of interest. If your file comes up, you'll never see it. You're out of chances." Hala threw the last bit on trying to make light of the situation.

"You know some people aren't going to be happy about it."

"I really don't care."

Excitement of getting a promotion was being washed out by the thought of Calvin and April's impending death. I hadn't been there long enough to be numb to it, and was starting to not only feel bad for the ones dying but also for myself. Hala gave me a few moments to think about it while she finished and snuffed out her cigarette. She had already made up her mind that I was going to do it, she knew that I wanted to do it, so she took my silence as a yes.

"Steven," she began," I haven't been entirely truthful with you."

My initial thought was 'no shit' but opted for the more polite. "About work?"

"No, about me," she replied dropping her head.

"You're not a man are you?" I said jokingly, but inside I was somewhat serious.

224

She smiled, but didn't laugh. "No, I'm not, nor have I ever been a man."

"Awesome. You'd make a shitty guy anyway."

"What's that supposed to mean?"

"I'm just saying, you're awfully girly."

"So. You made a crappy girl."

"What do you know about it?"

"That's what I'm about to get into, if you'd quit joking."

"Okay. Done." I crossed my hands in front of me on the table like I was preparing for math class.

"Thank you." she lit another cigarette. "As I was saying there's a lot you need to know."

"About work?"

"Will you just listen, and it is about work, but not really."

"I'm confused."

"Then shut your mouth and open your ears," she was joking but also mildly irritated.

I nodded.

She took another drag of her cigarette and on the exhale began speaking. "First thing you need to know is that you are Adam."

"Adam who?"

"The Adam. From Genesis."

"The band?"

"The Bible. Are you always this slow?"

"Like Adam and Eve, Adam?"

Hala confirmed with a nod. It took a moment to sink in. I've been around since the beginning. I wasn't entirely sure that I believed in the beginning, but I was being told that I was there. It was a heavy load. I reached across and grabbed the cigarette from her hand and took a drag.

Years had passed since my last cigarette, but my mouth and lungs remembered their parts. I pulled deep on the filter, filling my mouth with the warm smoke. As I handed the cigarette back I inhaled deeper to mix the smoke and oxygen in my lungs. I held it for a moment and exhaled slowly. The taste was worse than I remember, but the sensation was better.

While that news was shocking by itself, it still didn't explain anything except that I held the record for the maximum number of lives someone can do wrong. I tried to play it cool.

"Okay, so what does that have to do with work or Calvin or why you were so upset the other day?" I stole a smoke from the pack she left on the table.

She gave me her evil little smile, though there was a bit of pain behind it. "Calvin's our son."

Chapter 13

I struck the match to light my cigarette.

"So you and I slept together in a past life?"

"You could say that."

"I did say that. Quit with the games and riddles. What the fuck is going on?"

She lit another cigarette. It took her three drags to formulate what she was about to tell me. After those three, she snuffed it out, breaking it in the process.

"I'm Eve."

"Like, you were Eve?"

"I still am."

I downed my drink and waited to speak until the waitress came by with another. My biblical knowledge was limited to the creation theory, Noah's Ark, and a little about Easter. I knew about Adam and Eve, but only the part where she ate fruit and that's why everyone died. I had never heard anything about them having kids, I didn't know how they died, or why they were in such trouble, necessarily.

"By still am, you mean..."

"I haven't died."

"I thought that Adam and Eve both died in the Garden of Eden." I didn't want to associate myself with Adam.

"Not exactly. You were made mortal. I became death. Your punishment was to die. Mine was to watch it happen." She exhaled a large puff of smoke and wiped her eyes. She wasn't into a full cry, but it was near.

The million questions filling my head were clogging my mouth, leaving me to stammer incoherently until I gave up trying to ask questions and returned to my cigarette and beer.

A brief recap of the previous five minutes or less left me with the knowledge that I was the world's first screw up, I had an elderly black son who was about to die, a girlfriend who was about to die, I slept with my boss a few thousand years before I knew that I even knew her, and she was not only Death, but the biblical Eve. Being that I was only on my second beer, I already feared a proper hangover was on its way.

"So you've been alive for..."

"About four thousand years give or take, I guess. I didn't keep that close of a watch for the first couple of thousand."

"You look stellar for four thousand."

"Thanks."

"I take it that you don't age?"

"Nope."

"How does that go unnnoticed?"

228

Hala paused for a moment, trying to come up with the shortest yet most complete answer. "Other than co-workers, I haven't had a long enough relationship with anyone to notice. Everyone in our office knows what I am and just accepts it. You have to be able to accept a little of the fantastic to do what we do."

It was good enough for me. I had found myself believing a lot of new things; a person who didn't age didn't feel like that much of a stretch.

"Does Calvin know that he's our son?"

It felt like a bad joke, claiming Calvin as my son.

"No. He's only seen his current folder. And I don't want him to know."

"Why not?"

At first she looked at me like I should know better, but then she realized that I had been receiving a lot of new information and was hardly in a prime mental state. "Imagine you just found out you're going to die, but you've made peace with it because you're going to heaven."

"Okay."

"Now imagine that your boss comes up and tells you that she is your mother and the new guy at work is your father and that they are both probably destined for hell. How do you think that would make you feel?"

Hala gave me time to consider the situation.

"Like shit?"

"Exactly."

"Alright. Let's assume that I'm Adam, you're Eve, and Calvin is our son; what are you so upset about? You've been watching people die for thousands of years. Besides, we aren't exactly the same people we were then."

"You might want to call April. This is going to take a while."

I pulled my phone out of my pocket and began dialing April's number. Hala sat, hands crossed, waiting to listen to the conversation. Talking on the phone in front of other people was not in my comfort zone so I excused myself from the table and went to the restroom where I knew Hala wouldn't follow me.

"Hello," April answered sounding out of breath.

"What are you doing?"

"Finishing up packing," she made a grunting noise as she hoisted something heavy up, "are you done already?"

"Actually, no. I was calling to let you know it might take a little longer than expected."

"How much longer?"

"I don't really know."

"Why is it going to take longer?"

"I don't know. Hala just said it would. I guess there's a lot of information to go over."

"That's fine, but remember; this is the last night for us to engage in any activities in my apartment. Don't be too late or you might miss out on the fun."

"I'll try. I love you."

"I love you too."

It seemed like every conversation I had with her made her even more amazing. I knew she wasn't entirely comfortable with the situation, but she trusted me and wanted me to know that. I just had to try my best to not do what I was best at; fucking things up.

I returned to the table to find Hala smoking another cigarette and a full beer in front of my seat.

"Can I keep you out past curfew?" Hala asked while exhaling a thick cloud of smoke.

"A bit. I still can't be out all night," I took a sip and raised my glass, "and I certainly can't get too deep into this."

"Sure you can," she said with a devilish grin.

"We'll see."

We finally ordered a few greasy burgers from the bar menu. She had a standard cheese burger. I ordered the house special; a burger complete with a fried egg on top. Both had a side of fries. I drowned mine with ketchup while she was content with salt and pepper.

While we ate, our conversation drifted away from the issues at hand. I would try to get back on track and she would divert.

"It's bad for your digestion to talk about work while you eat," she claimed.

"It's rude to stall and keep secrets."

"Fine. Where would you like to begin?"

"How long have you known who I am?"

"Since before you took a leap off the American National Bank Building."

"How long before?"

"Not too long. A few weeks. This is how I always find you."

"See, what the hell does that mean? I can't even ask you a question without there being some sort of cryptic side note."

"Forget I said it, then."

"No, explain it, so we can move on."

She huffed. "I can only find you when your folder comes up, which means I only find you a few weeks before you are supposed to die. I've been doing this for a very long time."

"While I find all of this terribly flattering," which I did, "why have you been watching me die for a few thousand years? You couldn't move on to some other man?"

"That's what got us in this mess in the first place, sort of." Her gaze shot towards the table.

"Oh...my...God! Is any part of this going to be straight forward?"

"No."

232

"Then let's eat first, maybe I'll hear better on a full stomach."

She agreed, though my appetite had suddenly disappeared. I picked at my burger and ate a few fries, but at the first chance I got, I flagged the waitress down to take my plate and bring me another beer.

Hala took her time chewing. I couldn't tell if she was having fun with her confession fest or if it was troubling her at all. She appeared willing to divulge, but it felt like she was picking and choosing what bits to feed me. I was sure it wasn't the first time we had engaged in this particular conversation, but what I did know was that it was going to be our last. Of course, I probably thought that before too.

Before she continued I made her promise that she would be completely honest and start from the beginning. I conceded that she may have to skip some details in order to cover a few thousand years and have me back at home with my girlfriend before I got too drunk. She made me promise I would shut up and listen. Keeping those promises was the hardest part of the following hours.

In the beginning, there was just the two of us in the garden. Things were good. We had our plenty. After a few years though, things had gotten stale. As is common with most relationships, you can only spend so much time with each other before you just want to talk to someone else. That's what drove us to really explore the garden.

We set out on a journey and for days, we found nothing, just more garden. After almost a year we became discouraged and turned for home. We laid down for the night in a grove of flowers and trees that haven't existed for a few thousand years.

Apparently, while I slept, Hala was approached by another gentleman. He had been following us for a few days. They spoke for some time off in the bushes before he propositioned her. Only it wasn't for sex. He had an apple. We knew what the apple was. We knew we weren't supposed to eat it. He wasn't even shy about where he got it.

Hala was apparently quick to please the gentleman, or at least that's how it seemed to me as I listened. She partook of the apple. I had woken up and found them off in the bushes. It sounded like I didn't take it too well back then.

While she told me about what happened I became a little angry. I realized it was about four thousand years ago, but for some reason, I felt like I had been cheated on. There was no reason for my ego to feel bruised but nonetheless, it was.

"Let me get this straight," I interrupted, "you were the world's first cheater?" It was meant to be mean.

She took the meaning. "I wasn't cheating, we were just sharing an apple, but if I am the world's first cheater, then you, you became the world's first murderer."

"Who did I kill?"

"Most know him as the devil."

"You were off in the bushes with Satan?" I asked loud enough to draw the attention of a few of the other patrons.

"Yes, but it was just an apple; you went off and killed the guy with a rock."

I didn't want to talk to her anymore. I wasn't really mad at her nor did I have a right to be, but the conversation wasn't giving me a warm fuzzy feeling. On top of that, I could tell that before the night was up, I was going to end up drunk. Unfortunately, I wasn't any closer to saving anyone.

"Let's back up a step. You said I killed the devil?"

"Well, he wasn't so much the devil yet. He wasn't the devil until after you killed him. It's all very complicated."

"So how is it that I didn't go to hell for killing someone?"

"He loved you too much," she pointed up, " but that doesn't mean you get a pass for everything."

"How do you know all of this?"

"There used to be a lot more open dialogue. In the beginning there was communication, until we screwed everything up, well until I did. Then it got quiet. I still knew what I needed to know, who to collect, when to be at a certain place, all of these things were just ingrained in me, and the other Collectors."

"So you just know when someone is going to die?" Finally I got a break to turn the conversation to the things I needed to know.

"I used to. Back in the old times, I would make someone a Collector, they would collect, and that was that. We knew. As time has gone on, the intuition has faded and now I have to rely on a whole department of people to tell me where to be."

"How do you make someone a Collector?"

"I don't. Not anymore. It's more of a calling now. They usually find me, but that's another story for another time."

I gave her a pass.

"Did your intuition just disappear? I mean, what if you didn't do your job? What if you just let everyone go? Would people still die?"

"Eventually yes. But things get messy when you start messing with the system."

"How messy?"

"Let's just say there is usually a lot of suffering involved."

The longer I sat with Hala, the worse my prospects looked at saving April, or myself for that matter. I could delay her death, but it sounded like it was going to happen anyway and sounded like the longer I put it off, the worse her death would be. Also, hiding her folder was going to make my chances of not going to hell even slimmer. We were fucked.

"So there's no way to stop someone from dying?"

"Have another beer. I know we came to talk about work, but c'mon. You will have plenty of time to ask questions while you train under Calvin until he's...you know."

236

Her avoidance of the subject left me with a morsel of hope. Pushing the subject wasn't going to get me any further with her, so I decided to let the evening roll for a few more drinks. The only other work related item she mentioned for the rest of the evening was that I should start thinking about who I might want to take my place, since we would be down a sorter again.

It would have to be someone who was trustworthy and had a good work ethic. I immediately thought of Larry. Not only was he a good worker, he could be trusted, and since we were losing one African American, he helped us meet our equal opportunity employment quota. The hard part was going to be letting him in on what I do for a living without him laughing at me and telling me I was crazy.

Since talking about work was over, we switched to the same old topics everyone talks about. We discussed the weather getting colder and what the Farmer's Almanac said about the mild winter we were supposed to have. We argued over which was better; cats or dogs. I was a cat person, she was dog all the way. Her argument had something to do with Egyptians. As I didn't remember that particular time in history, I was far less biased.

Despite my limited knowledge on the subject, we talked about art. She was a fan of pointillism, I liked Garfield. The more time I spent with her, the more attracted I became. Perhaps it was the booze talking, but in my mind I kept thinking that we were the first couple ever. If we weren't meant to be, who was? Then my better reasoning would kick in and I would think about the wonderful woman I had at home.

I had agreed to this meeting to try and save April, not to become an adulterer. April and I weren't married, but I wasn't the kind of person that thought of it like that. For every impure thought I had about Hala, I would burden myself with five pounds of guilt. It was getting too heavy to carry around.

After my sixth or seventh beer and roughly as many cigarettes, I convinced Hala that it was time for me to go. She was quick to remind me that she drove and would have to take me to April's. She offered to have AAA drop my car off at my apartment, but I refused. In return I told her she could stay and that I could take a cab to April's.

"You don't trust me?" she asked.

"To get me there, yes."

"Then what's the problem?"

"You've been drinking too."

"Steven. I've had plenty of time to build up a tolerance. And that's not why you don't want me to drive you home. What's the real issue?"

"I don't entirely trust myself around you." On one hand, I didn't want to say that. On the other hand I did.

Hala gave me an inquisitive look. It felt terribly rehearsed, but that's just how those situations go. She had to play the game. Hell, she had the longest running streak of playing the game. It was unrealistic for me to think I had a chance.

"And why is that?" she asked. She was baiting me and I had just enough alcohol in me to bite.

"Seriously? Look at you?" I motioned my hands up and down to encompass her. "You're the first woman, you're ridiculously gorgeous, successful; shall I go on?"

"Well, what are you thinking?"

"I'm thinking a lot."

"Like?"

From the way she was leaning in, I knew all I had to do was nod, and I would find myself in her bed. The power struggle going on was arousing and frightful at the same time.

"I don't know. I'm drunk."

"All that means is that you are free to say what you want."

"No, that means I'm about to say something I'm going to regret."

Like a pro, she sat silently, giving me enough rope to hang myself. In my mind I was grabbing the rope, tying the knot, and slipping it over my head. Fortunately, the little angel on my shoulder took control of my mouth before I could say something stupid.

"I should go."

It wasn't what she wanted to hear. It wasn't necessarily what I wanted to say, but I said it.

"Are you sure about that?"

"No, but I'm going to leave anyway."

Hala didn't argue. "Fine, but I'll drop you off at April's."

I agreed despite the little voice in my head telling me it was a bad idea.

Hala was visibly irritated with me, though she was trying to cover it up. She kept asking me if I was sure and dropping not so subtle hints that I could change my mind at any time. I stuck to my guns, but barely.

Much to my disappointment, the alcohol was wearing off, and I could feel self-loathing and depression working their way up the back of my neck and settling in at the base of my skull. I had agreed to the dinner so I could find a way to save April and maybe even myself. All I ended up doing was finding out more about my past than I wanted, almost sleeping with my boss, and saving no one. At least it was more of a near fuck up than an actual one.

Hala refused to let me split the check as usual, and we gathered our things and left. She continued to talk all the way to the car. Like a good salesperson, she wouldn't discuss what she wanted directly, but instead continued to plant seeds and let them grow. It felt like a calculated move.

I wondered if this tactic had worked on me in previous lives or if I had just given in every time. Was it inevitable, or fate, or the design of some greater power that I was to sleep with her or was that my penis and alcohol talking?

240

Conversation on the way to April's was limited to me pointing and giving directions. Hala took the directions quietly. She knew what I was thinking. A few times I opened my mouth to talk about something else, but closed it before I could produce the words. I was trying not to be too cold to Hala, but her very existence was clouding my judgment. I focused my attention on the rain coming down. Ignoring her was the best chance I had at not being an asshole. I had been given a second chance in my current life by Death herself, and here she was temping me to do bad.

"Which apartment is it?" she asked.

"The one on the left," I pointed to April's apartment, "the one with the light on."

Hala shut her headlights off and pulled into the empty stall in front of April's window. The curtains were drawn.

"Look, I'm sorry I've been so forward tonight. I'm not normally like this. It's just that..." she paused and looked away from me.

"Just what?"

She looked back with the beginnings of tears in her eyes. "Nothing. It's nothing. Just forget I said anything. I'm sorry."

I looked over to make sure April's curtains were still drawn. "No, I'm sorry." I reached across and placed my right hand on her shoulder.

She cocked her head to the right and laid her cheek on my hand. Her tears were warm, but not as warm as her flush skin. She raised her head up and placed her right hand where her cheek had been. I glanced over to double check April's blinds. They were still closed.

Hala and I locked eyes and for a moment I almost gave in. I could feel my heart rate kick up, my breath deepen, and my guilt mechanism kick in. I tried to diffuse the situation with a hug. It was like trying to stop a fire with gasoline.

I leaned in and tried to tilt my head toward her shoulder. She did the same, but as I pulled back, she gently stopped my head with her hand and pressed her moist lips into mine.

It was the greatest kiss I had shared with a human being since Maggy Lowell in seventh grade, who happened to be my first kiss. There was no tongue, just lips. It was deep enough that tongue would have cheapened it. I had kissed plenty of women before, but this one was different, it wasn't lustful. It was the way you would kiss someone you love if you knew you would never see them again.

It lasted all of two seconds before I realized what was happening, or at least until I felt bad enough to stop. Our lips parted as I pulled back. I could feel her tears cool on my cheek and our lips struggle to separate. My eyes had closed out of reflex, and I opened them to see Hala staring straight ahead.

"Tell April I'm sorry," she said.

I said nothing, but instead opened the door and stepped out of the car. Hala backed out and took off, much faster than we had arrived.

Standing in the parking lot I had to take a moment to process what had just happened. That moment wasn't right then.

"What the fuck was that, Steven?" a voice yelled from about ten feet behind me.

I turned to find April in her pajamas, carrying her kitchen trash can over her head to shield the rain. She was coming back from emptying the trash in the dumpster at the end of her building.

Chapter 14

"I-"

"I what?"

"I don't know. I don't know what that was."

"I'll tell you what it was. It was you kissing your fucking boss."

"No, I mean, it wasn't supposed to be."

"What the hell is that supposed to mean?"

"I wasn't trying to kiss her."

"You weren't trying not to."

It was true. While I had technically tried not to, I knew what I was doing. I wanted plausible deniability.

"April, I'm sorry, I-"

"You need to call your new girlfriend and tell her to take you home." It was hard to tell if she was crying or if it was just the rain.

"She's not my girlfriend, April, can we talk? Not out here."

"Why?"

"I want to explain."

"Because there's a good reason you were kissing another woman in front of my apartment?"

She was right. There was no excuse. Nothing I was going to say was going to make it any better. I couldn't explain that I was Adam, my

244

boss was Eve, I was going to hell, and she was going to die if I didn't do something soon. Not only would I have sounded crazy, it wouldn't have explained the kiss.

"No. There's not. I'm sorry. I'll go."

April shook her head and walked past me. I hung my head in shame. As I stood there, I heard the click of her dead bolt locking. I fumbled through my pockets to find my phone to call a cab, but I couldn't find it.

Once again I found myself soaking wet and full of self-pity. Once again, it was my own damned fault. I started the long walk back to the office to get my car. At least this time, my arm was slightly less broken.

The six-hour walk back to the office afforded me plenty of time to reflect upon my current situation. Unfortunately, my current situation was a disaster of my own making. I spent all of my introspective time cursing myself, my penis, and saying 'Why me'.

About four hours in, I came across the American National Bank building. I paused to look up through the night and rain, but I couldn't see the top. I tugged on one of the front doors. I wasn't planning on killing myself; I just thought a different perspective might help. The locked doors told me to carry on.

Eventually, I found myself at the LDI building. I walked down the ramp to the parking garage and found my car. I got in and cranked the heater up, though I knew it would be a while before it warmed up.

I laid my head back and closed my eyes. When I woke up, my car was still running and I was sweating from the heater on full blast. The clock on my dash told me that it was just after 9 a.m. I took a survey of my surroundings and discovered the parking garage was still predominantly vacant. I turned the heater off and stepped out of my car to cool off.

Sitting on top of my car was my cell phone. I spun around to see if Hala was there, but she was not. The red indicator light on the front informed me I had missed a call. While dialing my voicemail I walked over to where I could see Hala's parking stall and it was empty. Relief and disappointment filled in the small places where self-loathing, remorse and anger left space in my head.

Had she been there, I didn't know if I would have just left or if I would have stormed up to her office and told her off. Not that I had any right to be mad at her. I was just as guilty. I strode back to my car, pretending I was glad she wasn't there.

To my surprise, the missed call was from Larry. It wasn't as pleasant as I had hoped it would be.

"Dude, what the fuck? April called and asked if I could help move her stuff into storage. She wouldn't tell me what happened, but I'm reasonably sure I can guess what happened. I'll be helping her move until about three. After that, I'm coming over to your place. You better be home and you better have a really good excuse."

I erased the message. All I really wanted to do was call April. I wanted to explain why I went to dinner with Hala in the first place. I wanted to tell her to just move her things into my place and I would apologize a thousand times a day until she forgave me. I tried her number, but the phone was off. I tossed my phone in my passenger seat and headed home.

When I arrived home, I closed all the blinds and curtains and flopped on the couch. I tried saying a little prayer to God, asking him to not let me fuck things up to the point of no return. I didn't hear an answer back, so I closed my eyes. Miraculously, I fell asleep within minutes

A firm hand pushing on my back woke me up. As promised, it was Larry. I could tell from his smell that he had either been helping April move or bathing in sweat and dust. From the fact that I couldn't see any of her things in my apartment, I was left to assume he didn't move her into my place.

I propped myself up into a seated position. Larry sat on my coffee table in front of me and dangled my keys, indicating that I had left them in the front door. I grabbed them and laid them on the arm of the couch. I was getting an honest look of disapproval from him. It wasn't a look I had ever seen from him, nor did I ever want to again. You know when your true friends give you that look that you've made a terrible mistake. As if I needed reminding.

He gave me a moment to let the fog lift before he spoke. "You know I've got your back, right?"

I nodded in the affirmative.

"Then I expect complete honesty."

"Sure."

"No, not sure, yes."

"Yes."

"What the fuck happened? One minute, you're in love and she's moving in, and everything is great, and then I get a call, from her no less, that she isn't moving in with you. I can only assume that you did something stupid."

"I didn't mean to."

"But you did."

"Larry, it's not that simple."

"I hope it isn't. It would be a damn shame to throw away a girl like April on some stupid, meaningless shit. Was it your new boss?"

"Didn't April give you all the details?"

"She didn't tell me shit. She said that you had a lapse in judgment and she needed to reevaluate your relationship. She's not even mad at your dumb ass. She's hurt."

That made it worse. It's slightly relieving when you screw up and someone is genuinely mad at you. When someone is simply hurt by your actions, you feel like a bigger asshole.

248

"Did she say we're broke up?"

"No. She's going to call you tonight. But I asked her not to until I could talk to you first."

"Why?"

"You're my best friend, jackass. I want to make sure your head's in the right place before you fly off and do something worse," he said, slapping me in the shoulder hard enough to make it sting.

"Thanks."

"No problem. Now get me a bottle of water. I'm thirsty."

Usually I would have told him to get it himself, but considering he took time out of his day to have a relationship intervention with me, it was the least I could do.

I returned with two bottles of water. "Now get off my coffee table. I have a couch for a reason."

He relocated to the opposite end of the couch from me and opened his water.

"Seriously. What's going on?"

"A lot more than you want to know, but you're about to find all that out. Do you like your job at LaRose?"

My question immediately piqued Larry's interest. He relaxed his shoulders slightly. I began by explaining that I had a job offer for him. Talking money was always a good way to get Larry to listen.

Initially, I avoided the subject of what I actually did, but focused on the fact that I was receiving a promotion and I needed someone to fill my place. I talked briefly about the unique team he would get to work with, though I left any mention of Bruce out.

"What's the pay like?" he asked.

I could tell he was already interested.

"Much better than LaRose, but there is a bit of a catch. You can't really ever quit."

"Why?"

"Let's not focus on that right now. Just keep the thought in mind."

Larry milled the thought around in head. He trusted me, loved new business opportunities, but didn't like being locked down. I felt I at least had to tell him the catch before I told him what I did. It was the fair thing to do.

"What aren't you telling me?" he asked placing his water on the coffee table.

"I really can't talk about what I do unless I know you are on board."

"What, do you guys do some illegal shit? Wire fraud, international espionage, stuff like that?"

"Do you even know what that stuff is?"

"No, but if you do, then we have a problem."

"It's nothing like that. It's complicated though."

"Would you rather talk about April, which I haven't forgotten about by the way?"

He had a damn good point. I didn't want to explain that situation until he had an idea of what I was up against. I was either going to have to drop the subject or come clean. Dropping it was going to keep me in the same situation I was in, but coming clean put me at risk of looking like a crazy person and was surely going to damage my score.

My score didn't matter at that point. I had gotten nowhere by keeping things to myself. The time had come for me to face the reality of what was happening and that there was no way I was going to save anyone or solve anything by asking procedural questions during lunches with my coworkers. Holding on to the file wasn't going to work forever. I had to deal with it. I had to save April. If I couldn't do that, then I at least wanted to be with her until the end. I had no choice. I needed help.

I got up excusing myself, claiming that I needed to go to the restroom. It was a stall tactic, he knew it, but he wasn't going to call me on it. He was a good friend like that. He would call me out when I was screwing something big up, but little things he let go. We don't like discussing serious subjects, so we save it for the important things.

I stood in front of the toilet, pants up, counted to fifteen and then I flushed, picked the lid up and shut it so it could be heard in the living room. Washing my hands would have been a giveaway that I didn't actually use the restroom or it would have implied that I got piss on my hands, so I skipped it. Larry was up walking around my living room when I returned. He opened the curtains and looked out, shook his head and headed back for the couch.

"What are you doing?" I asked.

"Checking for Feds," he said mocking me.

"Find any?"

"Not yet."

"Then sit down. I want to come clean, but you have to promise to keep an open mind."

"You gay?"

"No. Now shut up and listen."

I gave him time to find his seat and get settled.

"I work for an office that determines who goes to heaven and who goes to hell and who gets reincarnated based on their overall rating calculated from the various deeds, good or bad, that they commit. I'm the reincarnation of the biblical Adam, my boss, Hala is Eve, and I'm on my last chance to get things right in my life or I go to hell. My immediate supervisor, the old black guy, is actually my son from way back when and he is about to die, so I'm taking his spot, so I want you to take my spot. To make matters worse, April is going to die if I don't do something soon. I went to dinner with Hala last night to try to find a way to save April and instead of fixing anything I fucked everything up."

252

I paused to make sure I had come completely clean.

"Oh, and I broke my arm when I threw myself off the American National Bank building and hit a window washing unit."

Larry's face was expressionless. I could tell he was thinking about what I said and whether it was safe to laugh or if I was insane and he should play it cool. His mouth opened and closed a few times before any actual words came out. When he spoke, his words came out slowly like he was hand feeding a tiger.

"Have you been drinking?"

"Not since last night. Look, fuck it. Forget I said anything. I need to call April and see if I can fix this mess before it's too late."

"Are you high? Look, I know you're going through some shit. There's been a lot of change in your life, and that can be hard on anyone. We can get through whatever this is."

"Don't fucking do that to me. I know it all sounds like bullshit. I just told it to you and it still sounds like bullshit to me, but it is what it is. I wish it wasn't. I should be dead. I should have been dead a long time ago, but I'm not, so I have to deal with this shit. Sorry I mentioned it."

Larry took even longer to process what I told him. I could tell he wanted to believe me, but was having a hard time coming to terms with it.

"You are serious about all that shit? About heaven, hell, April, you trying to kill yourself?"

"Yes, but forget about it. It was a mistake to tell anyone about this shit."

Larry paused again. He was trying to see if running it through his head one more time would make it any more believable.

"You were serious?"

"If you ask one more time, I'm going to throw you out of here. I've got too much going on to deal with doubt from my best friend. I get it, it's hard to swallow, but I'm not crazy."

He wasn't completely sold on the idea, but he was at least going to indulge me. That's all I needed.

He spoke carefully. "Assuming you are serious, we have a lot to get done. Your shit is all fucked up."

"That's what I've been trying to tell you."

Whether he actually believed me or not, remained to be seen, but he was at least going to humor me. He asked me to start at the beginning, more specifically the part where I broke my arm. I gave him the condensed version of my tale. He knew about my accident in high school and understood how that could make me feel suicidal. He did, however, threaten to kick my ass if I ever tried some stupid shit like that again. I promised I wouldn't.

After that, he wanted me to explain in detail how I messed things up with April. He stressed that April had told him nothing. If he was going to take my word on everything I had just divulged, I had no choice but to take him at his. I began by emphasizing my love for April, despite what the situation looked like.

I had every reason to believe that the entire conversation would make it back to April. I knew it, Larry knew it, but we didn't talk about it. Larry, while mad at me, was there for me.

"As I said before, I was at work a few weeks ago and I got this guy's folder-"

"Folder for what?" Larry asked.

"When we get a folder for someone, that means they are going to die. Using codes, we tally up their score and that decided where they go next. Anyway, this guy's folder said that he was going to kill April."

"Jesus. How?"

"Hit and run. That's not important. What's important is that she's going to die if I don't do something."

"What can you do? What if you had that guy killed?"

I was certain he was joking, and while the thought crossed my mind for a moment, I decided I just wasn't going to respond to his suggestion.

"Anyway, I met with Hala to try and find out if there was anything I could do. That's when things got all screwed up. She started talking about how she is Eve from the Bible, I'm Adam, my old black boss is our love child, and she's been following me and watching me die for a few thousand years. I felt bad for her, and honestly, a little flattered."

"You didn't sleep with her did you?"

"No. It wasn't like that. I mean, I could have, but that's not the point. She just kissed me."

"That's it?" he asked, downplaying the severity of the action.

"Why did you even tell April?"

"I didn't. She did it in front of April's apartment."

"Shit."

That summed up the situation. It was comforting to know that Larry was on my side. It was going to take his help to get April back, fill in my spot at work, and keep me sane in the meantime. I hadn't even begun to consider how awkward work was going to be on Monday, but I had to keep going. I had to get as much information from Calvin as I could before he died and do everything I could to save April. That still left the problem of my soul's future, but I was going to have to put that on the back burner so that my current life wouldn't become a living hell.

"Well, I have no idea what to do about people dying, going to heaven, hell, or any of that stuff," Larry said standing up, "but I know relationships. I'll do what I can to help you mend with April, but I'm afraid I've got nothing on the other end of this mess." It was his way of being involved without having to commit to believing the more fantastic portions of my tale. I was grateful for any help.

"Thanks."

He slapped me on the shoulder. "I'm going to go. I'll run some damage control for you with April before she calls you. Just don't do anything stupider. And let me know when you want me to start, it won't hurt my feelings to leave LaRose on short notice." Even if he didn't believe anything I told him, he still believed in opportunity.

"Do you even believe in heaven or hell?" I asked. I was expecting more flak from him about the job.

He shrugged his shoulders and opened his palms. He left and I resumed my spot on the couch and closed my eyes to go back to sleep. Sleep came faster than I thought it would. I dreamt of the Eden Hala described, but it looked a lot like the San Diego zoo I visited with my parents when I was twelve. Instead of being there with Hala, I was with Natalie Portman and we were eating dinosaur eggs from a cast iron skillet over a camp fire. Besides the bizarre circumstances, it was quite peaceful.

The peace was ruined when my phone rang. I woke up to the sound, but it took me a few rings to realize what was going on. I was disappointed; Natalie and I were getting ready to go for a swim. By the time I got to my phone, I had missed the call. My caller ID didn't recognize the number. I hoped it was April. It rang three times before anyone answered. My hopes sank when a guy answered the phone.

"Hello," a masculine voice answered trying its best to sound tough.

I tried anyway.

"Is April there?"

"Is this Steve?"

"Yes. Who is this?" I asked trying to match the tough guy act, but I was still too groggy to pull it off.

"Clint. April's friend, Jennifer's boyfriend. And you've got a lot of nerve calling here," he apparently had some idea of recent events.

"What are you talking about? You called me."

"What do you mean?" he asked, struggling with my previous statement.

"He means, I called him," April said from another phone on the line. "I've got this Clint. Thank you."

"You sure?"

"Yes. Thank you."

"Okay. Steve, I'm not done with this conversation."

I decided being a smart ass wasn't going to help my situation, so I just stayed quiet until I heard the click of him hanging up.

"Hello," was the best opener I could come up with. I should have told her how sorry I was, apologized all over myself and promised her it would never happen again. I didn't have the balls to go down that road yet.

"Hello." She was as uncomfortable as I was.

"Did you call?"

"Yeah."

A long silence filled the few seconds before I could figure out what to say. "I'm sorry."

"Save it. It's too early for you to be sorry. Right now you just feel like an asshole."

I couldn't fault her logic. It was still that time after you fuck up where you just wish you could make what you did go away. It takes time for a person to suffer long enough to feel like they are truly sorry. One day certainly wasn't enough for what I did.

"Fair enough. Are you staying with Jenny?"

"Yeah. For now. I need some time to think about things."

"Where does that leave us?"

"I don't know yet," she said. "You hurt me pretty bad."

"I know. I'm an asshole. I'm..." I wanted to say sorry. When you can't say it, you have to actually think about how you feel, no canned apologies. "I understand. Take as much time as you need; I'll be here."

"Okay. I'll call you when I'm ready to talk about this," April said.

"Alright. Please do. I'm ready when you are."

Then came the moment where we would normally say 'I love you' and hang up, but I couldn't. I could hear her breathing on the other end of the line. I waited hoping she would change her mind and talk. She spoke before I could muster up the courage to say anything else.

"Bye."

The line clicked and she was gone.

I rolled back over and tried to go back to sleep. It was a futile effort. The scene from the night before played over and over in my head.

When rationalizing it failed, I started trying to justify it. It was failing just as miserably as my efforts to doze off. I turned on the television and started watching cartoons.

By the time I started feeling tired, the sun was coming up. My head was pounding, my eyes were dry and I had no desire to leave my apartment. I turned off the TV and shuffled into my room. With the door shut and the blinds drawn I was able to shut out enough light to finally get to sleep. The last time I looked at my alarm clock, it read 8:46 a.m.

I woke to the sound of my cell phone ringing again. It was in my living room, so I sprung out of bed to rush to it, hoping it was April, ready to talk. It turned out to be the last person I wanted to talk to; Hala. The thought of answering crossed my mind, but instead, my finger pressed the ignore button and sent her to voicemail.

I brought the phone back to bed with me, but put it on vibrate. It shook once letting me know I had a voicemail, which I ignored as well. Sleep came much easier. Ignoring Hala felt like a step in the right direction, whether I wanted to or not. No one else contacted me for the remainder of the weekend.

Monday I was up earlier than usual. It was to be expected considering I had logged about as much sleep in two days as I had in two weeks. The early hour combined with my overall demeanor set me up for a bare minimum effort Monday. I hadn't shaved in four days, so I had a bristly layer of stubble. I showered, but didn't try terribly hard to fix my hair. Breakfast consisted of a cup of coffee and a piece of bread. I didn't even feel like toasting it or covering it with butter.

I drove to work in silence. Traffic was light at 4 a.m. On the way in I contemplated checking my voicemail from Hala. I decided against it. Whatever she had to say, it could wait until work.

The parking garage was empty as usual at that hour. I parked one floor down from my usual floor, not wanting Hala to be aware of my presence when she arrived. It was admittedly a juvenile act, but I made peace with that.

I took the elevator to the lobby and took the stairs up to my floor in an attempt to avoid human contact. It was a successful plan, but ultimately tiring. The stairwells were poorly lit during off-peak hours, making the hike slightly creepy. Other than the sound of my heavy breathing, the only thing I could hear was the sound of my shoes stamping on each stair.

Arriving at my floor, I paused to catch my breath and wipe the sweat from my brow. Half of the lights in the hallway were on, dimly lighting the path to my office. The lights in the office were off, so I flipped the switch and waited for them to warm up and stop flickering before I stepped fully into the office.

I dropped my things at my desk and snuck a peek inside Calvin's office just in case he was sleeping. He wasn't. I returned to my desk and powered up my computer. I opened my drawer and pulled out April's folder. Was there something in there that I could use to get back together with her?

I pushed the thought from my head. Invasion of her privacy wasn't the place to start. It wasn't a big deal when it was someone I didn't know. It was just another name, another folder, and another score. I placed the folder back in my desk.

"Care to talk about it?" a familiar voice said from my left.

I jumped in my chair and turned to see Calvin taking off his knitted scarf and hanging it on the coat rack just inside the door.

"About what?" There were so many *its* in my life, I wasn't sure which one he was referring to. I couldn't decide which 'it' I least wanted him informed of; the Hala it, April's it, or that I was his dad it.

"Whatever brought you in here before me. It must be bad."

I wasn't sure if he was playing ignorant or honestly didn't know what was going on. Given his track record, I chose to believe he didn't know what had transpired over the weekend.

"Oh, nothing I can't handle," I lied.

"I don't buy it, but we'll just pretend I do," he said with a grin. "Let's not waste any time then, I suppose I don't have that much left."

Hala had apparently told him I was going to be taking his place. It made me curious as to what else she divulged. Five in the morning wasn't the time to get into it, though it was bound to come out before the end of the day.

He motioned for me to follow him to his office after a brief pause to wipe the corners of his mouth. He shuffled past me, filling the air with the smell of black coffee and plain oatmeal. The smell suited him. Inside his office, he flipped on the lights. All the files had been neatly organized and most of his personal effects were cleared out. It appeared he was already gone.

"What's the deal, Calvin?"

"I came in this weekend and got things cleaned up for you. I'm not gone yet, but I'm sure it's coming soon."

"Why do you say that?"

He wiped his mouth, "I'm assuming you mean other than my folder coming up. It's Hala. She's been acting queer lately."

"Queer?"

"Strange you knuckle head," he said shaking his head. "I saw her here Saturday evening, but she barely spoke to me."

I didn't immediately mention the events of Friday. My ego wanted to believe Hala was acting strange because of me, but Calvin's assumption seemed equally reasonable. I checked his expression to see if he was goading me. His face told me nothing. Calvin took some time to organize his belongings before settling into his chair.

"Well," he said with a clap, "where do you want to start? Have any questions for this old man?"

"What if I got someone's folder and I don't want them to die?" I asked and immediately broke out in a flop sweat.

He smiled. "You talking about the folder in your desk?"

"How-"

"You're always opening that drawer and looking at that folder. I doubt you even realize it."

"Have you looked at it?"

"No, no. It's none of my business. Well, at least it wasn't. Can't really ignore it now."

I was afraid I had jeopardized everything. I thought that surely Calvin couldn't know about it and not tell Hala. My fears were put to rest.

"This stays between us, right?" Calvin asked.

I nodded my head.

"I don't know how much help I can be but I will try my best. Bring me the folder and I'll see if there's anything I can do."

I jogged to my desk and grabbed the folder. Handing it over to Calvin proved harder than I thought it would be. I extended my arm across the desk, holding the folder. I was sure he noticed the tight grip I had when he reached out to take it. He forced a small cough signaling that I needed to let it go.

I watched as he opened the right hand drawer on his desk and gently placed the folder inside.

Chapter 15

Having shared the burden of April's folder with two other human beings gave me some relief, despite the massive hit I was sure my score took. The situation hadn't actually improved, but it felt more manageable. Calvin insisted on turning our focus to training me to take his spot, as it was almost time for my coworkers to show up. He mentioned that he thought Hala would be joining us. To my surprise and good fortune, she didn't.

"What about religion?" I asked. It wasn't a subject I really wanted to talk about but it seemed relevant.

"I'm shocked it took you this long to ask."

"I'm not exactly a quick study."

"Is there any particular place you want to start or do you want the 'from the beginning version'?"

"If your time is as short as you say it is, then we should start with something in the middle."

"You're stealing my 'old' jokes," he said with a grin.

He rapped his hands on his desk while trying to find a place to start. I watched as he scrolled through topics in his mind. He would stop, consider, shake his head 'no', then move forward. It looked like he was debating with himself.

"I'll start by saying that there aren't necessarily absolutes, but you should be used to that by now." Somehow I felt that he was talking about me and April in an oddly encouraging fashion. "Religion helps, but you don't get the big points simply by believing. You get points by doing. There are a lot of 'bad' people," he made air quotes with his arms resting on his desk, "that go to church and a lot of 'good' people who don't."

"But there is a difference between faith and going to church, right?"

"Absolutely. But the important thing is how you act outside of the church. Beyond that, it's really up to you as to who you align yourself with. Interesting tidbit; most of the part-time Collectors are preachers and priests."

"Really?" I hadn't heard much about other Collectors, so I was intrigued.

He explained that it had been that way for a very long time. Just about every hospital had one. Prisons had them. They had a long history of being present in military engagements. They were there to provide spiritual support and performed burial rights among other duties. It made sense that they would be in a prime position to collect. I could have listened to Calvin talk about them for hours, but my coworkers started to arrive, so it was time to return to my normal duties. I felt like he partially avoided the religion question, but I felt he gave me a more interesting bit of information. Maybe not as helpful, but at least entertaining.

266

Calvin decided it best to not make it obvious I was taking his spot until Hala announced it to everyone. He was sure everyone knew his time was limited. "After all," he said, "I'm old as dirt, it's not that big of a shocker."

I returned to my desk just before eight. Bruce took notice that I was just getting to my desk, but said nothing to me. My other coworkers said good morning as they got up to get coffee and use the restroom throughout the morning. That was how it went the rest of the week.

Hala had all but disappeared. The rest of my coworkers continued warming up to me, except Bruce of course. Judah even invited me to a party he was having that weekend, but I respectfully declined saying that I hadn't seen my girlfriend in over a week and we needed some alone time.

He made a gentle thrusting motion with his pelvis while still seated and simply said, "I get it," and slapped me on the back.

Calvin continued training me and I continued processing folder after folder. In that one week, I sent seven people to hell, seven to be recycled, and only three to heaven. It wasn't my best week. I also managed to squeeze in a few Legacy files. Calvin assured me daily that he was working on April's folder. As much as it bothered me to not have her folder in my hands, I was relieved that it was in his.

Larry, who rarely used text messages for anything, sent me almost two dozen throughout the week. Some of them asked simple questions, like if I saw a movie his girlfriend made him rent or who I thought was going to win the Sunday Night Football game. Others were attempts at jokes, asking if I sent anyone to hell that week. I knew he was just making sure I was okay, but he was trying not to come off as too concerned. Every now and again he would send me one advising me on how to apologize to April or telling me that I would get her back, but he would make sure to follow it with a joke.

Thursday night he sent me a text asking if April had called me. I replied with a no. He responded, assuring me that she would and to be patient.

Friday night came and I found myself alone. I waited for April to call, but she didn't. I spent the evening in my apartment with the lights off, the television off, and fell asleep in my work clothes sitting up on the couch with my head in my hands and an empty stomach.

I woke late Saturday morning with a dark cloud over my head. I was beyond self-loathing and was well on my way towards projecting my personal disappointment on to everyone else. Rationalizing why my shortcomings were someone else's fault wasn't much of a stretch. It started with Hala. If she had let me die, none of this would be happening. If she had been honest with me about everything up front, while I was sober, I could have handled it better. April should have known better than to let me go with Hala. She should have invited herself or vetoed the whole thing altogether.

As I sat brooding on my couch, the phone rang. It's amazing how three little rings can change your whole outlook when they are from the person you want to talk to most. I hopped up and jogged over to the phone. I knew from the personalized ring tone that it was April.

"Hello," I said trying not to sound overly anxious.

"Morning," April said. She sounded like she had just rolled out of bed.

"Long night?"

"Yeah, I guess."

I didn't have much of a right to ask her what she had done the night before, so I avoided it for the moment. My worst fear was that she had gone out on a date. The rules of our situation weren't clearly laid out, leaving me to assume that she could do whatever she wanted, while I had to be on my best behavior.

"How's work going?" she asked.

"Fine. I've just been working with Calvin, learning that position. How's LaRose?"

"It's okay. I'm thinking about quitting."

"Why?"

"I think I just need a change. My job is depressing."

"Where are you thinking about going?"

Her hesitation to answer made me uneasy.

She sighed, "I think I might move back home for a bit."

That was the last thing I wanted to hear. If she moved back to her parents', it meant we were through. Even worse, it meant that she would be collected by a different office. I desperately wanted to tell her to stay. I wanted to tell her why. Doing so would likely make her think I was crazy and send her away faster. All I could do was try to mend things in the hopes she wouldn't leave.

We talked for about ten more minutes. I wasn't about to mention the Hala incident and neither was she. The status of our relationship didn't come up, leaving me with more questions than answers. My focus was to regain her trust and not fuck up any more than usual.

After our awkward goodbyes, I reclaimed my place on the couch and moped for an hour. I decided it was time to get into hard-core self-pity. I left to go to the liquor store and came back with an eighteen pack of beer. I cracked the first one open and guzzled it. I smiled briefly, not out of joy, but because I knew I was achieving a goal.

As the bottles emptied and stacked on my coffee table, I became more agitated. My pacing began on the fourth bottle. I would travel from the couch to the kitchen, back by the couch and into the bedroom, then back. Only the sound of my breathing and weak floor boards filled my apartment.

By beer six, I was talking my way through the turn my life had taken since my most recent suicide attempt. First order of business was trying to rationalize why I had even tried to kill myself in the first place.

Part of me knew I had served my time, that I wasn't the same stupid kid from back then, that it could have happened to anyone. The thought that my dead friends were the lucky ones crossed my mind.

As soon as it popped in to my head, I immediately felt ashamed, or at least more ashamed. It made me feel like a crazy person. I should have felt remorse, not jealousy.

When I couldn't think about my friends anymore, I moved on to more recent affairs; Hala. Although I found it difficult deciding where to begin with her. Was I supposed to start with when we met at the American National Bank, or should I still be mad at her for fucking the devil? Maybe she was the devil. I knew better than to think that, but my eighth beer was telling me otherwise. Had she not screwed up way back then, I wouldn't be in this mess now. No one would.

While I tried to lay it all on her, it didn't serve my goal of self-destruction to let her take all the blame. I knew what she wanted. She never made it a secret. Going to dinner with her was a bad idea and I knew it. I wanted to be there, or at least some part of me did.

I slammed yet another bottle down on the coffee table with a thud. Its empty brothers and sisters rattled together. I had worked myself into a full-blown guilt frenzy and was starting to lose control of my faculties. I walked into the kitchen looking for a hidden beer, but there were none.

I placed both hands on the sink and before I could react, I threw up all over my faucet. I groped around for a towel and wiped my mouth.

My hand dug into my pocket and pulled out my cell phone. I was going to call April and work things out. It rang twice before going to voicemail. Instead of hanging up, I lifted the window in my kitchen and side armed my phone across the street.

A car alarm near where I thought I threw my phone went off. I supported myself as best I could as I slid down to the kitchen floor. The cold tile felt good on my sweating back.

I could see the clock on the coffee pot from my place on the floor. It read 10:07 pm. With nothing left to drink and the room spinning, I closed my eyes and passed out. I didn't wake up until almost 10 a.m. on Sunday.

My head was pounding before my eyes had a chance to open. My apartment smelled like booze and throw up. My mouth tasted even worse. In the process of sitting up, my back popped from top to bottom. I rolled over onto all fours before standing. I managed to get to my feet after a few deep breaths.

The apartment looked like a crime scene. My clothes were scattered throughout the various living spaces, a cluster of empty bottles occupied the coffee table, while random bottles could be spotted next to the television, on the floor and window sills.

The vomit was still all over the sink and faucet and remnants of it lingered in my facial hair. I grabbed a handful of ibuprofen from the cabinet above the fridge and a glass from my cabinet. Fighting the urge to vomit again, I used a hand towel to turn on the faucet and get some water. I downed the pills, the water, refilled the glass downed it again and then refilled it again and headed to the couch.

I leaned my head back and tried not to move for about an hour until the headache went away. When it became bearable, I got up, took a shower, and began the long process of cleaning my apartment. I decided it was time for a top down scrub. I pulled everything out of every drawer, took all of my laundry to the laundry room and got it started, reorganized my cabinets and even lit a scented oil burner to get rid of the vomit and booze smell. Unfortunately, 'Christmas Joy' was the only oil I had; a scent my mother got me the previous year to get me in the spirit of the season.

Whenever I came across April's clothes or things she left over, I developed a lump in my throat. I sat all of her items by the door in a well-organized pile. While cleaning the fridge, I came across the Fresh Start card I received from Dr. Vasanta. I crumpled it up and dropped it on the kitchen floor to be swept up later.

By seven o'clock, it looked like a brand new apartment. I had cleaned out a drawer in my dresser specifically for April's things so they weren't sitting out in the open being a constant reminder of what I had screwed up. I filled a glass with water and sat down for the first time since I started cleaning. Mid sip, someone knocked on my door harder than was appropriate. It was startling.

My hope for peace and quiet was shattered. I sighed and slowly stood up. The knocking continued only slightly louder and more hurried.

"I'm giving you to the count of three before I knock this door down!" Larry yelled through the door.

"I'm coming, chill out!" I yelled back.

I unlocked the door and Larry barged in. He had a confused look on his face when he saw the condition of my apartment, like he was expecting to walk in to some gruesome scene. He sniffed a couple of times, noticing my 'Christmas Joy' scent.

"Did you get a Christmas tree?"

"No, it's a scented oil."

"You know it's not even Thanksgiving, right?" he asked still examining my apartment.

"Did you come over to critique my choice in fragrances or was there something else on your mind?"

He turned finally turned to look at me. "I tried to call you last night, but you didn't answer, and your phone has been going to voicemail all day. I was just making sure you weren't doing something stupid."

"Like?" I knew what he was getting at, but I enjoyed watching him get uncomfortable about serious topics.

"Like nothing. Why didn't you answer your phone?"

"If you must know, mother, I can't find my phone." It wasn't a complete lie. Technically, I couldn't find it.

"That's odd, I found this phone in the street," he said digging in his jacket pocket and pulling out a handful of broken electronics. "It looks a lot like your phone, or at least, it did."

"Weird," I said holding my hands out for him to drop the pieces in. "Can I get you something to drink?"

"No, I have to get going. I just told April I would come check on you." His eyes widened like he had just let some information slip that he wasn't supposed to divulge.

"She asked you to check on me?"

"No," he hesitated, "I meant in general I would check on you."

Larry was starting to make me look like a good liar.

"Was she trying to get ahold of me?"

"Look, dude, I wasn't supposed to mention that she called me. She was just worried about you because you weren't answering the phone. That's all. She didn't want to make it a big deal."

"Did she say anything about moving back in with her folks?"

"She mentioned it."

"And?"

"And I told her I thought it was a good idea," he said confidently.

"You what?" I asked, though I knew what he said. "You fucker. Why would you say that?"

Larry patted me on the arm and asked me to sit. I refused, but he sat. He explained it was all part of his plan. First, he thought I needed time to figure out what I really want and with her there, I would be too distracted. Secondly, absence makes the heart grow fonder. His thought was that April would move back with her folks, hate it and be extremely anxious to come back. In the meantime, I had to turn my situation around.

"That's all great, but there is one tiny little problem," I said.

"What's that?"

"If she moves back with her parents, she's going to get collected by another office. You can't move away from death. I need her here."

"Fuck. I'm sorry." Larry looked at the floor, waiting for some encouraging words to form. I didn't say anything to make him feel worse because I knew he was trying. I gave him time to think. "Okay then, you've just got to fix it by moving day. We can do this. If all else fails, I'll sabotage the moving van."

It wasn't a good plan, but it was all I had. He left with little else to say. I was okay with being alone for the evening.

I resumed my spot on the couch and half watched Sunday Night Football until bed time. I went to bed in the middle of the third quarter and slept better than I had in weeks. My body must have known I needed it. At least until just after four in the morning. I woke with my eyes wide open. Instead of fighting it, I got up, showered, and headed in to work.

When I pulled into the parking garage, I noticed Calvin was already there, as was Hala. I took the journey up the elevator, through the lobby, and through the other elevator up to the office. The lights were already on

276

when I opened the door. I placed my things on my desk and powered up my computer. When the desktop came up, I headed towards Calvin's office.

Approaching it, I could hear Calvin talking and then Hala. I couldn't hear what they were talking about and I thought it would be bad form to try to listen in. I knocked on the door frame and peeked my head in. Their conversation stopped and Hala turned and noticed me. It was the first time I had seen her since the kiss.

Calvin wiped the corners of his mouth and smiled. Hala looked at the floor and looked back at me. She didn't know how to react and neither did I.

Calvin broke the tension. "Good morning, Steve. Here to catch the worm?"

"Yeah, couldn't sleep. Good morning, Hala."

"Good morning, Steven," she said heading towards the door.

"Oh, you don't have to go," I said. "I've got plenty of folders to work on."

"Thanks, but I really must. I've got an early collection this morning." She faced Calvin. "We'll talk later." She shot him a reassuring but sad smile. When she walked by me she placed her hand on my shoulder and let it slide off as the distance between us grew.

Calvin pretended not to see it.

"Everything okay?" I asked.

"Depends on what you mean by everything," Calvin said, folding his hands on his desk.

"What do you mean?"

"It's going to be this week."

I could tell that he was talking about him being collected. There wasn't much to say that would make that situation any less uncomfortable. I stared at the floor while Calvin stared at his desk.

"Well, no point in moping about it now. We've got work to do. These souls aren't going to relocate themselves."

He started talking about the basics and then elaborating on a specific point with a story of something he had run into before. That morning it was about special transfers. Occasionally, he would get a file from someone who lived in this region, but was traveling and collected in another region. It wasn't so much of a big deal if someone from the Midwest region was collected on one of the coasts. The coastal office would just go ahead and process the relocation there, but when someone was collected in a foreign country, that office usually doesn't understand the economic and environmental factors that the soul was subjected to.

When Bruce, Judah, and Phyllis showed up, Calvin excused me from the training session. He wanted to bring everyone into his office individually and talk to them about what was coming. He said Hala would be in later to explain that I was taking his spot. He followed me out and called Bruce in first. The door shut behind them. I couldn't bring myself to ask him about April. He had enough on his plate for one day.

I started in with Jerry Betts' folder; it was the top one on my desk. Jerry started out a good young adult. He had volunteered, donated to charities, and was a consistent tither, but on his thirty-fourth birthday, he had killed someone in a bar fight. The penalty for that killing had been lower than usual, which led me to believe he didn't intend to kill that person. Jerry had spent some time in jail, but when he got out, he had really turned things around.

I couldn't tell what he was going to die from, but his final score gave me hope. Eleven years after his time in prison for murder, Jerry was on his way to heaven. I pulled out a notebook and copied down some of his more unique deeds and their score value. I thought a cheat sheet for my future might not be a bad idea.

After about an hour, Bruce emerged from Calvin's office and fetched Tao. Throughout the day, one person would go in and then come out looking like they had been crying. They would grab the next person without saying a word and return to their desk.

At lunch, everyone went their separate ways, except Heather and Jordan who went to the cafeteria together. Judah and Phyllis hadn't heard the news yet, but they knew something was up. When they asked me about it I told them that Calvin made me promise not to tell anyone and that they would know by the end of the day. They weren't happy about the answer, but they understood.

By the time second break rolled around, everyone knew. Even Judy from human resources had been through Calvin's office. Just before the end of the day, Hala showed up and stepped into Calvin's office for a few seconds. She came out with Calvin in tow.

"Everyone, can I have your attention?" she said.

Slowly we all gathered in the center of the room. For the most part all eyes were on the floor. It was a dark day at the office. Calvin cleared his throat and started things off.

"Now I've spoken to all of you about what's coming, and I just wanted to say in front of everyone that it has been an honor to work with you. Some of you I've known forever, some of you, just a brief period, but I feel like we are all family. I will miss you all. That being said, Hala has a small bit of business to tend to because at the end of the day, these folders are the most important thing."

Hala put her hand on his shoulder. "Thank you Calvin. It really has been a joy working with you." Hala turned to address the group. "I know a big question on everyone's mind is who is going to fill Calvin's spot."

Murmurs could be heard throughout the group.

"I am pleased to announce that Steven will be taking the position of Recycler."

A few half-assed claps could be heard through the room. My eyes turned slightly up and to the left to check Bruce's reaction in my peripheral. Of everyone, I expected the most retaliation from him. He was stone faced. I wasn't really hoping he would be clapping, but I was looking for some reaction so I would know how to handle him. He gave me nothing.

Hala continued. "Does anyone have any questions?"

"I do." Calvin said raising his hand. "Who is bringing the cheesecake for my going away party? We can have it on Wednesday. Don't worry, I'm going to keep working until it's done, but better have the party sooner than too late."

His question elicited a few sniffly chuckles from the group. Hala sent the department home fifteen minutes early. She walked out of the office immediately, but Calvin stayed by the door shaking everyone's hand or giving them hugs as they left. I took my time gathering my things to make sure I was the last one to leave.

"I think that went over quite well, Calvin said sticking his hand out.

I shook his hand. "I'm going to miss our early mornings."

"As will I. Now go home, get some good sleep tonight."

I nodded and walked out of the office. A cough caught my attention about fifteen feet down the hallway, in the opposite direction of the elevators. Hala had been waiting for me. I checked over my shoulder as if I thought April might be watching me. The look on Hala's face made it clear that she saw my check and it didn't please her. Feeling childish, I approached her.

"I'm not going to rape you in this hallway, Steven."

"I know. Sorry."

"Can we do this without it being weird?"

"Yeah, sorry."

"Glad to hear it. I take responsibility for what happened."

I wasn't sure if that was supposed to make me feel better or her feel worse, but I wasn't going to let her be the only one soaking up all the guilt.

"It was as much my fault as yours, but I'd rather not talk about this right now."

"Me neither," she said.

"So is this work related?"

"Mostly. Can we talk in my office?"

I hesitantly agreed. Hala had proven that there was almost always an ulterior motive with everything she did. I wondered if she had always been this way or if it took someone thousands of years of practice to become so clever.

Chapter 16

Hala led the way to the elevator. I couldn't help but watch her walk. Even when I was mad at her and didn't trust her I couldn't help myself. Had I always been so enthralled with her?

She waited for me to enter the elevator. I posted up in the back. She turned immediately inside the doors and hit the button to the top floor. Her back faced me but I could tell she wanted to turn to speak. Instead we both looked up watching the floor numbers light up and go dark until we were at the top.

Her receptionist had already left for the day and Andy's office door was shut. We had the floor to ourselves. My imagination started to run away with me until I realized that Hala was waiting for me to step out of the elevator.

"Don't worry. It's safe," she said.

I followed her through the big double doors into her office. To my surprise, it was in shambles. There didn't appear to be signs of a struggle, at least not physically. It seemed that she had been holed up in there for a few days and housekeeping hadn't been by to tend to the cleanliness. The kitchen area was a mess, empty glasses hid like Easter eggs around the room. Random articles of clothing were draped over chairs.

From where I stood I could just see into the bedroom attached to the office and it looked much the same. The large desk at the far side of the office matched the rest of the room. I could see the contents of a number of folders strewn across the top surface as if she were frantically digging for something and didn't know where to find it.

"Everything okay in here?" I asked.

"It will be," she said, "it will be."

"See, now what does that even mean? This would be so much easier if you would just be honest and open with me."

"I was once. Look where that got me."

"So, what's this all about?" I said, moving a jacket from one chair to another so I could sit.

"Your folder. It came in."

The lump in my throat contradicted the relief I was trying to feel. "You mean..."

"No, not that you're going to die; the correction."

The ominous feeling I used to get before my parents would open my report cards settled into the back of my neck. My immediate reaction was to ask to see it, but I knew that it wasn't going to be that easy. It never was with Hala.

"What's the catch?" I asked, taking a defensive posture.

As expected she told me that she was going to have to review the folder for accuracy before she could let me look at it. When I asked how long that was going to take she responded vaguely saying it could take a few days. I let that slide because I knew that she was struggling with the idea of collecting Calvin.

"How are things with you and April?" she asked out of the blue.

Initially, it pissed me off and I turned to leave, until I realized she didn't mean it maliciously. A few deep breaths put me back in a calm mind so I could respond.

"They aren't so hot. She's moving back in with her folks for a little while."

She didn't respond. I didn't expect her to. When she did speak again, it wasn't about April.

"Saturday is the day."

"Pardon?"

"Saturday is the day I collect Calvin." she said pouring herself a drink out of a decanter. She nodded to me as if to ask if I wanted one. I shook my head side to side.

"Why so quick?" I asked.

"That's just the way it is sometimes. It always seems to come faster when someone knows it's coming."

"How do you know when you're going to collect someone?"

She pretended to not hear my question. "Will you be with me?"

"When you collect Calvin?"

Hala had been collecting souls for thousands of years and now she needed me there for support. Had she asked Calvin if he wanted me there? I would think that most people would want their death to be a fairly private affair. I had always been alone when I tried to end my life, anyway.

"Have you considered having someone else collect Calvin?".

"All of my other Collectors are busy that day."

"So hire another Collector."

She laughed halfheartedly. "It's not that easy. I can't just hire a new Collector."

I refrained from responding to keep myself from asking more questions.

"Just think about it."

I nodded my head and left. I didn't look back. Despite the tension between us, I was afraid I would fold if I saw her crying, and I was trying to think about the situation rationally.

The locks on the doors clicked while I waited for the elevator. She was going to be locked up in there for another evening. While I felt bad, I felt worse for myself and even worse for April. The elevator door opened and I stepped inside. I considered going back to see if Calvin was still in his office, but chose to head straight for my car. I needed to get home and have a drink.

I reached for my cell phone to try to call April when I remember that my phone was in twenty pieces in the bottom of my trash can at home.

That drink was going to have to wait. I wasn't saving anyone without a means of contact, so I headed out to get a new phone.

Two hours later I was on my way home with a new cell phone an emptier wallet and an even worse disposition. I plugged my new gadget in when I got home and could hardly stand the wait for it to charge the appropriate amount so that I wouldn't ruin the battery.

By nine o'clock the battery showed a full charge and the six-pack I brought home was gone. I pulled the phone from the charger and dialed April's number. While it rang, the pacing around my apartment began. By the third ring I had traveled from the kitchen to the bathroom and was heading back into the living room.

She didn't answer. I immediately knew to expect a restless evening. I prepared for bed even though I knew it would be a waste of time. A quick shower and a pair of running shorts made me look as though I was going to bed. It was at least worth a shot.

I eventually fell asleep around 12:30, but when my eyes cracked open at 2:37 I didn't bother trying to go back to sleep. Instead, I got dressed and started a pot of coffee. While I waited for the coffee to brew, I tried to remember how long I had been wearing my cast.

I counted back and realized it was time for that thing to come off. The smell emanating from it told me that I had waited far too long . I had become so used to having it on that it had taken a back seat to my other priorities. By 3:30, I was in the emergency room of Benton County General

Hospital. I approached the lone nurse running the admissions desk. She was in her early twenties, and quite the looker, most likely just out of nursing school. It was the only reason I could think of why a pretty young lady would be working that shift.

"Can I help you?" she asked, obviously distracted by the ten other things she was trying to do at the time.

"I wanted to see if I could have this cast removed," I said holding my arm up high like it was show and tell.

"Do you have insurance?"

"Yes."

"Is this an emergency?"

"Well, no, I guess not."

"Then insurance may not pay for it."

She still wasn't looking at me. I was trying my best to stay calm, but it was getting harder by the second. It was becoming clear why she was on third shift.

"Can I still have it removed?"

"Yes, but it is something you should have done at your primary care physician's office."

"Well, I'm not at my primary care physician's office, am I?" I replied in a snarky tone.

Apparently, that was all it took to get her attention.

"I suppose not. Fill this form out and place it on the desk when you're finished."

I responded with a half-assed 'thanks' and snatched the clipboard from her. I filled out all of my information and returned the clipboard to the desk. The nurse acknowledged me returning it, but let it set on the desk untouched for fifteen minutes. I suppose that was fair, considering the tone I took with her; though she did deserve it.

While I waited for her to enter my information into the system, a vagrant who had come in to warm up struck up a conversation with me.

He was a man probably in his early fifties, but looked nearly seventy. As my grandfather always said; 'It isn't the age, it's the mileage'. This man's odometer had rolled over a few times. He was completely bald on top. Had it not been for the dirt, his head would have been shiny under the fluorescent bulbs. He had a crown of wispy white hair that draped almost to his shoulders. The smile he wore resembled that of a poorly maintained horse. I couldn't tell if it was neglect or genetics, but all of his yellowed teeth seemed to shoot forward and out, at least where he had teeth.

He was wearing a pair of dingy khaki pants, untied work boots and a rugged military coat. The clothes had been on long enough that the dirt had become glossy. He smelled a bit like rotten fruit.

The conversation he started was primarily one-sided. I actually wasn't sure if he was talking to me or at me. When he began speaking it was as if he started mid-sentence. Perhaps he just forgot to say the first part out loud.

"That's all I'm saying," is how he began.

I smiled and shook my head in agreement.

"They want to talk about how smoking gives you cancer. What about the dyes in the food?" he chuckled."I mean, they sell popsicles to children, but they want to stop selling me a cigarette. Do you know what they use to color popsicles?"

"I don't."

"Erythosine. It's a food coloring, red number three. Do you know what Erythosine does? It causes cancer. They say it only causes it in lab rats, but how many lab children do they have? It isn't that they've never tested it on children, but they never published the results. That's how they get you. They tell you a little bit, to get you worried, then they give you the good bits of knowledge so that you feel better about what they are selling you. They make you trust them by making you think that they are looking out for you, when all the while, it's part of their big plan to keep shoving their Popsicle down your throat. I'd rather smoke myself to death. At least I know they are bad for me. I know they are addictive, that's what makes them so good."

Before he could start the next portion of his rant, a security guard came through the front door and approached us. At first I thought it was the guard I ran into when I first broke my arm. I was relieved to see that this guard was older and wiser.

"Time to go, Buck," the guard said, looking at my new friend.

He was obviously a regular around the hospital. Something told me that they called him Buck because of his teeth. The irony would have been too cruel if that was his real name. He didn't argue with the guard. Instead, he stood up, straightened his clothes and led the way out the door.

I spent the next hour watching drunks and one pregnant woman cycle in and out of the emergency room. Finally, after the drunk crowd was tended to, I was called to the back. The nurse took me directly to X-ray, where they checked my arm, and then they sent me to an exam room where I waited for about another hour. That hour went by quicker than the previous two, mostly because I fell asleep on the bed. Even the crinkly paper sheet wasn't going to keep me awake.

I woke to the sound of the door clicking shut behind the doctor. I sat up on the bed and wiped the drool from my cheek. The doctor bade me good morning and grabbed my arm. He rotated it a few times and shrugged his shoulders as if he was expecting something exciting to happen and was let down. Ten minutes later I was signing papers and walking out the front door. They let me keep my cast, though I wasn't sure why I kept it. Perhaps it was just another reminder of the stupid decisions I had made in my life.

On my way to work I stopped at a gas station to wash my arm off. They wiped it down at the hospital, but I could still pick up a light cast smell. After all my pit stops, I arrived at work at my normal scheduled time. Most of my coworkers already had their workstations powered up and were just starting on their first folders of the day.

I fired up my computer and proceeded to work on a legacy folder. After a few minutes Calvin sent me an email asking if everything was alright. He had become so accustomed to me being in a few hours early that when I was just on time there was cause for concern. I explained that I just had my cast removed.

He replied to my email asking if I wanted to get some more training in. Instead of going back and forth I got up and walked into his office, leaving Leroy Mancini's legacy folder on my desk. He was already dead, so I figured he wouldn't mind if it took me a little extra time to enter his folder in the system.

Calvin was seated in his chair and had his back to me. He was running his old hand over the map on the wall. It was best not to interrupt his train of thought, so I quietly took a seat. He repeated a zone designation out loud to himself seven times before he turned around. He noticed me when he turned around and I could see that it caused him to forget the number. His shoulders slumped lower than normal and he turned back around to look at the map.

"A7, A7, A7," he said loud enough for me to hear. I think he was hoping I would remember it if he didn't. As it turned out, that was exactly the case. He spun around in his chair again, "What was that number again?"

"A7. Rough morning?"

"Just not feeling well," he said wiping his brow and then his mouth. "What about you? Everything alright?"

"All things considered, yeah," I raised my arm above the desk so he could see it.

"Promise me you won't do anything stupid like that again after I'm gone."

I placed my right hand on an imaginary bible and raised my left. "Scout's honor."

"Well, let's get to it then."

He started off with another story from his past before making his point, only he was much slower about it than usual. I could tell he was struggling to stay focused and every time I would ask him what was wrong he would tell me that I should mind my own business. Unsure that I caught his sarcasm he would follow-up by saying that he was just kidding and that he was just tired. He knew he wasn't fooling me, but he stuck to his story and I was inclined to let him. We worked for a few hours without a break until he finally stood up and mentioned something about his old prostate and we paused for a restroom break and a coffee refill.

I stopped by my desk, allowing him to get a head start on the restroom. If we had left at the same time I would have been there, relieved myself and been back before he made it to the urinal. No point in bringing attention to how slow he moved.

The blinking light on my cell phone told me that I had an unread text message. I flipped my phone open. It was from April.

Hate to ask, but can you help me load some things up on Saturday?

Shit. She couldn't have picked a more inconvenient day.

What time?

I waited for a few seconds hoping for an immediate response. Calvin was coming out of the restroom before I received a response, so I put the phone back in my drawer and headed to the restroom.

On my way back from the restroom I stopped back by my desk, but there was still no response. In an effort to be proactive, I sent Hala a message asking if she knew what time she need me on Saturday. Yet again, I was offered no immediate response. I tossed my phone back in the drawer and headed back to Calvin's office. Bruce gave me a sour look for using my phone during business hours. I pretended not to notice.

Back in Calvin's office, he was patiently waiting for me. He asked me if everything was alright. I remind him that I asked him that all morning and just like him, I was fine.

"Now let's get some work done. I'm not getting any younger," I said with a smile.

We trudged through the rest of the day with only one more restroom break. By the time we realized that we skipped lunch it was almost time to go home, so we pushed through. While everyone else was gathering their items to leave, Calvin was still lecturing me on zone G8 and how it has become unstable. He tended to avoid zones like that because the neighborhoods ran the spectrum of really good to really bad, and he didn't like leaving that much to chance.

The notebook I had jotted all of Calvin's knowledge in was getting more work that day than any prior to it. An unspoken sense of urgency was put on the day.

Most of the employees made it a point to pop in and say goodbye to Calvin. They didn't know when his actual last day on Earth was, so they didn't want to miss an opportunity to tell him goodbye.

Around 5 p.m., Calvin stood up and announced that he was spent for the day. I could have told that from the weary look on his face. It was bad when we started, but it was even worse by the time we finished. His usually youthful eyes were dull and his face looked more wrinkled than usual. Looking at him gave me the same feeling I had the day I realized that my parents were getting old. Even though you see them every day, there's always one day when your perspective of them changes. That was my day for Calvin. I felt pity for him, whether he wanted it or not. I told him I would walk him out, and that I was not asking. He didn't have the energy to argue.

"You're a good kid," he said.

I gathered my things and took the journey to the parking garage never more than arm's length from Calvin, just in case he collapsed. He surely thought I was being paranoid, but he didn't say as much. His car was just near the elevator, so after he got in his, I meandered around the parking garage waiting for him to drive off. Once I felt secure that he was on his way home, I got in my car and checked my cell phone.

April's reply was first. It simply stated 'early'. Hala's response was second and it said 'not sure, afternoon some time.' It wasn't ideal, but at least I had some wiggle room. I sent Hala a message letting her know that I had some things to do in the morning, but should be able to be there. I waited until I got home to call April.

"Hello?" she answered. It certainly wasn't the 'Hey, honey' I was hoping for, but it was less awkward than the last few greetings.

"So, you're packing things up on Saturday?"

"Yeah, I quit LaRose today. Since I won't be making any money, I don't want to mooch off of Jenny and Clint."

"Ah. Are you sure you want to do that?"

"No, but it's what's happening."

"Is there anything I can do to keep you here?"

"I just need to get away for a while. Can you help me or not?"

296

"Yes. I'll be there early. I've got something I have to do that afternoon but I'll come back after it's done."

"Does it have to do with her?"

"It has to do with Calvin, but yeah, she'll be there."

The line went quiet but not dead. I knew that she wouldn't be happy about me meeting Hala but it would be worse to lie to her. I desperately wanted to explain the situation to her, but telling her that I was going to be with Hala for moral support while she collected Calvin's soul didn't seem like the best idea.

"Are you two..."

"No," I cut her short, "absolutely not."

"Then don't go."

"I have to."

"Why?"

Because it was the right thing to do, because a long time ago, Calvin was my son, because while I loved April I couldn't deny that there were some feelings for Hala, and I wanted to be there for her and Calvin. None of those reasons were going to make any sense to April.

Her asking me not to go was the first opportunity she had given me to try to right things with her and I didn't want to pass it up. It was time for me to sack up and be honest with her.

"I promise I will explain everything when I come back on Saturday."

"What do you mean everything?"

"I know I have no right to ask this, but, please trust me on this."

"Why should I?"

"Because I love you and don't want you to go."

The line went silent again. I wasn't sure if it was the right thing to say or not, but she stayed quiet for a few seconds. It affected her, I just didn't know how. She was too stubborn to let me know. I didn't deserve to know anyway. Having a little anxiety was getting off light if it meant I could mend things with her.

"Don't make me regret trusting you," she said.

Chapter 17

Calvin's 'going away' party was much more upbeat than I would have imagined it could be. A few of the girls had gotten together and decorated the office with Happy Retirement banners, which was morbid and amusing at the same time. Heather baked a chocolate cake and iced it with the words 'Good Luck Calvin'. Not sure what luck he was going to need, but the sentiment was nice enough. The guys brought soda, chips, and other store-bought snacks. Judah brought Gribines, a Kosher snack made from chicken skin and onions. I related it to Jewish pork rinds. It was the first Kosher thing I had seen him eat since I started. I chalked it up to Hanukkah approaching in a couple of months. Judy from Human Resources brought a number of assorted homemade dips and crackers. I couldn't tell what any of them were made of, but they were all amazing in their own unique way.

I brought the ice cream for the cake. I didn't really know what everyone liked, so I purchased a little of everything. I started with my favorite, mint chocolate chip, then the standard vanilla and chocolate. Concerned that it wasn't enough, I also picked up some Rocky Road and a tub of Black Walnut.

The festivities kicked off around 11. Hala pulled Calvin and I out of his office and told everyone to get their snacks and such from the break room fridge if necessary. She also told everyone to log off of Compass for the day. There was to be no more work until Thursday.

Matthew and I moved the Legacy files to the floor so everyone could put their treats on the tables. It felt good being able to use both arms effectively, so I had taken every opportunity I could to lift, carry, push, or pull heavy objects since my cast was gone.

Once we finished laying out the snack buffet, Calvin wasted no time starting the line to get food. At his age he couldn't afford to be modest. Following his lead, the short line formed quickly and before long, everyone had a heaping pile of carbohydrates.

Initially everyone ate in relative silence with only a few words spoken, mostly about how good the cake was. I think the quiet got to Calvin.

"Come on people," he said, "I'm not dead yet, let's act a little more lively."

His comment drew a few concerned looks.

Judah was the first to respond. "Do you have any good stories that you haven't shared with anyone? You know, anything wild or crazy you want to get off your chest?"

Calvin cracked a smile and wiped the ice-cream remnants from the corners of his mouth. "I'm an old man, Judah, I've got nothing but stories and arthritis."

For the next two hours Calvin regaled us with tales from his much wilder youth. He had hitchhiked along the West coast when he was just over twenty years old. His parents had died when he was younger and left him only an inheritance of one hundred dollars, which he said he was immensely grateful for. It was that money that had helped him travel from Kentucky where he was born to San Francisco and back.

We had to remind him to stop and eat his ice cream before it melted. From the excitement in his voice I could tell this was a story he hadn't shared with many people, but had always wanted to. The only person who didn't seem shocked by the story of adventure, women and violence was Bruce, but then again, Bruce was the one who had processed Calvin's folder. It was old news to him.

During Calvin's tale I snuck a few glances at Hala who had positioned herself towards the back of the crowd. She was fighting tears and smiling at the same time. This story was one that Calvin hadn't even shared with her. Although he was the 65th incarnation of her son, she still felt that maternal bond, and she was feeling like her grown child was finally confiding in her. It was as happy as it was sad.

I used needing a refill of chips and queso as an unnecessary excuse to work my way back to Hala.

"You okay?" I whispered.

"I will be. Just please be there on Saturday."

"I will."

Calvin finished his tale in just under two hours. It was good enough that no one had noticed. I don't think anyone knew that there was so much to him. Most everyone knew him as the super nice old guy who was at work before everyone and left after everyone else had cleared out. When someone is old the whole time you know them it is difficult to remember that they were once young and foolish like everyone else.

Calvin's story changed the mood of the entire gathering. At first it was as if we were poorly trying to make light of the situation, but after the tale, it truly seemed like a celebration of a man's life. The only one who appeared to be struggling with it was Hala.

She had her game face on, which she had perfected a long time ago, but I could tell that she was still about five degrees off-center. She would join in conversations, but her eyes would constantly turn back to Calvin. I knew this because my eyes kept turning back to her. My knight in shining armor complex was in full steam ahead mode. Not that there was anything I could do to fix the situation, but I wanted to comfort her.

Judy made it a point to seek me out. I could tell she was being personable but also had some professional intentions. It was only the second or third time we had spoken since I started. The fact that her office wasn't directly inside our bullpen made her seem like a bit of a recluse, though I got the impression that it was a misunderstanding brought on purely by the geography of the office.

"How are you handling all of this?" she asked.

I assumed she was talking about Calvin. "Well, it kind of sucks, but I suppose there's nothing I can do about it."

"You don't like the job?"

"Oh, no, the job is great. I thought you were talking about the Calvin thing."

"Oh, I'm fully aware of that sucking, though after a while you kind of get a little numb to all the death around here." She trailed off at the end of her sentence, leading me to believe she was thinking about someone dear to her that she had lost.

"Care to talk about it?"

"Hmmm, oh, no. I was just thinking about my grandpa. He was a little older than Calvin is now when he died."

"Did he..."

"Recycled. He was an old vet. He did a lot of good things, but also his fair share of the bad. Kind of a drunk, but who could blame him? Anyway he was my male role model after dad ran off." She rolled up her right sleeve and exposed a tattoo just above her sleeve line. "This is the same tattoo he had."

Wrapped around the cap of her shoulder was a four-inch tall naked brunette with bright red lipstick sitting cross-legged on top of a silver bomb. She was facing left and had one of her high heels slightly kicked off. Her right hand was on her hip and her left hand was waving an American flag far out to the left, leaving her bare breasts exposed. It wasn't the type of tattoo I expected on a woman, but for Judy it felt appropriate.

"Nice. That looks good." My response didn't really do it justice.

"Yeah," she rubbed the tattoo before putting her sleeve back down, "I like it."

"I'm sorry he's gone." I felt like I had to say something.

"Me too, but it's okay. I don't feel like he's really gone. I know Calvin recycled him somewhere nice; he'll have a good life and a better shot this time around. He'll get it."

"I bet he will."

She smiled briefly, but then remembered that she had actual business to talk about, so she abruptly changed subjects. "Some time after you officially take Calvin's spot you need to come see me. There will be a bit of paperwork to take care of. Don't worry, no more gold ink."

I chuckled to myself thinking about how I turned my penis gold, but decided to curb my smirk so that she wouldn't have to ask what I was laughing about. "Sounds good."

We chatted for a few more minutes until Matthew showed up and joined the conversation. I was about three sentences into a half-hearted conversation with Matthew about his kids' Halloween costumes when Hala raised a Dixie cup to the sky and asked for everyone's attention. It was a welcome break from discussing the intricacies of a homemade Dora the Explorer costume.

Hala cleared her throat and moved towards Calvin. He was sitting in a chair next to Phyllis, who had him completely enthralled in whatever she was talking about. The fact that he was an old man didn't change that he was still a man and susceptible to the charms of a much younger woman.

"Calvin," Hala said, "I've known you for what seems like forever. To be honest, forever just wasn't long enough." She looked over at me briefly, then back at Calvin. "I think I can speak for all of us when I say that you have changed all of our lives. I guess what I really want to say is thank you."

Calvin nodded in appreciation. He was smiling, but from my vantage point I noticed a tremble in his chin. It could have just been his old age, but the gloss in his eyes said otherwise. We all raised our paper cups and toasted.

Shortly after the toast, Hala dismissed everyone for the rest of the day. Matthew, Tao, and Judah were quick to escape. The rest milled about hoping for a chance to tell Calvin their feelings before he was gone. While awkwardly stalling for time I found myself in a conversation with Bruce.

Bruce started. "He has always been a good guy."

"I can only imagine."

"You've got big shoes to fill."

"I doubt I'll ever fill them quite as well as he did, but I'll try."

"Do you want my advice?"

I hesitated while I decided if he was being friendly or his usual self. "Sure."

"Don't be afraid to ask for help." He left it on that note and walked away, seeing a break in Calvin's queue.

I decided that I had stolen enough of Calvin's time, so I waved to him as I headed for the exit. He acknowledged with a nod. Hala had made her exit a few minutes before me, and I expected her to be waiting in the hallway for me. A strange sense of disappointment came over me when I walked out to an empty hallway.

Snow began to fall as I drove home. It was earlier in the season than usual and it wasn't terribly cold, but it was a reminder that winter wasn't too far away. There was no accumulation, so it didn't hinder my progress. After dropping my things off at home, I pulled out my larger winter coat a few sweaters I didn't wear anymore and some old boots, threw them in a bag and went for a walk. I intentionally left my cell phone at home.

There was a Goodwill store about eight blocks from my house and I wanted to donate some of my winter things. Every point counts. They were closed by the time I got there, so I took the bag around back and placed it by the receiving door. I made a note to ask around at work and see if leaving donations near a donation center counted towards your score.

Something about the start of winter always put me in an introspective mood, or at least more so than usual. Something about recent events made that mood even more intense. I didn't walk directly back to my house. I took a round about way back, so I could take in the falling snow. The big soggy flakes fell and settled in on the fabric of my coat. After a moment they would melt away leaving only a dark spot on the cloth.

It took almost an hour for the cold to get to me. My toes began burning and the tip of my nose became more sensitive. I rubbed my nose with the palm of my hand to buy myself a little more time. A small park tucked away in a neighborhood near my house presented itself as a good place to have a seat and watch the snow fall. The flakes were heavy and wet, and the park was quiet, allowing me to hear the flakes as they landed.

I located a wooden park bench next to a wall of boxwoods and sat down. The seat was cold through my pants, but it quickly absorbed my heat, making it much more comfortable. As I sat, I tried to craft a clever poetic phrase for how this setting was comparable to mine or Calvin's or April' situation. It took about fifteen minutes for me to come to realize that I wasn't a poet.

I headed home just as it was getting dark. Hanging around parks after dark wasn't fashionable anymore. Thanks a lot criminals. There were no missed calls on my phone when I returned home. It was relieving to be ignored for a change.

In contrast to how pleasant Wednesday turned out, Thursday was quiet and awkward. No one spoke, no one looked at each other, and everyone ate lunch separately, even Heather and Linda. Hala came down early in the morning and left with Calvin. He didn't return until it was almost time to go home. He didn't look at anyone as he passed through the office. I drove home in silence and was in bed early.

Friday was tense at work. Everyone knew what was coming and somehow Calvin's imminent death wasn't as well received without cake and ice cream. An occasional sniffle could be heard throughout the office and it wasn't just the women. Judah even made it a point to mention that the weather was really bothering his sinuses, though I wagered that no medicine could be found on his person, his desk, or in his system. I didn't have much room to judge. More than once, my 'allergies' caused me to wipe my eyes so I could better focus on the monitor in front of me. Calvin appeared to be the only one not bothered by his fate.

At random intervals throughout the day, a hint of humming could be heard coming from his office. He walked around to everyone's desk and asked them how they were doing, grabbed up completed folders and returned to his duties. He was either totally at peace or in complete denial. Either way he seemed truly happy. He even had a little more pep in his step.

Personally, his chipper disposition made it harder on me. I didn't want the guy to suffer, but it was always easier to deal with a person's departure when they had struggled with something for a long time. It always makes people feel better when they can say 'He's in a better place

308

now' or 'At least she can rest now'. With Calvin, we would be saying things like 'Plucked before his time' and 'He still had plenty of good years left in him'. It was selfish to consider such things, but I couldn't help it.

After lunch he called me into his office to go over the final details of me taking his spot. I assured him that Hala and I would figure it out. The last thing I wanted to do was turn the focus on me, but time was running short with April as well.

"Have you had a chance to look at April's folder? I know you've got other things on your mind, but you're the only other person that knows about this and I need a solution."

"Yeah, I looked at it," he said before wiping the corners of his mouth, "I've got good news and bad news."

I hated when people said that. It usually meant that there was mostly bad news with a some off topic thing they made up to soften the blow. I waved him on with my hand as if to say 'get to the point'.

He sensed my frustration and tried to get to the point. "First off, you've got a great gal there. She really scored high."

That was the good news.

He continued, "Unfortunately, there really isn't much that can be done. I think you should just process the folder before your score gets damaged. Enjoy what time you have with her, and just know she'll be in a better place."

I felt like a kid on Christmas morning who knew he was getting a bike but ended up getting a book. Calvin's answer to the situation wasn't what I thought it would be. When I entrusted him with it, I thought that he could surely figure out some sort of way out of it. My disappointment in the situation was overwhelming.

"Calvin, I can't."

He noticed my eyes welling up. I tried to wipe it away, but it was too late.

"Listen, son, I tell you what," he started, "I'll talk to Hala about it tonight. I didn't want to go down that route, but who knows, maybe she'll throw a dead guy a bone."

"Good lord, Calvin."

"Sorry, my sense of humor for the last twenty years has revolved around being old. Now I get a day or two to joke about being something more severe than being old."

"Fair enough, but are you sure that's a good idea? I don't want to endanger your score."

"I'm sure I can take it. It's your score that's taking a beating. Besides, do you have a better idea?"

I didn't.

"I'll do what I can, but if it turns out I can't fix this, the folder won't leave this desk."

I went home unsatisfied. I called Larry for a morale boost. He didn't answer right away so I left him a message regarding the promiscuity of his mother. While I waited for his return call, I called April to confirm our plans for me to help her move.

"Hello," she answered.

"Hey."

"Whatsup?"

"Are we still on for tomorrow?"

"Are you?" she asked, implying that she had some doubt.

"While I'm not thrilled that you're moving, I certainly don't want to miss a chance to see you."

"Good," she said, "what are you doing tonight?"

"No plans."

"Great. Let's get some dinner then."

My hesitation in responding must have given her the impression that I wasn't interested.

"We don't have to, I just thought that maybe we could reconcile some things."

"I would love to," I hurriedly replied.

We agreed to take separate vehicles and meet at Bucci's. It was nicer than the places we usually went, but I wasn't going to cheap out on one of the last few chances I had to convince April to get back in my life.

Bucci's was a sure thing for Larry; I was hoping for it to work for me too. On my way there I called Larry again, this time he answered.

"What?"

"Is that any way to talk to a friend in need?"

"How was I supposed to know you needed something? Your message implied that my mother was a woman of the night."

"Yeah. That means I have to ask your opinion on a matter."

"Which matter, the good girlfriend, the hot boss or the dying old man?"

"The first one. We're going to dinner tonight. She said she wants to reconcile some things."

"And? What's the problem?"

"And this might be the last time I have to be with her. Calvin said there wasn't anything I could do about her folder. He's going to talk to Hala about it, but I'm not holding out much hope."

"Shit."

The silence coming from his end of the line led me to believe that he was as stumped as I was. I hadn't expected to see April that night, and intended on telling her everything on Saturday after Calvin was gone. It was going to be too difficult to act normal, knowing that most likely she was going to be dead soon.

"Have you considered being honest?"

"Of course I've considered it, but she's going to think I'm loony."

"I can understand that."

"I'm serious."

"I know. I'm sorry. This isn't the time for joking. If you really want my advice, be yourself and just tell her what you know. Just wait until the van is almost full. That's when emotions will be highest for both of you. It'll mean more. On a side note, I'll take the job if it's still open. It has become abundantly clear that you need me around to keep you in check."

"Thanks. I don't really have a choice do I? I'll talk to Hala, assuming she's still talking to me by Monday. Later."

When I hung up I was in the parking lot of Bucci's. I arrived before April. She never was much of a fast driver. I took the extra time to prep myself. I turned on the dome light in my car and checked for stray nose hairs, straightened my eyebrows, and checked my teeth. Satisfied, I headed for the entrance.

Despite the chill, I waited outside for April to arrive. I watched her pull in and park. I thought it would be gentlemanly to meet her at her car door and open it. It became clear that she didn't notice me approaching her car because when I opened the door she jolted in shock. My chivalry was failing already.

I suggested we head in and let her lead the way. She probably knew I was looking at her ass, but she neglected to tell me not to, so I assumed I had free reign. At the door, I slid in front of her and grabbed the handle. I pulled the door open with my right hand and motioned with my left for her to enter. She nodded as she walked through. Upon entry we were greeted by the host. He was a small man in his early forties with a bald spot on top and a black thin mustache.

"Do you have reservations?" the host asked without looking up from his ledger.

I panicked immediately, having not thought to call ahead. One of the nicest restaurants in town on a Friday night and I assumed we could walk right in. The evening was looking like a total disaster.

April cleared her throat, "Yes, under Morrison, for two."

The fact that she put the reservation under my name was startling enough, but the fact that she called in the reservation and got it made me think that she had been planning it for a couple of days.

We were sat at a booth, not far from where Hala and I sat when I had my interview. Looking over the menus afforded both of us a chance to get acclimated before we started conversation. It was an unsettling feeling; not knowing how to talk to someone you had dated for months. We had talked on the phone since the kiss, but in person it was much harder.

"Any suggestions?" she asked.

"The veal is pretty tasty."

"Have you been here before?"

I forgot that I wasn't exactly honest about my lunch with Hala.

"No, I just heard from Larry that it was good."

314

It was good enough for her. I made a quick promise to myself to start being more honest with her if she stayed and lived. I felt like a drunk asking God to make the room stop spinning and vowing never to drink again.

We returned our attention to the menus. I knew I was going to order the veal, but I still hadn't formulated a topic for discussion, so I tried to look confused as I pretended to scan the menu.

"Any particular wine?" she asked with the same confused look on her face that I had. It became obvious that she was using the menu as a stall tactic as well. She was just being more vocal about it.

"Oh, I don't know, something red?"

"Sounds good. We'll ask the waiter for suggestions."

I closed up my menu and sat it on the edge of the table. April did the same, which alerted our waiter to come take our order. I insisted that April go first so I had a bit more time to think about what I was going to tell her.

She held a short conversation with the waiter about what wines go with veal and what his suggestion was. I nodded in agreement, though I wasn't listening and thus had no idea what was going on.

"And for you, sir?" the waiter said. Based on his tone and the look on April's face, it was the second time he had asked.

"I'll have what she's having," I replied, hoping that she had in fact, ordered the veal.

Left alone and out of diversions, one of us was going to have to eventually say something of substance. She obviously had an agenda. I couldn't hold it against her though, as I had an agenda of my own.

"Something on your mind?"

She beat me to it.

"I've missed you."

"I've missed you too, but it seems that something else is bothering you."

About a million things were bothering me, but it was too early to explain myself. I decided to start small. "Work has been crazy, with Calvin...leaving and the promotion, it's been a lot to take in."

"I can imagine." April bit her lip and appeared to be gathering some focus. "What if I said I had a solution to fix us?"

Her ability to muster up the courage to say what she need to say always impressed me.

"I'm listening."

"Why don't you quit your job and move with me? I can get us jobs. My cousin owns a tax service and I've already talked to her. We won't make as much, but the cost of living is way better back home."

Shit. It was the worst best thing she could ask. I wanted to reconcile and she was giving me a clean shot at it. Unfortunately, I couldn't quit my job and she couldn't move. On the other hand, I considered that if I couldn't save her perhaps I could move out with her to finish out whatever days she had left . Who was I to deny a dying woman, who I was in love with, one of her last requests? Asking Hala for a leave of absence would be incredibly awkward but worth it..

She must have sensed my hesitation. "Just think about it. I know it's a huge decision."

"It really does sound great, but I am going to need some time." I reached across the table and placed my hand on hers. She didn't shy away.

My hand sat motionless on top of hers. It felt like coming home after a long vacation. We both contemplated the dangers of wrapping our hands together. I was the first to ignore caution. I curled my fingers, gripping hers gently in case she recoiled. She reciprocated the grip, gave my hand a long squeeze and slowly let my hand go. It was comforting, but left us both retreating into our own thoughts.

There was a period of contemplative silence between us until the meal came. Fortunately, it arrived within a few minutes. My wine glass found itself empty quicker than I expected, but it found itself full again in no time. April was making sure I didn't go thirsty. In kind, I made sure her glass never dipped below half full. While we ate, conversation floated around how good the meal was or the change in weather. It was a forced casual.

As my belly filled and my blood alcohol level rose, I felt more and more relaxed. The strain to keep conversation to trivial topics was loosening quickly. The flirty touches across the table picked up intensity from both parties. By the time my plate was empty, it was beginning to feel like old times.

It was the best I had felt in a long time. During the course of dinner, I couldn't bring myself to bring up the truth of my situation, her situation, or what I did for a living. I didn't want to ruin the moment. It worked.

After dinner, we took my car back to my place. While it felt a little rehearsed, the way events were unfolding did not bother me in the slightest. All I had to do was keep my mouth shut and not screw it up. I turned my phone on silent and tucked it in the couch cushions.

Chapter 18

The next morning started moving day.

As I laid awake watching April sleep next to me I made up my mind that I was going to talk to Hala about taking leave while April lived out her remaining days. If I couldn't save her I could at least let her enjoy the remaining few months or weeks or days before the end.

If doing so meant no promotion at work or that my score was going to get worse, then so be it. I was starting to feel more and more like what I did in this life was too little too late. I might as well enjoy what time I had left with her.

I placed a kiss on April's forehead to wake her up, reminding her that we would have to get started if we were ever going to get her things packed and moved. She stirred and stuck out her bottom lip. She was as interested in getting out of bed as I was.

We took our time getting ready, though I had an eye on the clock. Hala was going to contact me a few hours before Calvin's time, and I couldn't help feeling rushed.

We stopped for a drive thru breakfast and headed back to Bucci's to get her car. With every moment we spent together I became more and more resolved in my decision. It was also starting to settle in that she wasn't going to be around much longer. I tried to suppress how that made me feel in an atetmpt to keep focused on the moment.

I followed her to her friend's house to begin packing and loading. We arrived to find Larry waiting on us with his Tahoe and an enclosed moving trailer. He was sitting on the front steps of the house holding a box of doughnuts and a box of coffee. Guessing by the sniffles he was over exaggerating he had been out in the cold for a while.

"Took you long enough," he said, "next time warn me if you're going to stop and make nasty before we move your stuff so that I'm not stuck out here freezing my balls off."

"You could have gotten back in the truck," April replied.

He looked at the truck as if the thought hadn't occurred to him. Disappointed in his own ignorance, he shrugged and handed off the doughnuts to April and the coffee to me. "Well, let's do this."

April failed to mention that her friend was out of town for the weekend. I was relieved to hear it, except that we had to load everything up by ourselves. I figured it could have been worse; I could have still had my cast.

It was amazing how she had managed to fit every item from a two level apartment into one garage and a bedroom. We started with the garage because it had the largest items and it was closest to the truck. Larry and I struggled to get the couch and her washer and dryer in the truck. None of us had the foresight to rent a hand truck.

About an hour into the move, April and I were in the middle of a quiet but pleasant coffee break. Larry had stepped inside to use the restroom and had been gone for a while, giving April and I some time to discuss the evening before. We tried acting like we weren't going to talk about it and let it be what it was, but it wasn't working for either of us. Between sips I would open my mouth to speak and quickly close it. April would look over at me as if she had something to say and when I would ask her what she was thinking she would reply with 'Oh, nothing'. It was the 'oh' that made it clear she was thinking the same thing I was.

Larry came out of the house talking on my cell phone. It took me a second to realize who he was talking to.

"It sounds like a great offer. I'll talk to Steve about it. Oh, yeah, here he is," he said passing the phone off to me.

I took the phone from him and stood up. I made it a point to stay near April so the conversation wouldn't look suspicious. She knew who it was and was trying not to look irritated.

"Hello," I answered in my best professional voice.

"She's right there isn't she?" Hala asked.

"Uh huh. Is it time?"

"Almost. Meet me at Calvin's place in about an hour. I'll text you the address."

"Okay."

"Thank you, Steven."

"No problem."

We hung up and a knot formed in my stomach. I was about to go watch someone die. Worse than just a 'someone', it was Calvin. He used to be my son, was my mentor at work, and part-time counselor, whether he knew it or not. Being there for his death was going to be as tragic as it was honorifing. I hoped that when I died someone would want to be there for me. I wondered who had been there for me in the past, other than Hala, of course.

I looked down at April who was still seated, patiently holding her cup of coffee waiting for me to tell her I had to go. She knew I had to go, but she wanted me to announce it, or maybe she was hoping I would say that I didn't have to go.

"I've got to go, but I will be back in a few hours. If you guys want to go get some lunch or something you can and I'll help finish up when I get back."

Larry caught my attention with a subtle nod. He mouthed the words 'don't fuck this up' before speaking out loud. "Sounds good. I could use some lunch after picking up all your slack this morning."

April rocked forward to meet me for a kiss, but the contact was half-hearted. While I wanted to ask what was wrong, I knew what the answer was and that there wasn't anything to be done about it at that moment. I bid my farewells and left. I watched April in my rearview mirror as long as I could.

Calvin's house was a few miles outside of town in a poorer suburb. It wasn't the ghetto, but it wasn't too far off. Considering what I was about to make in his position, it seemed odd for him to live in such a crappy neighborhood. It was the kind we would recycle someone in if their score was just a few thousand points over the bar.

His home was a single floor ranch style house surrounded by poorly maintained chain link fencing. The white paint over the asbestos siding had lost its luster at least a decade ago. The red brick that covered the bottom half of the façade was still in decent repair with only a few cracks in the mortar. Calvin's car sat in the driveway. Somehow it managed to look sad, as if it knew he was never going to start it again. Considering he had been its only owner in over two decades, I understood. As I headed up the driveway to the front door I patted the passenger side fender, as if to tell it that it was going to be okay.

Calvin seemed relieved that it was me ringing his doorbell and not Hala. Not that he wouldn't be glad to see her personally, but he wasn't particularly excited to see her in a professional capacity. The fact that he had made peace with his end didn't mean that he was looking forward to it.

"Come on in," he said.

"How are you holding up?"

"All things considered...pretty well. Can I offer you some coffee?"

"That would be great."

Only a small lamp was lit in the living room, making it difficult to see. The grey of the overcast day did little to brighten his dwelling despite a few open curtains. His decor was about what I expected. His living room was boxed in with a couple of worn leather couches. Dark wood end tables book-ended the larger couch that faced the television.

The television was the only thing that looked out of place. Against his dated burlap looking wallpaper hung vintage garage sale paintings and knick-knacks and a forty some inch flat screen television.

Calvin looked back as I followed him to the kitchen and noticed me staring at the TV. "I like my shows."

The kitchen was separated from the living room by a small bar. I stopped on the front side while Calvin proceeded into the kitchen and poured me a cup of coffee. He slid the cup across the bar top to me. The glazing on the outside of the mug looked like it was from the sixties.

I spun the cup by the handle to get a look at all its glory before taking a sip. On the back it said 'Gone fishin!' and had a painting of an old man passed out in a chair with his pole leaning against him with no bait on the hook.

"Good coffee," I said raising the cup after a sip. It was actually terrible coffee, but no need to be a dick.

"Eh," he said wiping his lips with his right hand after a small sip. "I haven't had caffeinated coffee in years, but I figure I might as well enjoy it now while I can. Sad really. This coffee is terrible."

We reconvened in the living room. I took a seat on the small couch. I let Calvin sit in what was clearly his spot, from the look of the broken down leather. The rest of the leather on both couches looked new.

Calvin's movements and mannerisms were more lively than usual. It wasn't a happy lively, it just appeared that he had gotten his second wind. The thought cross my mind more than once that he looked like he still had years left in him, not hours.

"What do you suppose people talk about before they die?" he asked me.

"I don't know. Life lessons, fond memories, love lost, the weather? I barely know what to talk about when I know I'm not going to..."

"Die?"

"Yeah. That."

"Well," he began before wiping his mouth, "let's talk about you before Hala gets here."

"What about me?"

"How you're going to get out of this pickle you're in?"

"Which one?"

"Well, I suppose the whole jar. Your folder came back, and it's bad, the girl you really want to be with is scheduled to die very soon, and the girl who really wants to be with you has been sabotaging your life since before Jesus was around."

I was with him on the first part, unfortunately I was with him on the second part, but the last bit didn't set well with me. It wasn't Calvin's typical style to be *that* blunt, and I certainly didn't expect him to speak ill of Hala, which I assumed was who he was talking about. I gave him my best confused dog impression and let him continue.

"As for the first thing, you don't have a lot of options. Just do the best you can with what time you've got. Maybe enough donations, rescued kittens and no more screw ups, and you just might make it into heaven, though you're looking at lottery odds."

"That bad, huh?"

"Seven suicide attempts tends to put a dark spot on your eternal resume."

"When was the seventh?"

"Remember that time you drank so much you had to have your stomach pumped?"

"Barely."

"Well, someone remembers," he said pointing up.

He proceeded to list off the previous six attempts, ending with my most recent failure. I had never stopped to really think about it, but for as many times as I had tried, it was a bit of a miracle that I was still alive. I was also starting to feel like an incredible asshole, listening to my rap sheet.

"You remember all of this? When did you get my file?"

"A few months before you started. Bruce was actually the first person to get your file. He brought it to me before you tried to kill yourself last time. I had to review it after Bruce checked it, because of your unique situation."

He paused for a moment. In five minutes he had spoken more than he usually did in a week. He wasn't winded, but rather gave pause out of habit. His hand crept up and cleaned the corners of his mouth. It gave me the opportunity to interject. He was talking so fast I hadn't been able to ask all the questions that were popping into my head.

"Bruce had my folder?" I asked, trying not to sound offended.

"Yeah and you're lucky he did. Not everyone would have been smart enough to know to bring the fact that you were on your last try to my attention. Most would have let you go straight to hell."

"Why didn't you let me?

"I was going to, but I brought it up to Hala and she took it from there."

"What exactly did she do to keep me from going to hell?"

"She chose not to collect you, and while that did work out in your favor, to a degree, that's why you are in this boat in the first place."

I was afraid that he was telling me things that I shouldn't know or things that might tarnish his score. That didn't stop me from listening intently. I kept looking out the window, hoping Hala didn't show up before he told me everything. Calvin seemed unconcerned.

"I don't mean to be rude, but how is any of this her fault?"

"Had you died in that wreck with your friends, you would have been well enough off. If you had died on your first suicide attempt, you would have been fine. Everything since then has had you so far below the bar that salvaging this situation looks damn near impossible. Not to mention what you're doing for April. Or were doing rather."

"Were? I haven't talked to Hala about it yet."

"I know," he said, "I did. I turned her over to Hala."

Fire coursed up my spine and settled into the base of my skull. I knew he was trying to do the right thing and that he might have to talk to Hala about it, but I wanted to be the one to deliver April's folder to Hala. It was difficult to be mad at a dying man, but I was well on my way, justified or not.

"Why? I was going to handle it."

"No, you weren't. And if you were, it was going to go against your score, holding onto it like that. Mine could handle it. You don't need any help digging your hole deeper."

He was right and that made me more angry. Unfortunately, I didn't have time to express myself due to a soft knock at the door. I looked over at Calvin. I could tell he didn't want to answer. I raised my hand to let him know I would get the door.

The short walk to the door was long enough to get me thinking about Hala and what Calvin said. I should have been dead a long time ago and hanging out in heaven with my dead friends and family. Instead I was standing in the living room of a dying man, waiting for death, in a life that had been riddled with disappointment and suffering.

I took a deep breath before opening the door. I wanted to put on my best game face. It wasn't the time or the place to bring up my issues with Hala. I began turning the knob to open the door, but Hala had already started pushing the door open.

She wasn't in her usual work attire. She was wearing jeans and a plain black blouse and a maroon overcoat that hung to just below her knees. Her hair was pulled back into a pony tail. Normally I wouldn't think about someone dressing casual on a Saturday, but it clearly wasn't her typical style. Apart from her wardrobe, I noticed that her makeup was applied recently, most likely to cover the puffiness around her eyes.

She didn't say a word. She started to head to Calvin but stopped just inside the doorway.

"Calvin, Hala's here," I said as if he were expecting someone else.

His lack of response made me think he was scared. At least that was until I heard Hala sniffle. I walked just past her so I could see her face. Her eyes were closed and she was mumbling softly. What she was saying was unclear, but I got the gist. I looked back at Calvin. His eyes were pointed in our direction, but he wasn't looking at us. He was gone. It had to have been an embolism as fast as he went, but I never asked.

"Calvin," I said again, hoping he would snap out of it.

"That's not going to help," Hala said.

She stepped forward and placed her hand on my shoulder. Her delicate touch felt uneasy. I could feel a tremor in her hand. I brought my hand up and placed it on top of hers. She wanted me there to comfort her, not the other way around. Despite the recent enlightenment from Calvin, I wasn't prepared to confront her yet.

"What now?" I asked.

It took her a moment to speak. She was having a hard time composing herself. I barely noticed the pause. My attention was still focused on Calvin, who was sitting on his couch. The shine had left his eyes and all that was left was an empty shell.

"Now I get to work," she said removing her hand from my shoulder.

"Can I do anything to help?"

"Just stay with me."

I nodded my head.

She opened the small purse she had with her and pulled out the score card from Calvin's folder. Digging further into her purse she retrieved an ornate golden pen. Holding the card in her trembling right hand, she looked up at the clock on the wall and scribbled what I assumed was the time of death on the card. The pen seemed to hold the same golden ink as the fingerprint pad I had to use at orientation.

She placed the card in her purse and pulled out her Blackberry. She typed a quick email and fired it off. I wanted to ask who the recipient was, but the timing wasn't appropriate. It was also the least important of the long list of questions I was forming in my head. Hala didn't know it, but she was on the verge of a full on interrogation. I just didn't want to do it standing over Calvin's dead body.

She placed the blackberry back into her purse and placed it on the ground. Hala began rubbing her finger tips together in preparation to place her hands on Calvin. She stalled, but it didn't look like fear or disgust; she was trying to remain composed. She took a step closer to him and looked back at me. I nodded again, assuming she was looking for encouragement. Perhaps it was just to make sure I was paying attention.

She carefully placed her hands on his cheeks and looked into his dull eyes. Under her breath she mumbled a few words of a personal nature and kneeled down beside him. She leaned in and kissed him on the forehead. She stood up and bowed her head in prayer.

I stood motionless for about two minutes while she prayed. Standing still for two minutes normally wouldn't seem so difficult, but standing idly by staring at a dead guy and his grieving mother made that time feel like an hour.

My feelings on the matter hadn't settled in just yet. Being Calvin's father in a past life didn't give me the same perspective on the event that Hala had. I was upset, but not as upset as I wanted to be or felt like I should be. That lack of sadness and my inability to do anything but wait was giving me too much time to think about what Calvin told me just before he died. In those two minutes I went from compassionate to asshole.

In my typical fashion I spoke without thinking. "How many times in this life were you supposed to do this for me?"

Her prayers stopped briefly. She heard me, and was processing what I said, but was trying to maintain her focus on the task at hand.

Her eyes came up before the rest of her head. Her gaze was not a friendly one. I had obviously hit a sore spot and at quite the wrong time.

"What is it that you want from me, Steven?" she asked.

"A little fucking honesty would be nice."

"Really? Do you really want honesty?"

"Yeah, I do. I was supposed to be dead and in heaven with my friends years ago. Why did you take that from me?"

"Take? From you? You can't even imagine what it's like to have something taken from you!"

"What is that supposed to mean?"

"You lost some friends, Steven, and you've made more. I've had my children taken from me for thousands of years, and I've had you, the one person on this Earth who I was meant to be with, taken from me seventy-six times, and I've been a direct witness to all of it. You're scared of going to hell; I've been living it for four thousand years," she yelled as a precursor to her tears.

"We are talking about my eternal soul. I'm sorry your life has sucked, I truly am, but I had a chance to go to heaven, and now it's gone. How does that even compare?"

She didn't respond. I didn't expect her to. I knew I was being selfish, but what's four thousand years compared to an eternity?

Without a word, I looked at Calvin as if to say goodbye, and then I turned and walked out the front door.

It took barely over a block for me to feel like a complete asshole. Was it really too much to ask to give her support and deal with my issues on Monday? Apparently. I got on the highway, cranked up the stereo and just drove. I wasn't ready to go back to April's. I drove in circles for the better part of an hour, taking one exit and turning around and getting back on the highway. Within that hour I still hadn't come to peace with what I had said. Even when I tried to justify it, my resolution quickly faded. On the way back to April's, I realized I was no better than Hala. Holding onto April's folder was no different than what Hala had been doing. I just hoped I hadn't ruined April's chance at heaven.

While I was driving around venting, April called. Initially I let it go to voicemail, but after I thought about it I knew I had to call her back or it was going to become a trust issue. I took the nearest exit and headed her way before dialing.

"Hey. I'm only way back now, what do you want me to pick up for lunch?"

"Actually, where are you? We need a break, so we will just meet you for lunch. Larry is starting to wither away."

"I'm on 90, near Lincoln. How does Burger Hut sound?"

"Terrible for me, but tasty. See you in about twenty minutes."

I pulled into the parking lot of Burger Hut and shut my car off. For twenty minutes I sat pondering the sheer volume of my poor decisions and how to deal with the consequences. Larry knew about my job, and it was time April did too. She needed to know about her file; she needed to know about me. I had held onto her file for so long she may have already missed her first planned brush with Hala, but she needed to know what was waiting.

While I attempted to put my thoughts in an order that would make sense to April I noticed Larry's Tahoe waiting at the intersection about half a block away, waiting to turn left. My thoughts quieted while I watched. The arrow must have turned green, because Larry started turning.

Coming from the north, a tan sedan came speeding through the intersection and slammed into the passenger side of Larry's SUV. The world slowed to a crawl around me. The Tahoe moved to the side unnaturally, like it was floating on the pavement, before the driver's side tires gripped and it rolled over onto Larry's side.

Glass exploded from the scene making it look like it was raining from the ground up. Billows of smoke came from the wheel wells of the car I could no longer see from my vantage point. I wasn't sure how it happened, but before I knew it I was already halfway to the scene.

Chapter 19

It felt like my pulse was trying to push through my throat. My breath was labored and I could feel the sweat forming on my forehead. Broken glass crunched under my feet as I approach the mangled vehicles. The smell of burnt rubber, antifreeze and gasoline filled my nostrils.

From my approach all I could see was the top of the Tahoe and the smashed in passenger side. I cut my hands on torn metal as I climbed on top of the wreckage. Coming over the side, I glanced quickly at the sedan that had caused the wreck. The driver was ejected through the windshield, and was lying limp on what was left of the hood. There didn't appear to be any other passengers. I didn't get a good look at the guy on the hood, but he seemed too old to be the guy who was supposed to kill April. My holding on to the folder must have changed something.

Secure on top of the rear passenger door, I dropped my head into the passenger side. I immediately got dizzy and wanted to vomit from nerves. April and Larry were pressed together. I could see Larry starting to jostle around. They were both covered in blood and glass. April wasn't moving.

"April! Larry!" I screamed into mess hoping to get a response from one of them.

Larry was slow to respond. "Steve?"

336

"Are you okay?" I pushed my right hand in to touch April's neck, trying to feel for a pulse. I couldn't feel anything but I also didn't really know how to feel for a pulse.

"Steve, call 911, man. This isn't good," Larry said.

"What is it?" I asked in a panic, assuming he knew something I didn't.

"Just call!" he screamed.

I wanted to help, but knew there was nothing I could do but make the call. I didn't have time to inquire about April more. I pulled my head out of the wreckage and started dialing my phone, when I noticed someone on the side of the road on their cell phone.

Looking on from the curb was Hala. She was looking at the other car, but when I looked over at her, we briefly made eye contact. I couldn't make out what she was saying on the phone and I had no reason to believe she was calling an ambulance. The 911 operator answered the phone and I told her there was an accident, the intersection and to hurry and I hung up the phone. The whole time I was talking I never took my gaze off of Hala. I wanted to make sure she wasn't looking in April's direction.

"Larry?" I yelled, still looking at Hala.

"Yeah?"

"Is April still breathing?"

A long pause followed my question. Larry could be heard trying to maneuver inside the wreckage. In my peripheral vision, I could see spectators starting to gather. One man ran over to the other car and stood dumbfounded at the lifeless body in front of him.

"Larry!"

"I think so, but barely. She bleeding everywhere."

"Fuck."

I could hear sirens in the distance. Panic was taking a deep hold on me. April was on her way out and all I could do was squat on the vehicle near her and stare at Hala. I needed to get Hala away from April. If she wasn't there to collect her, April could make it to the hospital and get help.

"Larry?"

"What? Are you going to get help or just sit up there and ask me questions?"

"Do you still carry that gun?"

"It's in the back, in a case, why?"

I hopped off the side of Tahoe and headed towards the back of the vehicle. The back glass had already been busted out, so I leaned in the opening. I cut both hands even deeper supporting myself looking for the gun. Larry pinned where he sat, continued asking why I wanted the gun. I ignored him.

I could only see the back of April's head from my vantage point. Her hair was matted with blood and was hanging to the side limp, a few inches away from Larry. It was almost too much for me to handle. Instead of dealing with it I quickly found the gun and slid backwards out the shattered window.

During my search, the sirens had gotten closer, leaving me short on time. It was still a little unclear to me how Hala did what she did, so I did everything I could to keep her from looking April's direction. I turned around and tucked the gun in the back of my waistband to not alert the crowd, but I needed Hala to see that I had it and at the same time imply that I was going to try to use it. All of this in the hopes that she would follow me before she collected April.

To get her attention I walked back around the Tahoe and placed myself between her and the dead guy lying on the hood of the car. As I looked him over, it brought back memories of my accident. Did my friends go this quickly? I hoped so. As I stared at the limp body on the hood, I noticed the soft look on the man's face. He must have been in his sixties, and probably on the back side of them. His gold-rimmed glasses were still on his face, but the glass in the left eye was missing. The right lens was cracked. Blood was coming from somewhere on his head of stark white hair, but I couldn't tell specifically from where. It channeled into the deep wrinkles around his mouth and eyes. With the blood gone, he would have looked like he was taking a nap.

My thoughts snapped quickly back as other motorists were starting to gather around, trying to help or at least get a good look at the mess; all I could do was pretend to try to help the dead guy and inconspicuously shift so that the handle of the gun sticking out of my pants became visible. I was banking on the fact that everyone else would be looking at the wreck and not at me. I could tell it worked when I looked back and Hala gave me a look of extreme disapproval.

I backed away from the wreckage, wanting desperately to be angry at the guy who caused the accident, but it just wasn't in me. I didn't work his folder, for all I knew he had been a great guy who wasn't going to make it home for dinner with his wife. I felt bad for the fictional family in the fictional back story my mind made up for him.

Sure that I had Hala's attention I ran back to my car in front of Burger Hut. I glanced back at Hala, who was still focused on the wreck, but was slowly walking backwards, presumably to her car to follow me. So far so good.

It was harder to get the key in the ignition than it should have been. I didn't realize it, but my hands were shaking violently. I was also crying. I wiped my face with my hands, not thinking about the cuts on them from the broken glass, so I had to wipe my face again with my shirt, smearing small streaks of blood on the front. Once I got my car started, I took off towards American National Bank.

Instead of using their parking structure, I parked my car a few blocks away. Depending on how things turned out, I didn't want any evidence I was there. I pulled into the parking lot of the small pedestrian zone and jogged off to the ANB building. Downtown was dead on the weekends, so mine was the only car there.

I tucked the gun into my back pocket as I jogged towards the building. My left hand stayed behind my back to keep the gun in place while I ran. I was never more aware of how out of shape I was, forcing me to fast walk the last block. As I approached the building it occurred to me that I hadn't told Hala where I was going, but I was sure she would know. If she didn't she would have called. The thought that she wasn't coming crossed my mind, but I pushed it aside. She would come.

The revolving doors to most office buildings downtown were closed on weekends, but there was always a normal door for those who worked outside the normal business hours. I pushed the door open and headed in. As luck would have it, one of the two security guards for the whole building was wandering the lobby and noticed me immediately.

Even though I had a gun, this guy was huge, and I didn't want the gun taken away from me and shoved up my ass. The guard was a mid-thirties white man with a shiny bald head. His uniform looked as though it was about two sizes too small, especially in the arm department. My appearance quickly set him on edge.

"Can I help you with something?" he asked reaching for his baton and approaching me faster than I was comfortable with.

"Oh thank God. There was a wreck about a block from here, and this was the first door I found open."

His eyes widened. From years of working security in a building where nothing ever happened, he was excited at the prospect of being useful. Fight or flight kicked in and he was all fight.

"Where at?"

"One or two blocks south near the alley of that one sandwich shop."

"Alright. You stay here and call 911. I'll go check it out."

He took a deep breath, gathering his courage and he bolted out the door with a smile on his face. I even found it in me to grin. I was well on my way to becoming the liar I always said I wasn't.

With G.I. Joe out the door, I headed for the elevators. The last time I had made this journey was supposed to be my last. I had made peace with dying, hell, I had wanted to. I was still okay with dying, or at least that was what I kept telling myself. April dying was what I wasn't okay with, as selfish as that may have been.

The elevator ride was much longer this time. It's more agonizing to worry about someone else's life than your own. I had to assume that April was still alive and that Hala was following me, otherwise this was the worst plan to rescue someone ever conceived.

The doors opened and I sprinted out, up the stairs, and to the roof. The wind was less of a shock this time around, except that it was much cooler than the first time. It was much closer to winter and the breeze had become much sharper. The air still smelled the same, lending the situation a bit of familiarity.

I found myself less interested in going near the edge than my first visit. I looked around for the rigging to the window washing unit, but it was nowhere to be found. Pacing back and forth around the door I came out of, I expected Hala to be bursting through the door at any moment.

Ten minutes passed, and I was still alone. After five more minutes I was starting to worry that my plan had failed. For all I knew, April was lying in a hospital bed dead somewhere and Hala was back at her office waiting for me to show up.

My fears were slightly premature. I could feel my phone vibrating in my pocket. It was Hala. I didn't want to be talked out of my mission, but my need for assurance that April wasn't dead yet prompted me to answer.

"Hello?" I asked curtly.

"Where the fuck are you?" Hala asked with even more irritation in her voice than I had.

"American National Bank. Roof."

I sounded like I was in the middle of hostage negotiations, though the only hostage I had was myself. Not the best bargaining chip.

"Why? I've been driving all over town looking for you."

"What do you mean why? It's where we first met. I thought you would understand the sentiment."

"I'm not getting into this with you. I'll be there in ten. Don't do anything stupid."

"Stupid?"

"Yeah, like try to kill yourself."

"Then you better hurry, and April better still be alive."

"She is, for now, but promise me you aren't going to do anything...foolish, or I will turn right around and head to the hospital."

I hung up. It probably wasn't the brightest thing to do, but it felt more dramatic. I thought she knew I wouldn't do anything until she got there, so I was reasonably confident that I had made my point. My phone ringing meant that I was wrong.

"What?"

"I said promise, not hang up. I'm not fucking around Steven."

"Seriously? It's not like I can kill myself if you're not here anyway."

"Yeah," she paused, "you can, it just won't be pretty."

I remained silent.

"I know. Just wait until I get there. Promise?". Her 'promise' sounded more like a command with a small question mark on the end.

"I promise."

She hung up the phone. If I survived this ordeal, I was definitely going to have to work on my timing.

As I waited for Hala to arrive, I began to get cold. The initial excitement of the day's events was wearing off and while I couldn't get

April out of my thoughts, my body was starting to absorb the cold and the wind. The arm I broke the last time I was on the roof started to ache. I tried thinking of other things to distract myself from the discomfort. The only thought other than April that kept my mind occupied was the thought of finishing the job I had started the day I first met Hala.

She said I could kill myself, but it wouldn't be pretty. While I didn't understand what that meant, it did mean I had the free reign to do it. Maybe if I did it, I would go straight to hell. Maybe I would float around in limbo if there was such a thing. Maybe she was full of shit. Hell had almost become a foregone conclusion for me, but at least I might be able to buy April some more time, even if I was dead.

As I contemplated the various scenarios of me killing myself, I realized that my plan had not developed much past the stage of getting Hala away from April. In that I had succeeded, but then what? Did I plan on just begging Hala not to do it? Was I going to make a deal and if so, what did I have to offer? My only bargaining chip was me. If I died, Hala would be alone. I wasn't feeling supremely confident that the day was going to end in my favor.

I looked skyward and began a prayer asking God for an answer. My request was interrupted by Hala opening the door to the roof.

"I wasn't done yet," I said still looking up.

"Who are you talking to?"

"Your boss."

"And?"

"And nothing. You interrupted."

"I can leave," she said grabbing the door handle.

"Don't," I insisted.

My order didn't come out nearly as tough as I had meant it to sound. It sounded needy. I cursed myself under my breath. Hala stood perfectly still waiting for me to finish chiding myself. She was staring me in the eyes. I could feel it, but I didn't want to lock eyes with her. She would know how out of sorts I was.

"Why are we here, Steven?"

"Because. I don't want April to die."

"Is that it? All of this because you don't want your girlfriend to die? If that's all this is about, I'm going to the hospital." She grabbed the door knob again.

"What else do you want from me?" I yelled desperately.

She paused. I wasn't sure if she was contemplating her answer or if she was taking a moment to relish the fact that she had me where she wanted me.

"What I want and why we are here are miles apart, Steven. If all this is just because you don't want someone to die, then this is a waste of both of our time."

"Is there a better reason?"

346

"Yeah, like, I don't know, maybe you love April. Maybe you want to do some courageous deed in a last-ditch effort to save your soul. Anything more than just because you don't want someone to die. You think you're the first person that didn't want someone to die? Did you even consider that I've been down this road a thousand times before? You've really fucked things up."

I hadn't. I hadn't thought anything through. My hesitation was my answer.

"Were you just going to kill yourself if it didn't all work out in your favor?"

"It crossed my mind."

"You know, you weren't always this selfish and weak."

It was the first time Hala had actually said anything negative directly to me. For the first time, I actually felt like I had mistreated her. At the very least I was using our relationship, whatever it was, as leverage for my own gains, never stopping to consider her situation.

"I'm sorry," I said, walking backwards towards the edge of the roof.

"For which thing?"

"Everything."

"That's great, but it still doesn't explain why we are here."

"Because I love her, Hala. I'm sorry, but I do. I know that's not exactly what you want to hear, but I do."

"It is and it isn't. Would I rather hear that we were up here so you could get me alone? Yes. Does it hurt? Yes. But I can't expect you to be in love with me after a lifetime of not knowing me, no matter how long I've known you."

"So where do we go from here?" I said as I sat down on the ledge.

Hala put her hands up, as if to say that she wasn't going to try anything. She walked slowly towards me and took a seat next to me on the ledge. Her hand crept over and she placed it on the gun I was still holding in my right hand. I let her take it. She placed it on the ground next to her feet.

"There is one way out," she said, "but I've got to be honest, I'm not crazy about it." Hala smiled at me. It was an eerily and calm smile.

"What? Anything."

"You could kill me."

"That's not funny, Hala."

"I wish I was joking."

"You can't die though."

"I said I couldn't die, that's true enough; I never said I couldn't be killed. Since I failed to collect you, it is within your power to collect me. In doing so, you would essentially take my place as Death. Unfortunately, you would have to kill me."

"How do you know it would work?"

I felt even worse than before for even entertaining the idea. The only comfort my conscience felt was because I wasn't the one that had brought it up.

"I've seen it happen. Back during the Crusades, there were so many dead that it was hard to keep up. I had a lot more help back then, but every now and again, one of my helpers would miss one by a few minutes, only to be slaughtered by the intended dead guy. Trust me, it will work, but you've got to kill me."

"I don't want to fucking kill you! Are you crazy?"

"Look, Steven, I want you to kill me. It will solve all of our problems. You won't die, meaning you've got a long time to right all of your wrongs, April's folder will go back to the main office, and I will get my chance to do something to repay you for taking your chances at heaven away for the last four thousand years."

"I can't."

"It's already been written, though admittedly I was hoping to avoid this outcome myself, but when your file came back, it wasn't alone."

"Yours?"

She nodded. Overwhelmed only scratched the surface of how I felt. All I wanted to do was save April, but what I was going to have to give up was more than I had bargained for. I didn't want to kill Hala, I didn't want April to die, and I don't want to go to hell. I wasn't going to get my way on everything.

Hala grabbed the gun at her feet and extended her arms out, offering the gun to me. When I refused to take it, she gripped the gun in her left hand and grabbed my right wrist. She lifted my arm and put the gun in my hand. I held it loosely. My hands were shaking, but I took special care not to drop the weapon.

Hala was smiling behind the tears that were preparing to run down her face. I felt my own start to well up. When I had full possession of the gun, she grabbed my other hand and placed it on the other side of the handle. Cupping my hands with hers, she stepped up so that her heart and the barrel lined up perfectly. There were no words to describe the look shared between us.

She leaned in and gave me a soft kiss on the lips. With my eyes closed, the salty taste of her tears were more powerful. I slowly opened my eyes. She had pulled back and was standing proud.

"Living forever gets lonely. Promise me you'll look for me when it's time."

"I promise."

As soon as the words escaped my lips, her thumb slipped over my trigger finger and pressed it. The gun went off and I started sweating. I quickly dropped the gun and grabbed Hala before she fell to the ground. Her blood was already starting to wet our clothes as we collapsed to the ground.

I immediately regretted not taking my life when I had the chance. Hala was there with me. I could have jumped or shot myself and she wouldn't have had a choice. That chance was over and gone.

As I held Hala's limp body, I expected a Hollywood moment. She was supposed to say something profound to make me feel better before she died. The police were supposed to show up and save her. She didn't speak. There were no police. She was dead.

Within seconds, I was hit with an overwhelmingly warm sensation in my chest, like a small sun had taken up residence there. It was Hala. In what felt like an out-of-body experience, I began praying. The prayer wasn't in English and I had no control over the words. They flowed from me for just over a minute. Not having control of my voice would have normally forced me into a panic attack, but somehow I knew it wasn't a bad thing. It was a welcome distraction from the meltdown I was headed towards.

When the prayer stopped, I was left alone with the wind and Hala's body. I laid her gently on the ground and stood up. She looked peaceful, aside from the blood. Her eyes were softly closed and her face was relaxed. I knelt back down and touched her cheek and said goodbye. I didn't want to leave, but I knew the guard wouldn't be gone for much longer and I didn't want to be standing over a dead body when he returned.

As I stood to leave, I heard the door behind me open. Panic hit me immediately and hard. It was the security guard from the lobby and he was pissed. Standing over a dead body was likely not going to improve his mood.

"What the fuck are you doing up here?" he asked slowly approaching me, arms at his side, ready to pounce.

I looked back to where Hala's body had been. It was gone, along with all the blood. Feeling my shirt, all of her blood was gone from my clothing, leaving only the blood that came from the accident.

The closer he got the more I backed up but within a few steps my heel kicked the gun that had not disappeared with Hala's body. The security guard's eye caught the gun sliding backwards, causing his face to lit up with excitement. I was fucked and knew it.

He charged me. Out of instinct I back pedaled even faster. I felt the ledge approaching. When I tried to stand my ground, I tripped over my own feet and began falling backwards, over the edge.

All this work for nothing was the first thought that rolled through my head.

The guard shot his hand out to catch me, but my shirt slipped through his fingers and down I went. The sensation of weightlessness wasn't as exciting as it was the first time. This time, my eyes were open, but I was facing the wrong way to enjoy the view.

Chapter 20

As gravity did what it did, I felt the wind flapping my ears, creating a whoosh, drowning out whatever the security guard yelled as I hurtled towards the earth. I hoped it was something along the lines of 'I'm sorry', but it was probably just 'oh shit'. It's what I was saying.

"Shit, oh, shit," were the exact words that came out of my mouth.

I barely had time to get the words out before something hit the back of my head. It immediately felt like my brains were going to fly out of my eye sockets. Fortunately, that feeling took a back seat to the feeling of the rest of my body hitting the same thing. The pain was short-lived however, as everything went black and I no longer felt a thing.

There was no bright light, no burning sensation, no bearded man dressed in white, nor was there a goat footed red man with a tail, horns and a pitch fork. When I opened my eyes I was greeted by a familiar face. It took me a moment to realize where I had seen the gentleman in front of me. When I figured out who was in front of me, I immediately knew where I was. The confusing part was that prior to that moment, I knew for a fact that Jesus' window washing unit had not been there when I arrived earlier.

"I don't think you should visit this building anymore, my friend; it's bad for you," Jesus said, standing over me with his hand out.

"Yeah, I think I'm starting to get that," I said.

"What the hell are you doing up here?" the security guard asked helping Jesus pull me to my feet and off the washing unit.

I didn't answer right away; partly because I was pissed at him for forcing me off a roof top and partly because I didn't have an answer that was going to make any sense to him. The advantage of Hala's body disappearing meant that I didn't have to explain a dead body. That didn't answer my question of what happened to the body, but that could wait.

"I was going to shoot myself."

"Couldn't you do that at home?" the guard asked. "I mean, not that you should, but why go through all the trouble to do it up here?"

Jesus chimed in, "He's been here before. He's not very good at killing himself."

"Thanks."

"What? It's true."

It was true.

"Seriously man, you scared the shit out of me, falling off the roof like that," the guard said.

"You were charging me."

"And you thought you'd take your chances with a forty story fall?"

The guard asked it with a grin on his face. He had been waiting for some action, something outside his daily duties of escorting skateboarders off property and checking empty offices. I had delivered the action and an ego boost to boot. I didn't have it in me to ruin his moment and tell him I tripped.

"At the time it made more sense. I mean, I was trying to kill myself."

"By the way, there was no wreck, but there was a car getting a towed down by the park. Looked like someone broke into it. That yours, by chance?"

"Huh," I said, trying not to seem upset, which I wasn't, at least not about the car. I was still in shock over Hala. "Well, I think I should get going-"

"The only place you're going is the hospital, buddy. You took a hard fall," the guard insisted.

I had planned on going to the hospital, but not for me. I needed to see April and Larry. I waved goodbye to Jesus, hoping to put him in my rearview once and for all. He waved back, but when I turned, he made a fake cough, suggesting that I was forgetting something.

"Oh, thank you for saving me again."

"That's not what I meant. Actually, I have your change from the first time."

Jesus approached me while digging in his back pocket. He pulled out a small carefully folded stack of bills and a receipt folded on top. He dug in his front left hand pocket and pulled out what amounted to thirty-seven cents. I reluctantly extended my left hand. He poured the change in my hand and placed the bills on top. I quickly removed the receipt and put the money back in his hand.

"Keep it. I think. I owe you more than this."

"If you insist. Oh, and don't worry about her, you'll get a chance to make it up."

He smiled like he knew the punch line to a joke no one else knew and then gave me a fatherly pat on the shoulder with his free hand. Before he turned, his hands carefully refolded the money and put it back in his pocket and headed back to his washing unit. He turned and smiled at me again as I watched him lower below the roof line.

I didn't have time to process what he meant.

The guard escorted me to the elevator and out the door. About every minute or so he would ask if I needed a ride or if I wanted him to call an ambulance. I politely and repeatedly refused. He didn't mention the gun left on the roof, nor did I. I assumed it was going to go in his private collection as a trophy. Larry didn't need it anyway.

The air outside the American National Bank was a bit warmer at ground level, but not much. Since all my adrenaline had been used up, I found myself much more sensitive to everything around me. I pulled out my phone to call a cab instead of trying to run back and argue with the tow truck driver, if he was even still there. I had every intention of calling Larry once en route. Unfortunately, I must have landed on my phone when I fell. It was mostly in one piece, but refused to power on.

I walked to the nearest trash bin and gently tossed the phone in. There were very few people walking downtown, most of the restaurants downtown were for the weekday lunch crowd, and all the bars were in the outlying areas, so I practically had the place to myself. I found it to be a perfect time to clear my head while I journeyed to the hospital.

Based on where the accident had happened, I assumed that April and Larry ended up at Benton County. I bent down in an attempt to touch my toes, stretching out for a long walk. My fingers reached about mid shin before I felt I was at the extent of my flexibility. With a deep breath I put my left foot in front of my right and marched on.

I should have spent the walk trying to put all the pieces of what happened together. I didn't. I was tired of thinking. I was tired of worrying. For the first time in as long as I could remember, I shut my mind off and just walked.

I arrived at Benton County hospital within a few hours. My legs were surprisingly fresh when I got there. Unlike my last visit to the hospital, I was calm and collected and in one piece. In contrast to the empty streets I had walked down to get there, the lobby of the hospital was full of people. One of those people was Larry, talking to his girlfriend. He didn't see me, so I approached him from behind.

"You look like shit," I said.

He turned and let out a slightly feminine gasp. "What the fuck was that all about?"

"Just handling business."

"You're being awfully nonchalant about leaving the scene of an accident with a gun," he said in a whispered yell.

"I had some things I had to take care of. How's April?"

I got a long stare from Larry. He wasn't going to get anything else out of me and he knew it.

"I'm fine thanks, but April is in pretty rough shape. They won't tell me much. I know they almost lost her on the way here. Hell, she was almost dead when they arrived." He pulled me away from earshot of his girlfriend. "Does this have something to do with your...job?"

"Sort of. It's a long story, but let's just say I got another promotion."

Larry didn't ask anything else. Instead he got me in contact with a nurse that could get me back to see April. The nurse prefaced my entering the room with a warning that she was awake, but heavily medicated and not in good shape.

Before I opened the door to her room, I hesitated. What if Hala had lied, and me becoming Death meant that I would inadvertently collect April the moment I stepped in the room? I decided I couldn't avoid her my entire life. With a deep inhale and a long exhale I opened the door and stepped inside.

The curtain was pulled around her bed, shielding me from immediate view. I could hear a slow drug out moaning. The kind you hear from drunks minutes before they pass out. I took the moaning as a good sign. If she was moaning she wasn't dead. She obviously wasn't terribly comfortable either.

"April?" I whispered.

"Steve," she answered from behind the curtain and through the pain.

"Yeah. It's me."

"Are you okay?"

"I'm not the one in the hospital bed." I approached the curtain and pulled it back. It made a swoosh sound as it folded up against the wall.

Lying in the bad was a battered and bruised April. Where they hadn't shaved her head to put in stitches were mats of hair, glued together with bits of dried blood that they hadn't cleaned off. Her eyes were puffy and her nose taped up. If she hadn't answered in the affirmative I might not have been able to tell it was her at all. The sight brought tears to my eyes.

"I'm sorry," I said.

When she spoke it was clear that she was in pain, but it was being well controlled by medication. Her sentences were drawn out and required deep breaths before each word.

"You don't have anything to be sorry for. These things happen. I'm just glad to be alive." She placed her hand on mine.

That was the best thing I had heard the entire day. It made me feel like I had made the right decision; fighting to keep her alive.

"Do you remember anything of the accident?"

"No. I remember we were going to meet you for lunch and then I woke up here."

The nurse and doctor entered the room. The nurse was a plain woman in baby blue scrubs, mid-forties ordinary blonde hair pulled tight into a shoulder length pony tail. The doctor was just under thirty. He was wearing a white coat and slacks and a pair Birkenstocks. His curly brown hair was intentionally unkempt.

The doctor grabbed her chart, asked her how she was doing. The nurse checked one of the machines April was hooked up to and adjusted a couple of dials. Satisfied with what she did, she wrote something down on a clipboard that hung from a wire hook on the machine.

"We're going to give her a little medication to help her sleep," the nurse said to me while the doctor continued looking over April. I leaned in and gave her a kiss.

"I'll be back later."

A few steps down the hallway, the doctor caught up to me.

"Are you April's husband?"

"Boyfriend. Why?"

"I don't wish to alarm you, but I feel I should let you know that she has extensive injuries and with injuries like hers there may be complications."

"Like what?"

"I should probably wait for her family to arrive and discuss this with them, but...April will probably never walk again."

It was foolish of me to think I was going to save April with no consequences. Unfortunately, I wasn't the one paying the price. I asked the doctor if he was sure at least three times before I truly accepted it. The hospital had already contacted her parents, so I didn't have to have that conversation.

The doctors kept April sedated until her parents arrived so they could tell them together. I had to sit quietly by and pretend I didn't know. I didn't even tell Larry. He knew there was nothing he could have done about the wreck, but that didn't stop him from feeling responsible. It was cowardice on my part, but I didn't want to be the one to make Larry feel worse.

When April's parents arrived, I ushered them to the room. Her mother was holding back tears, while her father was trying his hardest to stay positive. He gave me a firm handshake and thanked me for being there with his daughter. Her mother hugged me. It was uncomfortable at first, considering I had never actually met her, but after a moment it felt nice to have genuine contact with another human.

Larry and his girlfriend had left the hospital, leaving me alone with April's parents and a sedated April. Her parents posted up on either side of the bed, each taking a hand. This put me at the foot of the bed.

I rubbed her feet through the sheet. As I pressed my thumbs into the arch of the foot, I hoped to get some reaction. There was none. April was still too groggy to really understand what was going on, so she hadn't noticed the lack of sensation in her legs yet.

The nurse came in and gradually started weaning her off her medicine until she would be comfortable but alert. I continued rubbing her feet and sharing awkward glances with her parents. They asked if I knew how it happened and I explained in as little detail as possible.

When April started to wake up, I stopped rubbing her feet. I didn't want to be the one to give it away. The doctor seemed to know that she was awake and entered the room almost immediately following her eyes opening.

"How are you feeling?" he asked.

"I've been better. I could use a shower, maybe a spot of makeup, but other than that, fine I suppose," April answered.

She pushed herself up in the bed with her arms, trying to prop herself into a more upright position. Part way through the push she stopped. Her brow furled and she took a deep breath. April finished pushing her way up and looked at me, then her parents, then the doctor. I pretended to not know what she was thinking.

"I can't feel my legs. Why can't I feel my legs?"

The doctor took her hand. "I'm sorry, April, but due to complications during the accident, you may not regain use of your legs."

She smiled first, like it was a joke, but when no one returned her smile, her expression melted into a confused and angry scowl. Her parents shared the same look. They began firing questions at the doctor and he answered them the best he could, but kept reminding them that it was still very early and that they needed to run more tests. I sat back quietly and returned to rubbing April's feet.

As soon as the doctor had a chance to escape, he snatched the opportunity and disappeared, leaving the four of us alone to sort through everything. I had already gone through the shock of it all; I blended into the furniture while April and her family talked it out. My presence was noticed only by April who kept looking at me with helpless apologetic eyes. When she would look, I would mouth the words 'It will be okay' and 'I love you'.

As night came, they drugged April up enough to sleep well. I told her parents that I was going to go home and shower and that I would be back in a few hours. I called Larry and had him pick me up in his girlfriend's car. Instead of going home, something told me I needed to go back to the office. I wasn't going to leave Monday morning up to chance.

When Larry arrived I told him I would drive, he had been behind the wheel enough for one day. I didn't tell him where we were going until we arrived. I didn't want him backing out. He was surprisingly receptive to the idea of checking out the office. On the way over I told him of April's condition. It took some time for him to say something other than 'shit'.

We went in through the parking garage. At such a late hour on a weekend, the parking garage was empty; horror movie empty. Larry kept looking over his shoulder as we approached the elevators. Inside the elevators, we didn't speak. It wasn't against the law to be in the building after dark, but as it wasn't the norm, there was an international espionage feel to our visit.

The elevator doors opened into the lobby and we proceeded past the evening security guard with little more than a nod. Judging from his physique, he wasn't terribly excited to stop anyone from anything. Short of brandishing a gun in the lobby, nothing was going to separate the man from his chair.

The elevators in the back of the lobby were already open and waiting for us. We entered and proceeded to the office.

With a heavy breath I opened the door. The lights were out except for a few computer monitors that people had left on. Their soft blue glow illuminated the room only enough to appear creepy. I flipped on the light while Larry stood behind me, as if I was a human shield. I expected to see the Devil himself sitting in my former chair, but the lights revealed nothing. We were alone.

Larry didn't speak. Instead, he walked around the office looking for something fantastic. I could sense his disappointment in how ordinary everything was. I think he had expected some sort of magical place, not a standard cubicle filled office. He walked around examining my coworker's belongings.

I walked to my desk, hoping to find a clue about what to do. There was nothing. The door to Calvin's office was cracked. The light was off. I approached it with the same caution as I had the outer door. My hand slid in-between the door and the frame and carefully slid along the wall searching for the switch. Larry had taken notice and stopped staring at a picture Phyllis had on her desk showing her in her prom dress, a long black number with a slit that went on forever. He looked on from across the room waiting to see if some creature was going to pull me into the office and devour me. Instead, the light flipped on and I entered under my own power.

I heard the picture frame fall over on Phyllis' desk, and knew Larry would be right behind me. I worked my way around Calvin's desk, though I knew it wasn't really his anymore, I couldn't bring myself to think of it as anything else. I began digging through the drawers, hoping for a big glowing arrow pointing me in the right direction, though I still didn't really know what direction I was hoping for.

"What the hell are you looking for?" asked Larry.

"I don't know. Something to tell me what to do. Calvin is gone, Hala is gone, April is paralyzed, I just became Death; I'm just having a hard time with this. I need some direction."

"Do you want to explain any of that, or does this fall under the normal 'I will tell you later' category?"

"Yes."

"Yes what?"

"The second thing."

"Fine. What about this post-it? Does this help?"

Larry pulled a yellow square of paper from the top of the desk that I had overlooked. He handed it to me and written in Hala's handwriting was a simple note: 'My office. -Hala".

I left the drawer open that I searched through and hustled around Larry, darting for the elevator. Larry was confused, but was along for the ride, so he was just behind me. I honestly would have left him there if the elevator hadn't taken so long to arrive.

Inside the elevator, I felt antsy. I didn't know what I was going to find in her office, but the prospect of finding anything filled me with excitement and relief. Larry noticed my fidgeting, and while he would have normally said something he simply looked at me and nodded with a sort of proud approval, though I don't think he knew why.

I was out of the doors before they had finished opening. I stopped in my tracks. The stop was so abrupt that Larry ran into the back of me.

366

Sitting on the receptionist's desk was Bruce. He looked tired as though he had been waiting there all day.

Upon making eye contact he forced out a breath, letting me know that I had inconvenienced him in some way. He cocked his head to the left, towards Hala's office.

"What are you doing here, Bruce?"

"Making sure that you made it here."

"I don't understand."

"You will," he stood and started heading towards me but walked right past me to the elevator. "Oh, I'm taking some time off soon."

I waited until the elevator doors closed before heading into the office. The doors opened and unlike the office, the lights were on. It was the first location I had been since my arrival that I felt comfortable.

The office was clean. It was the kind of clean where you can tell the previous occupant didn't plan on coming back. A part of me hoped that Hala would be sitting behind the desk when we entered. She wasn't. I glanced around to make sure we were alone and headed to the bedroom. The door was closed, and just as cautiously as before I slowly opened the door. Larry stuck to my heels.

The lights were out in the room. I felt along the wall for a switch. I found a knob and turned up the dimmer. The lights slowly came up. The room was cleaner than the rest of the office. It had even been redecorated.

The decor was more masculine. Lying on the bed was a black un-hemmed suit. Pinned to the suit was a letter, folded into thirds.

"Can you give me a minute?" I asked.

"Sure, man, no problem."

Larry left the room. I stared at the letter for a few seconds before removing the stick pin. I sat down on the bed, next to the suit and unfolded the letter.

Steven,

I imagine by the time you read this, you'll have had quite the day. I'm sure I didn't answer all of your questions, but no point in looking back now. Either Bruce has delivered this to you or you are in your new office. Regardless, I want to reassure you that everything will be okay. I also have a confession to make. Forgive me for not saying all of this to you in person, but you would be surprised how hard it is to truly talk to someone you've known for thousands of years. That aside, there is business to discuss first. The suit you might be sitting next to is yours. I thought it might look a bit more professional, if you are going to run things. Bruce is aware of what needs to happen, so get with him on Monday. He's rough around the edges, but he takes the job very seriously. Furthermore, the training you received from Calvin was so you could train his replacement. Of course you can promote from within; that is your choice. Everything will take care of itself in time. The other Collectors have been called in for a meeting Tuesday so you can get an idea of who they are.

Now the confession. I would like to say that everything I did was for your own good, but it wasn't. It was for mine. I don't expect you to understand yet, but give it a few hundred years and I think you will. My folder and yours are in the top right hand drawer of your new desk. I asked Bruce to send April's folder back to the home office for a correction; since I know you are thinking about it. Take time to go through the folders carefully and know that I am truly sorry.

I can't expect you to feel the same way, but I love you. Always have.

- Hala

P.S. Take the phone from the desk. You're going to need it.

The letter finished with a lipstick kiss.

I read the letter six times before getting up from the bed. I went to the wet bar and grabbed a beer from the fridge. I tossed one to Larry who had taken his position on the couch. He looked at me cautiously as if he was waiting for me to fly off the handle or have a break down. Instead I waved him to scoot down the couch and I took a seat on the opposite end from him.

We didn't speak. The only sound in the room was the occasional held back belch and the sipping of our beers. We finished our beers at the same time and placed them on the coffee table.

"Did you find what you were looking for?"

"Almost," I said.

Since April's folder was sent back, that meant she wasn't supposed to die yet. If that was the case, why did Hala let me go through with everything? I knew the answers would be in my folder and in Hala's. I glanced over at the desk then back at Larry.

"Got time for one more?"

"Always."

I went back to the fridge, my new fridge, and grabbed another round of beers. Larry graciously accepted his. I took mine over to what used to be Hala's desk. The top of the desk was clean. The only items that were out were a lamp, a laptop and a large desktop calendar. The chair let out a whoosh as I lowered myself into it. I placed my beer on the calendar. I didn't want to start a habit of sitting drinks on the wood.

Before I opened the drawer with mine and Hala's folder, I looked over at Larry who had found the remote and turned on the television. He

370

must have known it was going to be a while. I grabbed the knob of the drawer and pulled back slowly. The desk was old enough that it didn't have rails with rollers. Opening it took more effort than I expected, as if the drawer didn't want me to see what it was hiding.

Inside the drawer was a single padded postal envelope and underneath that was a cluster of them rubber banded together. The individual package was approximately an inch thick with the padding. The bundle contained six packages of about the same size. All of the packages had been opened.

I pulled the top one off. Inside was a manila folder. It had my name on it and stuck to the front was a post-it note that said 'read first'. Out of curiosity, before I read anything, I opened the bundle of packages. All six volumes were Hala's.

The sun was coming up by the time I finished reading through my folder. Larry managed to get drunk over the course of me reading. We didn't really speak until the bottles were empty. Based on how much I drank, I should have been feeling something, but I wasn't. I couldn't tell if it was just that my body couldn't process the alcohol and everything else it had been through or if it was a side effect of being a Collector. Every now and again, Larry would ask how it was going and I would respond with 'fine'. It was a good enough answer for him. Eventually he just passed out on the couch.

The truth was that I was fine. It was liberating looking back at everything I had ever done in my life. Most of it I had forgotten, but plenty came back to me when I saw it in print. Some of the deeds were fond memories; others not so much. The death of my friends was my fault, Hala's death was my fault, even changing April's fate was my fault, and it was all there in front of me. Everything I had ever felt guilty about on paper.

It was freeing, but in the end, my score was just a reminder that I was still a long way from escaping hell. Hala knew it. She knew that there was little to no chance I would have made it to heaven in this life time. A thousand donations and rescuing orphans from burning buildings on a weekly basis and I still wouldn't have squeaked over the line. She bought me an eternity to redeem myself.

Hala's folder was going to have to wait. I needed to get back to the hospital before April woke up. I drove Larry back to the hospital, giving him a little more time to sleep off the beers. I woke him up when we pulled into the parking lot. He wished me good luck, which didn't seem to fit the situation, but was comforting nonetheless. He also gave me a weird side armed hug before I got out of the car and he took the driver's seat.

Epilogue

By the time I walked back in the room, April's parents were sleeping in separate recliners next to her bed. April was awake and staring at the ceiling. The faint morning light coming through the closed blinds reflected off the stream of tears running down her cheek. They weren't from pain. She looked at me when I entered the room and quickly looked away.

I approached and put my hand on her shoulder. "I'm sorry."

"You don't have anything to be sorry about. You can't help life."

"You say that, but..." I trailed off, not knowing how to start the conversation I was about to have with her.

While her parents slept, I started from the beginning. I told her about trying to kill myself. I told her about my first meeting with Hala and more importantly why. I explained the nature of my relationship to Hala, what my previous job was. I left out the part about becoming Death. I didn't want to tell someone who had just been paralyzed that I was going to live forever. April's tears dried up and she wore a look of disbelief and curiosity as I recanted the tale.

When her parents would stir we would stop talking. They were late sleepers, so they stayed asleep for quite some time, affording us time to progress our conversation in whispered voices, though it was a fairly one-sided conversation.

The hard part was trying to explain that it was my fault she was likely wheelchair bound for the rest of her life. Before I could finish, her parents stirred and finally woke up. We gave each other a we'll-finish-this-discussion-later look.

April told us that she was tired and asked me to take her parents down to get some breakfast. I gave them time to brush their teeth and smooth down their hair and we headed out of the room and into the hallway. No sooner than we got to the elevator, the phone I picked up at the office beeped three times from inside my pocket.

I glanced down to see an appointment reminder on the screen.

10:37a.m. Sandra Worth - Benton County Hospital - rm. 714

It was obvious what it was, but it didn't immediately settle in my head that it was something I had to do. On the quiet elevator ride down to L1, it dawned on me that I had to be in room 714 in forty-three minutes to witness a death. My nerves were surprisingly quiet.

I sat with April's parents and enjoyed pancakes from the cafeteria, while we spoke hopefully of April's condition and how strong she was. At 10:28 I excused myself from the table and told her parents that I had a couple of phone calls to make and I would meet them in the room later.

By 10:46 I was back in April's room. Her parents were on opposite sides of her bed, rubbing her numb legs. Sandra Worth had been collected and at her final destination, whether it was heaven, hell, or back on Earth, I didn't know, but I knew I had done my job. It was easier than I had expected. All I had to do was witness and pray and get out. The closest analogy I had was the old question; if a tree falls in the forest and no one is there to hear it, does it make a sound. Well, if someone dies and I'm not there to witness, it just doesn't happen.

I stayed at the hospital until I had to go to work Monday morning, except a small cab ride to the impound to get my car. I swung by my apartment and headed out. My new suit was still in my new office, so I threw on an old pair of pants and a T-shirt for the trip to work. I couldn't bring myself to park in Hala's spot. Since I was about two hours early, I parked close, but I didn't feel bad because I came by it honestly.

To my surprise, I wasn't the first one in the office. Bruce was already at his desk working diligently.

"Morning," I said.

"It sure is."

Already the conversation was feeling a bit like talking to an ex-girlfriend after a year of no communication and she finally wanted her DVD's back. There was a high degree of tension, but you both knew you had things to discuss. It was clear I was going to have to pull things along.

"I'm not entirely sure what you know, but I think we have a lot to talk about," I said.

"Depends on what you're talking about."

"About here, work, Hala..."

"I know a bit about that. I worked her folder."

"So you are aware-"

"That you shot her?"

"Basically."

"Yeah. I knew that," he said. "But I also know why. Hala explained nearly everything to me a few weeks ago. I'm going to tell everyone that she had to take an immediate transfer to the home office and that she regretted not being able to tell everyone goodbye. I don't think the others would understand like I do."

"Where does that leave us?" I suddenly found myself concerned about how Bruce felt about me.

"You're the boss. It doesn't need to be more complicated than that."

"Do you want Calvin's old job?"

For the first time, he cracked a grin. It wasn't a big smile. His face probably wasn't acclimated to smiling, so even a grin was quite the statement.

"Sure. I should have gotten it in the first place. Now I suppose you want me to help you explain this to the rest of the crew."

"Nah. I think I've got this one."

We continued talking about the way things were going to progress over the next few days. While we talked, I received another meeting alert on my phone.

Collector meeting: 7 p.m., Personal office.

I put the alert on snooze and continued on. My coworkers filed in over the next hour, clueless as to the events of the weekend. They all looked towards Calvin's old office, checking to see if he had passed over the weekend. Their faces turned to the floor when they saw that he was not in.

I took the first part of the day to stop by Judy's office. She too had already been informed of the events of the weekend. I began to wonder if I was the only one who didn't know what was going to happen.

"No," Judy reassured me, " Hala had to tell me; there's a lot that goes into changing the head of a company. Legally speaking anyway. I've been working on the paperwork for a week."

My initial reaction was to be upset that she had known for a week, but I knew that privacy and secrecy were just going to be the beginning of what I had to get used to in this line of work.

"So how much of Hala's business were you aware of?"

"Hala didn't have a lot of people to confide in, but I would like to think that I was one she could. She told me a lot. Let's just say that I knew who you were well before you started here."

The thought of pressing her for more information seemed futile and insulting.

"I'm going to assume I can trust you the same way if that's alright with you."

"I think that would be great." She paused for a moment and let me get to the door. "It doesn't necessarily mean anything now, but she really wanted the best for you."

"I know. I just wish I deserved everything she did for me."

"She thought you did."

Around first break, Bruce gathered the group's attention. I began by confirming that Calvin had passed. I then informed the group that Hala had taken a transfer to the home office and that Bruce would be taking Calvin's spot and that I had become a Collector and would be taking over Hala's spot. There were a few murmurs and confused looks.

Bruce stepped up and assured everyone that while it was a lot of change, things were going to run as usual. While that was immediately satisfying for the group, I knew I had to speak up. For once, I didn't mind being in the spotlight for a moment.

"I know that this is a lot to take in, believe me. I wasn't expecting any of this either, but I promise to do the best I can and I know Bruce will do an excellent job in Calvin's place. If any of you need anything, let me know and I will do everything in my power to help."

It wasn't exactly a *Braveheart* speech, but it was good enough.

That night I met with a small group of Collectors from my region. The group consisted of a few men ranging from forty to sixty years old, and as Calvin had said, they appeared to be clergy of some sort, and two young

378

women in their early thirties. One was a heavy smoker, the other was a heavy eater. The last person to the meeting, twenty minutes late, was a young man in his early twenties. He looked like a dope fiend and came in smelling heavily of weed.

We didn't exchange names. They basically showed up, we talked about Hala's departure and how things weren't going to change. They didn't seem to understand much beyond their essential job function, so I didn't get into much detail before ending the meeting.

I wouldn't see any of them again until years later when I had to make special trips to collect them. Unlike me, they were mortal. In time I would come to envy that about them.

For the next month, my days were split between being at the hospital with April, collecting souls, occasionally volunteering at the soup kitchen downtown, and trying to manage the office. I talked Bruce into hiring Larry to fill his old spot. Shockingly, they hit it off immediately and some days it was hard to tell who had been friends with Larry the longest.

It wasn't long before I had to explain to April why I wasn't aging, a point I left out the night I told her what I did at the hospital. I made her a dinner and spilled the last bits I had held out. I knew my score was going to take a hit, but it was long overdue and worth the cost. She took it better than I had expected. Instead of being dismissive or doubtful, she was curious. I answered her questions until well past sunrise the next morning. Satisfied with my answers, she never asked me about my work again.

April never regained use of her legs. It never dampened her spirits, however. She was still the same woman I had fallen in love with, and I never left her side. We married two years later. Due to complications with the accident, we couldn't have children. It bothered April, but she treated it like everything else; if she couldn't change it, she wouldn't dwell on it. Besides, we had Larry's children and grandchildren to spoil.

Eventually, the time came when I had to start collecting those around me. It began with Tao, about fifteen years after I took the job, and slowly worked its way around the room. Most of my coworkers went to heaven, some got another shot at it.

When it came around time to collect April again, she was nearly seventy. It still didn't seem like it was enough time though. She was remarkably brave. As soon as I saw her folder come through the office, by way of Larry, I told her. I expected a lot of tears from her. Instead they all came from me.

The night it was to happen, I took her out to her favorite restaurant and then we went home and put a puzzle together, something we had become fond of doing together over the years. I helped her into bed and cuddled in behind her.

"I'm sorry if I ever did anything to hurt you. I love you," I said.

"You have nothing to be sorry about. You've given me the best life a girl could ask for. I'm glad things worked out how they did. And I love you too."

She rolled over as best she could and gave me a kiss. It was the last time we spoke. At 4:03a.m. I kissed her on the forehead and sent her on to heaven.

Larry carried on for almost a decade longer. He had moved into Bruce's spot after Bruce passed away. He made everyone promise not to let him know when his folder came through and to pass it directly on to me when it was time. His time came on a Thursday over lunch.

He usually ate lunch at his desk and that day was no different. When I stepped into his office, he must have been able to tell from the look on my face.

"It's time, isn't it?"

"Lunchtime?" I asked, trying like hell to keep my composure.

That was how we dealt with difficult situations, so it confirmed it in his mind.

"Well, shit," he tapped his desk nervously with his wrinkled hand, "if I had known I would have brought a better lunch."

"Sorry."

"No worries. I'm old. But before you do your voodoo, I have something for you."

He opened up his top right hand drawer and pulled out a big thick rubber banded stack of dusty folders and plopped it on the desk in front of me.

"I know you haven't looked at this for a number of years because of April and all, but here. Besides, without me around, who's going to keep you in line?"

Lying in front of me was Hala's folder. Underneath that was the folder of the woman she had become on her second chance. Larry had been keeping track of her since he first got hired on. She was in her forties, married, then divorced with two late teen children. From the look of her current folder, she wasn't headed to heaven this round, but she wasn't going to hell either.

I was going to have to pay her a visit. After all, living forever gets lonely.

Made in the USA
Coppell, TX
07 September 2021

61976388R00213